TANGLED IN TROUBLE

USA TODAY BESTSELLING AUTHOR

HARLOE RAE

Howdy, readers!

First of all, thanks for choosing to read *Tangled in Trouble*. It means more than you know. Byron and Frankie have an incredible story to share. Settle in for a wild ride!

While *Tangled in Trouble* is a standalone, there are two other published novels in the Cloverleaf Meadows series. It isn't necessary to read Buckled in Barbwire and Saddled in Secrets to enjoy or understand Tangled in Trouble in its entirety. However, you may notice the mention of the main characters from those books since they are part of the Benson family world.

Also, there are trigger warnings to be mindful of—mostly due to Frankie being a baddie with a dark past and one helluva knife collection. I love to go into a book blind, but if you want to be prepared, you can find the list of warnings at book.harloerae.com/tangledtriggers.

Thanks again for supporting me and my books. I hope you love this one!

xx
Harloe

NOVELS BY HARLOE RAE

Reclusive Standalones
Redefining Us
Forget You Not

#BitterSweetHeat Standalones
Gent
Miss
Lass

Silo Springs Standalones
Breaker
Keeper
Loner

Quad Pod Babe Squad Standalones
Leave Him Loved
Something Like Hate
There's Always Someday
Doing It Right

I'd Tap That (Knox Creek Standalones)
Wrong for You
Yours to Catch
Score on You
Headed for Home

Cloverleaf Meadows (The Benson Family)

Buckled in Barbwire

Saddled in Secrets

Tangled in Trouble

Total Standalones

Watch Me Follow

Ask Me Why

Left for Wild

Lost in Him

Mine For Yours

Screwed Up (part of the Bayside Heroes standalones)

To the morally gray baddie that lives inside all of us. May you always hold your chin high as the grumpy alpha male whimpers in your clutches.

Also, to those who see beyond the jaded defensive mechanisms that cover scars of many shapes and sizes. Without you, the darkness would never see the light. Thank you for making a difference.

PLAYLIST

"Dirty Work" | aespa (featuring Flo Milli)
"Somethin' 'Bout a Woman" | Thomas Rhett & Teddy Swims
"Gone" | Bebe Rexha
"Half a Man" | Dean Lewis
"Dark Horse" | Katy Perry & Juicy J
"Truck Bed" | Hardy
"Excuse the Mess" | Ella Langley
"Wings" | Birdy
"Ain't Thinkin' 'Bout You" | Greylan James
"Shake It to the Max (FLY) – Remix | MOLIY, Silent Addy, Skillibeng, & Shenseea
"Never Enough" | Loren Allred
"Make You Mine" | Madison Beer
"Tears" | Sabrina Carpenter
"Simple" | Florida Georgia Line
"Skin & Bones" | RAYE
"Times of My Life" | mgk
"River" | Leon Bridges

Listen on Spotify!

TANGLED IN TROUBLE

PROLOGUE

THE CHAIR CRASHES TO THE FLOOR AS I LAUNCH TO my feet and stab a sharp fingernail at the asshole beside me. "You're on my shit list."

Jaxon chuckles. "A coin flip never fails."

I roll my eyes. "Not for you."

"Just get it over with. The boss will reward you."

"With another bullshit job," I spit. I'll believe his promise of a raise when I see it.

"That's the name of the grifter game, Franks. You're just waiting for the next big hustle to land in your lap. Might as well earn a little extra on these side gigs until it arrives," he says.

Which is sad but true. Our days are spent obeying James Keller's command. We've been blindly following his orders since I was old enough to remember. He runs the crew with a harsh, unforgiving fist. If I refuse to do as he says, I'll probably get kicked out onto the streets. Honestly, the moments when I wonder if I'd be better off are happening more often. Much like now.

"Walker," I sigh and turn to my brother. "Will you do it?"

"Busy." And by that he means snorting whatever drug is chopped up in front of him.

Disgust slithers through my stomach like a venomous snake. "You and your nose could use a break."

Walker's bleary eyes struggle to focus on me. "Oh, yeah? Well, I think you could be more useful. Get on your knees for a few rich fucks and make us some real money."

"I'm not a whore," I seethe.

My brother scoffs. "Not yet."

A permanent escape from this hell beckons to my dwindling spirit, but it's futile. I can't see beyond the rancid shack we're forced to share. "Why do I even bother?"

Jax nods at the excess powder on the mirror. "You could get a hobby to dull your senses. Eventually, you'll stop caring about the details."

That suggestion turns my stomach. "I'd rather deal with Bianca Benson."

"Get on with it then and quit your bitchin'," Walker mutters before bending for another bump.

My middle fingers lift to bid them farewell. "So much for being family. I hate both of you."

I kick at the horse stall like an unruly mare, pissed that I'm the one stuck on this assignment. Bianca is a spoiled rich girl who caught the wrong type of attention. Once the boss discovered that she's important to his son, the sparkly rodeo princess got a target placed on her back.

A long sigh passes through my lips. Colton is another complication entirely. Why the boss insists on dragging my cousin back into the crew after he abandoned us seems ridiculous. Even for a shady group of misfits such as ourselves. But I don't make the rules. I'm just expected to follow them.

My eyes narrow to showcase my annoyance for the woman in front me. I still can't believe I'm the one confronting her. At a kid's therapy camp, no less. The boss better keep his word and pay up.

Bianca returns my glare, as if this pampered brat has anything to complain about. Her attitude has been nothing but a headache. Why my cousin cares about her beats me.

I shrug, rolling her hostility off my shoulders. "You'll want to hear what I have to say."

The youngest Benson snorts like a champion sire asked to breed with a Shetland pony. "I don't see how that's possible."

That makes two of us, but I have a job to do. "A little birdie told us that you're having trouble leaving town on your own. We can help you escape."

"Ohhhh," Bianca laughs. "The cowboy criminals want to make me disappear. Convenient."

"Is that what you're calling us?" I flip my hair at the endearing title, trying it on for size. "I'll have shirts made."

"That'll have you dressed more appropriately at a family-friendly facility." Her gaze scours over me in disdain, as if I'm manure stuck to the soles of her expensive boots.

It doesn't bother me that much. I'm used to this judgment from the likes of her. "Bitchy, huh? Makes sense."

"Excuse me?" Bianca bristles and straightens her short stature.

"Don't get your thong in a twist," I huff. "That's just what Colton sees in you."

"Guess he has a type," she launches in return.

And the friendly portion of our chat is over.

Fire licks at my skin, preparing to deliver a real message. Talk is too cheap for her expensive taste. A single step slices the distance between us in half. I wonder how hard she'll cry if I pull her hair a little bit. The thought almost makes me smile.

But then a blur of motion launches at me. I don't have time to react other than to brace for impact. Fuck, I'm caught off-guard. That never happens. It allowed Bianca's reinforcements to pummel me. She deserves more credit, but I won't be the one to admit that.

My body flexes into a weapon as I assess the situation. Except this attack feels… gentle? That can't be right. A glance down steals the breath from my lungs.

There's a small child latched onto my legs. I think she's

hugging me. My eyes widen while I slowly lift my hands. Shit, am I surrendering? My heart is pounding too fast. It feels like I've been compromised.

I've stared down the barrel of a gun more times than I care to count but never flinched. An unexpected hug from this little girl is what's going to do me in. Instinct tells me to push her away, but that seems unnecessarily cruel. Even for me. My empty gut churns on a feast of nerves. I don't know what to do.

Another person arrives on the scene, but I can't look away from this tiny human. She's gazing at me with such adoration. It's unsettling but pleasant. Warmth threatens to cradle my frozen heart.

Her pretty face nuzzles my leather pants. "She's a superhero, Daddy."

Daddy? Her father must be nearby. Why isn't he detaching her from me? I'm a stranger, not to mention extremely dangerous.

In my peripheral, I watch a very tall man look me over. "She's something."

My breath sputters. What the fuck is happening?

The little girl clings to me like we're family. Or maybe she's stuck. There's a gooey residue on her cheeks and fingers. My upper lip curls. That's going to leave a stain.

Which must not be permanent enough damage for this small child. She blinks at me, revealing her genuine soul and intentions. "Will you be my mommy?"

Something strange happens to my stomach. Almost

like it flips over onto itself. I might be sick. She's asking me to be her mommy? Is this a joke?

But nobody is laughing. My heart pounds faster as I wait for someone else to react. Nothing happens other than her tiny arms proving their mighty strength. Maybe I'm being tested. I definitely can't hang around for another shot to be fired.

With more care than I've ever given in my life, I pluck the kid off me. A squeak from my biker boots announces my retreat. My shoulders hike around my ears while I disappear into the cheerful crowd. Dammit, I'm never one to flee.

Defeat tries to weigh me down as I rush toward my Harley. Forget the raise. The boss can find someone else to handle that level of dirty work.

CHAPTER ONE

Three weeks later...

"**D**addy!" Ronnie squeals while rushing down the bus stairs.

I lower to a crouch, spreading my arms wide to welcome my little girl home. "Hey, cupcake. How was school?"

"Amazing! I colored a rainbow and sang a bunch of songs and played with my friends outside." Her unbridled glee brightens the cloudy autumn afternoon.

"Wow," I breathe. "You were busy."

She beams at me. "Uh-huh, kindergarten is awesome."

I release the uncertainty trapped in my lungs. It's a good day. Maybe even great. Those have been rare as of late.

Shortly after Ronnie's fifth birthday, my little girl went from happy and carefree to quiet and withdrawn. The reasons vary depending on who I've sought advice from. Some say it's a phase. Others claim it's delayed grief. A few are extremely concerned about her mental health. It's been an emotional challenge, to say the least.

"Ready for a snack?"

Rather than answer, her bottomless green eyes search mine. "Have you seen her?"

And there's the fucking punch in the gut I'd been expecting.

The reminder of who restored my daughter's smile sours my own mood. It's the same question she's been asking me since we first saw that mysterious redhead at Camp Cloverleaf two weeks ago. For whatever reason, my daughter sees something significant in that woman. Something worth idolizing. Meanwhile, I'm tangled in trouble and conflicted beyond measure.

"Afraid not," I mumble.

"Did you look really hard?"

"She's nowhere to be found." My tone is brittle but soft.

"Doesn't she miss us?"

"You can't miss someone you don't know," I murmur quietly.

"That's not true! I miss Mommy, but I never met her."

"Should we look at her photo album? I can find some videos too."

Ronnie visibly sags in front of me. "Not right now."

Pain wheezes from my lungs in a strangled sound. My young child has the power to completely obliterate me. I slump against the ground, glancing at the sky for answers that aren't there. It's moments like this where I feel the loss of my wife as if she just passed yesterday. Nina died during childbirth. She hemorrhaged and the doctors couldn't stop the bleeding. There was nothing they could do except give me the miracle we created. I've been stumbling through parenthood alone ever since.

Words fail me, which is nothing new when it comes to this situation. Rather than try to piece together a pitiful explanation, I wrap my little girl in a fierce hug. Ronnie flings her arms around my neck, accepting the embrace. Maybe needing it, much like I do. We take deep breaths and hold each other close, and slowly, our combined pain loses its sharp edges, smoothing into a dull ache. We'll get through this together.

After several moments, I gather the courage to pull away. I trace a line down the slope of Ronnie's nose, ending with a tap to her chin. It's our sign of love and comfort. She rolls her eyes, but then repeats the motion on me. That small move is like a glimmer of light flickering in the shadows, alerting me that not all is lost.

"You're right," I admit. "Your mother is a part of you. Way down deep. You'll always carry her with you. This woman you saw just once is different, though. She doesn't even know who we are, cupcake."

My little girl grunts. "But she's gonna be my new mommy."

"Ronnie—"

"Nuh-uh, that's a sad voice." Her bottom lip pouts out. "That's how Auntie Bee sounds. I don't like it."

"Well, I don't like seeing you upset." With my thumb and forefinger, I turn her frown upside down. "We've tried looking. I think it's time to forget about her."

"No!" My five-year-old stomps her little foot. "The superhero lady is special. Once she knows me, she's gonna wanna be my mommy."

I flinch at the determination in her tone. "We've talked about this. That woman is a stranger, cupcake. You can't keep saying she's going to be your mom."

"Yes, I can." The stubborn glint I'm becoming very familiar with gleams in her green eyes. "I feel it in here." She points at the spot on her chest—right over her heart—where I've always told her our love comes from. "She's gonna be our family. We just gotta find her."

This type of innocent insistence is impossible to argue against. I'll admit, I was struck by the lioness in leather at first too. That was before I found out who she works for. Ronnie isn't so easily dissuaded. It's almost laughable that my daughter thinks the dangerous woman is an adequate replacement for her mother. But the heart wants what it does. There's no logic.

"You don't even know her name," I say gently.

Ronnie tips up her chin. "That's why we gotta find her. She'll tell me once we do."

I hang my head, rising to stand and steer her toward the house. Her shoulders curl forward as she follows my lead. The fight seeping out of my daughter's small frame threatens to cleave me in two. Her obsession with this bad influence is getting out of hand.

Although, the woman's identity is no longer a mystery. I haven't revealed that discovery to Ronnie in fear she'll become more relentless. The leather-clad criminal doesn't deserve her adoration.

Francesca Keller is Colton's cousin and deeply involved with the cowboy criminals, as Bianca affectionately refers to the group of crooks wreaking havoc around town. Colton cut ties with his father's crew years ago when Frankie was still a teenager. That's why he didn't consider her as a suspect for the one who confronted Bianca at Camp Cloverleaf. He also didn't think Frankie's brother would try to permanently remove him from the equation, but that's a different story.

What's important right now is convincing my daughter to forget she ever saw Frankie.

"Want to visit the auction barn with me? It's packed full of pretty ponies for the sale this weekend. Maybe I'll buy you one," I offer with entirely too much enthusiasm.

Ronnie exhales heavily. "I don't want a pony."

My palm thumps my forehead. "What was I thinking? You're ready for a big horse. There are plenty of those available too."

She kicks at a pile of fallen leaves. "No thanks."

The urge to throttle Frankie and her terrible influence trembles through me. As if my dad falling victim to their dirty deals wasn't bad enough. His gambling addiction buried him in a debt so deep that he willingly stole from his own family. I haven't seen him for months, but I'm still cleaning up the mess he left behind. The last thing I need is my precious daughter getting caught in their trap.

The spark in Ronnie's mood has dimmed completely by the time we reach the front door. Even a rowdy greeting from her two dogs can't chase off the gloom. Darla and Dottie shower her face in sloppy kisses, but my little girl barely acknowledges them. The pair of Shepherd mixes follow her to the chair near the bay window. Their heads rest on her legs once she sits down and stares outside. She absently pets them while waiting for the impossible. It's the same routine as every other afternoon since Francesca Keller darkened our path.

Once again, I find myself cursing that woman's name. Nothing good has come from the ghost of her presence. I'm beginning to believe she fled with the rest of the cowboy criminals. With their leader six feet under and several others behind bars, the remaining crooks scattered. For all I know, Frankie is halfway across the country in search of a fresh start. That's for the best. If only I could explain that to my daughter in terms she'd accept and understand.

Failure is a lead weight on my shoulders. I want to be enough for Ronnie, which is selfish, but our dynamic was working until earlier this year. She needs a female role model, especially as she gets older. There's an unfortunate shortage in that department.

My mom's visits are nonexistent. She prefers to stay away from Cloverleaf Meadows where the bad memories of my father haunt her. My cousin Bianca does what she can, but she has her own shit to deal with. Between work and raising a child, I've never found time to date. It's not as if any random woman will do the trick regardless.

A sigh thick with hesitation spews from me. There's another option.

I clear the tightness from my throat. "Remember what Dr. Laurel said in your last session?"

The mention of her new therapist earns me a side-eye. "Dr. Laurel is old."

It takes great effort to stifle a chuckle. "She's been doing this a long time. That's why she has great ideas for us to try."

Ronnie's flat expression isn't easily swayed.

I walk toward her and crouch down to her level. "Dr. Laurel believes you're attached to this… superhero lady because you want a connection like a daughter should have with her mother. She suggested a trusted adult to hang out with you after school or when I'm at work. Someone similar to Auntie Bee, but you'd see her more often. This person could be your nanny. Would you like that?"

Ronnie perks up. "Can the superhero lady be my nanny?"

"Ronnie…" I sigh.

The momentary joy leeches out of her. She sniffles and drops her gaze, done with me and my worthless attempts to lift her spirits. Guilt stabs at me until it's difficult to breathe.

"She's free to apply," I compromise.

A groove appears between her eyebrows. "What's that mean?"

"If she wants the job, she has to come get it." The odds of that happening are slim enough to offer it without concern.

"Here? At our house?" Ronnie points at the plush carpet beneath her feet.

"That's part of the requirement."

"You're using too many big words," she huffs.

"Whoever we find to be your nanny will be the perfect fit. You'll love spending time with her."

"I only want the superhero lady. She's gonna take my sadness away." A serene glow transforms her features.

"That's what I'm afraid of," I mutter.

"Huh?"

I'm beginning to loathe this so-called great idea. "She might be too busy doing superhero stuff."

Ronnie blinks quickly. "But I wanna love her forever."

"That's very sweet of you. We'll have to wait and see if she finds us."

"But I've already waited a really long time." The whine in her voice chips at my hardened heart.

"You've been very patient," I agree. "And there are so many others who would love to be your nanny right away."

My little girl is already shaking her head. "I only want the superhero lady to be my nanny. And then she'll love me like I love her and wanna be my mommy too! Please find her for me. Please, please."

It's not ideal, but it's progress. Better than her referring to Frankie strictly as her new mommy. A win is a win, after all.

"I'll try my best, okay?" If only to end this madness.

Ronnie smiles, granting me a temporary reprieve from the darkness. "Okay! Thanks, Daddy."

My lungs fill with warmth and hope. I'll track Frankie

down just to make my little girl happy. Maybe Bianca can provide some helpful insight.

"Anything for you, cupcake."

And then she launches herself at me like the cheerful child she was too many months ago. "I love you. So super much. You're the best."

Heat stings my eyes and I squeeze my lids shut. "Love you too. You mean everything to me." Which is why I refuse to fail her again.

One way or another, Frankie is going to face my daughter and expose her true colors.

CHAPTER TWO

A LOUD BUZZ FILLS THE CLAUSTROPHOBIC ROOM. My brother appears in the narrow doorway, escorted by an armed guard. A faded gray jumpsuit dulls Walker's already pale complexion. He blends right into the dingy walls of the visitation area like a shit stain on concrete.

The fluorescent light flickers from above, threatening to burn out. It would do us all a favor, but the stench would remain. I wrinkle my nose. This place reeks like stale piss and corruption.

Walker's muddy brown stare is flat as he shuffles forward. Dark circles hang heavily under his eyes. Neglect coats his jaw in thick stubble. It matches the disheveled mess that his hair has already become. As he drops onto the chair on the opposite side of the bulletproof glass, I can practically hear his spirit dying.

I lift the phone to my ear, waiting to speak until he's clutching his own receiver. "You look like shit, bro."

His expression hardens into stone. "Did you come here to ridicule me?"

"Nope, this is more of a courtesy call. To make sure you're… taken care of."

Walker raises his cuffed wrists. "Can't even take a shit in peace."

I've spent enough nights in jail to have personal experience. My petty crimes aren't worth mentioning compared to his, though. "Probably won't for many years to come. That's what happens when you're on the hook for attempted murder. You're lucky it wasn't considered premeditated or you'd be facing a life sentence."

My idiotic brother was high on who knows what and convinced himself that after our boss died, his estranged son—our cousin—would return to take control of the crew. That delusional state drove Walker to send Colton a message. I only went along for the ride to make sure my brother didn't do anything too stupid, as if assuming Colton would actually want anything to do with his past life wasn't bad enough.

He's still in the hospital recovering after Walker's trigger finger slipped while under the influence.

"Innocent until proven guilty," my brother drawls.

I scoff across the tapped line. "Is that what the judge told you?"

"You'd know if you bothered to show up to the trial."

"Initial hearing," I correct.

"Same thing."

My grip on the phone tightens while I picture hammering some sense into his thick skull. "It's really not."

That ignorance is just one reason why he'll rot in county before getting transferred to a more permanent cell. But he's not ready to accept that.

"Gonna bail me out?"

Laughter bursts out of me. It's the humorless kind that's reserved for especially stupid scenarios. "Never took you for a comedian."

Walker narrows his eyes at my theatrics. "Not tryin' to be funny."

"Well, I sure think your optimism is a joke. The judge said no pre-trial release. That means no bail, brother."

"Why not?"

"Is that a serious question?"

His empty gaze gives me the answer.

"You're being charged with attempted second-degree murder, moron," I state. "They're not letting you out, especially after you ran from the police. Talk about a flight risk."

"Don't have to be a bitch about it," he grumbles.

"You almost killed Colton," I hiss.

That shot still rings out in my nightmares. I almost flinch from the memory, especially when his glare pierces me, but I refuse to expose a weakness. I just give my brother the glower he deserves.

Walker grunts. "Go fucking figure. You're taking his side."

"As if that wasn't obvious when I didn't flee the scene with you."

"My own sister ratted me out," he sneers. "Un-fucking-believable."

I palm my forehead, trying to block his stupidity. "You incriminated yourself. There's no denying it."

Which is further proven as he chomps on nothing but his guilty conscience. "Pretty proud of yourself, huh? Got off without so much as a ticket. Is anyone coming to my defense?"

The hollow pang in my chest is an unanswered echo. "Wouldn't know. They're all gone."

Walker goes deathly still. "What'd you mean?"

"Cops raided the compound after you shot Colton. Everyone scattered. Haven't heard a peep and it's been nearly a week."

That makes him go quiet for a long moment. "Nobody stuck around?"

"Not that I've seen. Jax didn't even bother to say good-bye." Which should've hit me harder than it has.

If anyone stuck around after all hell broke loose, I would've put money on Jax. That money would've been lost. The three of us were as thick as literal thieves and often teamed up together. Trust is impossible in our line of work, but we relied on each other when it counted. At least until my brother went on a rampage and my so-called friend took off without even giving me a middle finger salute.

All I've ever known disappeared practically overnight. They were my family. We took care of each other, as best as a pack of criminals can. I suppose ditching each other comes just as naturally.

After the initial shock of abandonment wore off, a detached numbness spread. I'm upset but not devastated. In the following days, I've realized this is a blessing in disguise. For the first time in my life, I can choose my path.

"Well, shit." Walker almost sounds remorseful. "What're you gonna do?"

I straighten my shoulders. "For now, I'm planning a wedding."

He eyes me skeptically and for good reason. I might be trying to go legit, but party planning is an extreme. It wouldn't belong in my wheelhouse even if I got a complete personality transplant.

"Who's getting married?"

My voice drops as I whisper, "Can you keep a secret?"

Walker looks ready to choose his jail cell over finishing this conversation.

"Colton and Bianca," I chirp before he can holler at a guard.

His eyes bug out. "You've gotta be shitting me."

I allow my smile to stretch to obnoxious proportions. "And their upcoming nuptials have made me realize anything is possible. Who knows what tomorrow might have in store for me?"

My brother has proven that the path we were on leads to a dead end. I want more for my future. And maybe I'll finally get it.

Walker guffaws, as if I'm the disappointment. "Aren't you a ray of gloating sunshine?"

Rather than stoop to his level, I exhale softly. I'm choosing to use this as an opportunity for a fresh start. "Don't be jealous. I'll send you a letter from wherever I end up."

CHAPTER THREE

Byron

Thy irritation I've been swallowing for the entire two-hour drive crawls up my throat when we arrive at our destination. What I'm sure is a lavish farmhouse barely registers. My gaze is locked on where Bianca and Colton are practically glowing while strolling down a makeshift aisle. Their expressions reflect the type of unconditional bliss that can only mean one thing.

"We missed it," I grumble.

Chance winces from the passenger seat. "Sorry."

I grip the steering wheel tighter while parking behind my uncle's truck. "Don't apologize to me."

My younger brother blinks in what I imagine to be confusion. It pairs well with the theme of his behavior. He's reckless and irresponsible and it's gotten worse lately. This is precisely why the burden of my dad's betrayal fell solely on my shoulders. It's up to me to prove that Chance and

I aren't like him. We want to escape the shadow that our father cast over us.

It sure would be nice if my brother's actions could at least support that message. Just this week, I gave him the simple task of finalizing a delivery for the auction barn. The hay wagons showed up this morning rather than tomorrow as planned. More often than not, I feel like firing him from the family business. But the kid has to learn eventually. His rodeo career will only get him so far.

Just as I'm about to harp on him about prioritizing bulls and broncs over our legacy, an unforgettable shade of red catches my eye. I'm not surprised to see Colton's cousin at his wedding. After a brief discussion with Bianca earlier this week, I was informed that the happy couple chose to forgive Frankie for her past crimes and believe she's planning to straighten out. It sounds like petty theft was her specialty. That's easy enough to keep an eye on.

Which is why the sight of her doesn't aggravate my upset. Instead, the confirmation that she's somewhat redeemable soothes the beast. It's a risk I'm willing to take for Ronnie's sake.

I squint to get a better look. Frankie is wearing a… pink dress? A chuckle almost slips free. That's a sight I'm going to appreciate up close and personal.

"Let's go congratulate the bride and groom." And confront a certain bridesmaid.

On cue, Ronnie chooses that moment to wake up. Her afternoon nap stretched to cover the whole ride. My little girl rubs her eyes before glancing out the window. Any lingering drowsiness evaporates instantly.

"Puppies!"

That goes to show how out of character Frankie's outfit is. Ronnie doesn't recognize the ex-con or even spare her a glance while racing across the yard. My daughter has thought of little else other than that woman, but Bianca's pack of dogs steal the scene. Maybe not all hope is lost.

Only one way to find out.

I tug on my tie, striding toward the newlyweds with an excuse already perched on my tongue. Frankie is talking as I approach. It gives me a better opening than I could've planned.

"Not to barge in, but time is of the essence. I need a place to crash," she tells them. "Your house is about to become the honeymoon suite and I'm not dealing with that."

The urge to smirk overpowers me. "You can stay with us."

Frankie whirls to face me. Shock blanches her expression as if I appeared out of seemingly nowhere. In the next second, her eyes narrow. "Do I know you?"

"No, but you're about to get a thorough introduction." But first I tip my cowboy hat at my cousin and her groom. "Congrats on getting hitched. Sorry we're late. Chance had trouble at the auction barn."

But my brother and his problematic work ethic are no longer a concern.

Without further delay, I return my gaze to the redheaded enchantress. Her dark tattoos and nail polish contrast with the cheerful color of her dress. It's a striking combination.

"Now, where was I?" A pleased rumble rolls out of me as I give Frankie another once-over. "You've been haunting my dreams, darlin'. My daughter is convinced that you're a superhero and we need you in our lives. She won't listen to reason. Don't fuck this up."

She's already shaking her head, having the audacity to pretend there's nothing between us. "Definitely have the wrong—"

"Daddy, you found her! You found her!" Ronnie is running full speed toward us, but her sole focus is fixed on the woman she's been obsessing over.

Recognition pinches Frankie's features as she braces for impact. "This is gonna hurt."

I grunt. "She's harmless."

"But I'm not."

Frankie doesn't get the chance to elaborate. My little girl crashes into her, wrapping them in a familiar embrace. An uncomfortable warmth spreads across my chest. That sensation strengthens as Ronnie gazes longingly at her new favorite person.

"Why are you wearing a costume?"

Frankie squishes her lips to one side while scrutinizing her uncharacteristic ensemble that's currently being crushed by a child's love. She gestures between herself and the other bridesmaids. "For… cohesion."

My daughter gives her a questioning stare.

The redhead waves her raised hands, struggling in more ways than one. "It's Paisley's fault. She wanted us to match."

A soft grin relaxes Ronnie's features. "Paisley is Auntie Bee's best friend."

"Um, yep."

"And she's married to Brody."

"That's what I heard." Frankie's arms are still lifted at an awkward angle.

"He's my first cousin, once removed. Auntie Bee is too." Ronnie rises onto the balls of her feet to reach higher and then drops her voice. "She's not really my aunt. It's just a nickname."

"Oh, okay?" The fierce redhead nods slowly as if reassuring herself. "That's… interesting?"

"Uh-huh, and guess what?"

"What?"

Ronnie giggles. "Paisley moved into Brody's room and turned everything pink! It's soooo super pretty."

Frankie's wide stare studies her dress again. "Makes sense."

I scrub a palm over my mouth to stifle a chuckle. These two are just too damn adorable. Ronnie hasn't chatted this freely with anyone for months. The fact Frankie is floundering only adds to my entertainment.

My little girl suddenly gasps. "Do you wanna see my room?"

The woman still firmly in her clutches gulps audibly. "Umm…"

"You're gonna come home with us, m'kay?"

"Oh, I don't think so."

Ronnie pouts. "Why not?"

Frankie looks at me as if I'm going to save her from this

situation. I snort and cross my arms. Her mouth begins to move silently, forming a few words. If I'm reading her lips right, she's going to kill me.

Her focus lowers to my daughter. "Uh, well… I'm a stranger? You shouldn't invite strangers to your house."

That triggers an immediate response. My polite little girl straightens and thrusts an open palm forward. "Hello. My name is Veronica Benson. You can call me Ronnie. I'm in kindergarten at Cloverleaf Meadows Elementary. It's nice to meet you."

The redhead gapes at her proffered hand before giving it a gentle shake. "Hi, Ronnie. My name is Francesca Keller. You can call me Frankie. It's nice to meet you too."

Ronnie appears very satisfied with the exchange. "Now you can see my room. We aren't strangers anymore."

Meanwhile, Frankie's jaw is hanging slack. "How old are you?"

"Five, but I'll be six in February."

"You're really smart, huh?"

My daughter crinkles her nose. "I dunno."

"You are," Frankie confirms. "Take my word for it, kid."

Ronnie bounces on the soles of her shoes. "Does that mean you want the job?"

Startled green eyes lift to me before returning to the only one giving her answers. "What job?"

"Since I can't have you as a mommy"—Ronnie rolls her eyes like that's total bullshit and she smells it—"you're gonna be my nanny."

"Your nanny?" Frankie sputters. "Me?"

"Yep!" My little girl resumes bombing her with affection, holding tight enough to probably hurt. "We looked everywhere, but couldn't find you. I'm never losing you again."

"Ohhhhh, no." Red hair whips in the breeze as she shakes her head wildly. "No, no, no."

Ronnie just nods. "Daddy said I get to pick who hangs out with me. I told him I only want the superhero lady." She catches Frankie's bewildered stare and whispers, "That's you."

The shocked woman opens and closes her mouth, soundlessly searching for an escape. "I don't have any experience with kids."

"You're about to get plenty of it," I interject.

Frankie gawks at me. "You're encouraging this?"

"Can you blame me?" I jut my chin at where Ronnie is gazing at her with pure admiration.

"Yes! I'm not fit for the role."

"My daughter says otherwise. I have my doubts, but your rap sheet isn't that terrifying, darlin'." I shrug, completely unbothered.

"Quit with that," she snaps.

A grunt of agreement trips out of me. "Yeah, you're more of a menace."

Ronnie tilts her head. "What's a menace?"

"Trouble," I answer while keeping my determined stare set on the problem. "Are you going to deny her?"

"This isn't fair." Frankie motions to the position she's been put in.

I let my earlier chuckle tumble free. "Little menace, you of all people should know life ain't fair."

CHAPTER FOUR

Unknown Sender: Make your decision yet?

Me: Depends who's asking...

I ROLL MY EYES AT MYSELF. AS IF I DON'T KNOW. ONLY one insistent little girl, along with her extremely attractive father, are waiting to hear from me. Not that I actually planned to contact them. After wiggling my way out of Ronnie's grasp, I spit out the first noncommittal response that came to mind and took off in the opposite direction. That's twice I've run from them. It's pitiful.

Much like my attempt to blend in with the locals at their beloved cafe. They all stare at me like I'm a stain on this town. My tattoos and leather might as well be a neon sign, labeling me a fraud. I should slink back to the wrong side of the tracks, but I won't give them the satisfaction of scaring me off too.

Byron: Ronnie won't take no for an answer.

My stomach knots. I might not be a kid person, but knowing I'm going to disappoint that innocent child doesn't sit well. That doesn't mean I'm fit to be her nanny.

Me: Tell her I left town.

Byron: I don't make a habit of lying to my daughter.

Me: Not my problem. How'd you get my number?

Byron: Bianca gave it to me.

Betrayal burns my cheeks, which has nothing to do with the shameless leers everyone is aiming at me. Whispers lash my ears, telling me what I already know. I glare at the screen and toggle over to my thread with the traitor.

Me: You gave Byron my number?!

Bianca: Against my better judgment.

Me: WTF

Bianca: Sorry, cuz. Ronnie is determined.

Me: I'm not nanny material!

Bianca: You won't hear me argue, but my opinion doesn't matter.

Me: I have a criminal record!

Bianca: I wouldn't brag about that. Not that it matters. The job is yours. Good luck.

I drop my phone onto the table. It clatters loudly, masking my groan of frustration. The noise draws even more eyes toward my spot in the corner. Unease creeps up my spine and tries to curl my shoulders inward, but I refuse to cower. Instead, my chin lifts as I return their unwanted attention. Most look away while others scoff as if my reaction is unreasonable. I'm expected to let them treat me like an outcast on display.

This is what I get for trying to blend in. I know better than pretending my presence will go unnoticed. Sip in the Stacks is where all the locals gather to discuss the latest gossip in Cloverleaf Meadows. I'm serving myself up as easy prey for them to devour. A grin tugs at my lips as I lift my mug and take a sip. Momentary bliss fills me, proving the extra hot caramel latte loaded with whipped cream is totally worth it.

Byron: Well?

Me: Not gonna happen.

Byron: Figured you'd say that.

Me: You'll find someone much more suitable.

Byron: And what're you planning to do? Wait around for another free ride to swoop in?

I flip off his message. Such a pretentious ass.

Me: Let Ronnie down gently for me, okay?

There's an uncomfortable pinch in my chest as I turn my phone over, ignoring any additional attempts he might send to persuade me. Ronnie will forget about me soon enough. That's the way it goes. I'm not worth the trouble.

Which is why I've been left to fend for myself. A lonely pit yawns in my gut at the reminder. With nowhere else to go, I decided to park on Main Street for the day. For some pathetic reason, I thought a few of them might circle back to look for me. Jax was the closest thing I had to a friend. He could've at least said goodbye. But then what?

My gaze skitters out the window, watching the town do normal afternoon things. Holiday lights are strung up on lamp posts, twinkling in anticipation of the festivities. Traffic flows through the intersection without a hitch. Fallen leaves drift on what I imagine is a strong breeze. People rush along the sidewalk to avoid the late November chill. The view is picturesque and calm and it's obvious I don't belong.

That realization strikes deep, carving at what's left of

my identity. Maybe this is what lies ahead. I've rarely had anything to look forward to. But that doesn't feel quite right. I'd be lying if I said that little girl's persistence hasn't warmed my frozen heart. Nobody has ever cared enough about me to be so relentless. It's nice to be wanted, even if she doesn't realize I'm the worst choice.

Fuck, I'm a mess. My mood is more unstable than Ronnie's decision-making skills. I lower my head until it rests on the table. Just for a moment to gather clarity. A sign pointing me in a general direction would be great.

"Howdy, menace."

My neck cracks as I lurch upright. Byron Benson in the flesh towers over me like a dark knight. Gloom evaporates, replaced by shock and something else. Something thrilling. The sight of him takes my breath away. I flap my lips soundlessly in an attempt to form words. It fails miserably.

Once again, I'm caught off guard. It's a small comfort to see I'm not the only one. Every set of eyes is locked on him. Byron commands the room by just entering it. Masculine energy pulses off the walls, filling the entire space with his presence.

There's no looking away from his hypnotic stare. I'm caught in the trap he's set, unable to even blink. His attention doesn't leave me either. Even shadowed under the brim of a cowboy hat, eyes the color of semi-sweet chocolate swirl with unwavering promises of pleasure.

Attraction thrums in my veins, spreading steadily until I'm consumed. He's just so… large. Broad and manly and gruff. The width of his shoulders expands the thermal flannel he's wearing to its limit. I know from experience he fills out a suit much the same.

Heat rises in my cheeks. What would it be like to get trapped underneath all that bulk as he thrusts into me? The emptiness in my core clenches, desperate to be stretched and stuffed beyond capacity. My throat goes dry. It's been too long since I've felt that.

Byron takes the seat beside me as if it's saved for him. "Happy to see me?"

I force a smile, but the edges lack a certain sharpness. "You wish."

"Who else put that blush on your face?"

The acknowledgment burns my face hotter. How humiliating. "You caused a scene strutting in here. The gossips can't pick their jaws up off the floor."

His lips quirk to one side. "Nah, they were expecting me."

"Oh?"

"I'm a sucker for the scones." He hitches a thumb at the large display case near the front.

A snort escapes me. "I bet you are. That doesn't explain what you're doing at my table."

"You didn't answer me." He taps my phone that's still face down.

"Think I did."

Byron leans toward me and drops his voice. "Not with what I wanted to hear."

My brain crackles. Fuck, he's too close. His cologne is cool and crisp like a winter forest. The fresh scent overpowers the strong aroma of coffee, making my mouth water for an entirely different reason.

I stare at him, getting pulled under the dark surface of his eyes. The shades of brown are warm and inviting. It's like the comfort of a trusted embrace, as if I know how that feels. Everything else fades away until it's just me and him in neutral territory. That allows me to regain my composure.

The fluttery expression I give him is coy. "Sorry to disappoint, stud. My answer won't change. You're better off with anyone else."

"What if I… sweeten the deal?" Kinky sex practically drips from Byron's tone.

I squirm in my chair. Shame is quick to douse the flames. Dammit, he snared me again. He's undefeated when it comes to me. This man needs to get taken down several notches.

My palm finds his leg under the table, squeezing gently. Byron just about jolts straight out of his seat. I allow my grin to spread at the victory.

"Problem?"

He tugs at his collar. "Just unexpected."

"Isn't this what you had in mind?" I drift my touch higher along rigid muscle and worn denim.

Byron rests his hand over mine. "Knock it off."

My pride shrivels into a raisin. How dare he reject me. I rip myself away from his hovering proximity. My back bumps the wall when I put as much space between us as my corner seat will allow.

A thought occurs to me while I recover my dignity. "Did you know I was here? Or are the scones really that good?"

"I put out an alert on our town's message board. The responses have been rolling in since you sat down an hour ago." His shrug isn't apologetic in the least.

Misguided betrayal threatens to choke me. "They gave you my location?"

"Without batting an eyelash." He waves at them in gratitude.

And that's my cue. I begin collecting my things, slugging the last of the delicious latte. Byron's watchful gaze devours my rushed movements. He leans back in his chair, clearly not planning to leave.

"Got somewhere else to be?"

My legs manage to hold me steady under the weight of the crowd's scrutiny. "Far away from you and your informants."

That gets him on his feet. I duck around him, rushing for the door. A solid grip on my elbow slows me down.

"Not so fast, little menace. Do you have a place to stay?" Concern softens his voice.

The fact he overheard that conversation at the wedding needles me. "None of your business."

Byron follows me out into the late autumn chill. "I'll find you."

My hurried steps slap the sidewalk. "I'd prefer if you didn't."

"Don't care what you want. You make Ronnie happy. That's all that matters."

Frustration spikes into a thorn that demands a target. I whirl on him in a fluid motion. Whatever he sees on my face has him retreating backward into a narrow alley. The wind doesn't touch us here, but a cloak of privacy does. It gives me the confidence to reclaim what's mine.

My hips swing as I approach him. "What makes you happy, hmm?"

The brick wall halts his escape, trapping him for a change. "Will that change anything?"

As if I'll answer that. "Who takes care of you?"

His jaw hardens. "Don't fuck with me."

"I'm more interested in fucking you." Mutual desire pulses between the short distance separating us. "How long has it been?"

Byron glares, but doesn't move otherwise. "You're crossing a line."

"Says the man who tracked me down at a cafe."

"That's different."

"Is it?" I press my body against his. "How were you planning to sweeten the deal?"

The brown in his eyes brightens. "A signing bonus."

"Money is nice, but predictable. Let's see what else you can come up with."

"What do you want?"

"Control," I breathe. "Let's forget the boundaries. Just relax. Enjoy yourself for a moment."

He trembles against me, which is confusing. But then I feel the unmistakable steel of his arousal. My smile is predatory and victorious, like slipping on a favorite push-up bra.

This game boosts me to a blissful state I've rarely reached before.

"Do you like this?" I grind my hips along his cock.

The bob of his Adam's apple is telling. "No."

"Liar," I whisper against his lips.

"You're doing this on purpose."

"Of course," I scoff. "It's a bit of payback for putting me on the spot. But maybe you'll get something out of it."

Byron's breathing is labored. "You're catching me at a weak moment."

"How does it feel?" I have personal experience with the pressure he inflicts. It's only fair he gets a taste.

My cheek caresses his. The coarse friction from his beard is gasoline on the fire and I'm going to watch him burn. Specks of gray are buried in the dark bristles, giving a nod to our difference in age. There are probably a solid ten years separating us. My bottom lip gets trapped between my teeth as I wonder if he knows what to do with that gap.

"Stop," he rasps.

I go still. "Do you actually mean that?"

His head jerks to the side, confirming what I already knew. That grants me permission to cup the bulge nudging into my torso. A throb greets my daring exploration.

My mouth curls in satisfaction. "I have an almighty Benson in my grasp. Who would've thought?"

He shifts in my hold, pushing closer. "Don't let it go to your head."

"Wouldn't dare, but I'm not going to waste this opportunity either."

"You're a witch," he mutters.

"Been called worse." My heart races as I grip him tighter. "Such a big boy."

"Don't sound too surprised," he grits through clenched teeth.

"I'm not. Your ego and influence are larger than average. It's only logical that you'd be blessed with a cock to match. I bet you've never wanted for anything."

His eyes flash. "You don't know shit about me."

"Tell me. Do you want more?"

His nod is sharp. "But it doesn't mean anything."

"Just a quick release. In return, you'll let me go."

The strain in his neck highlights his fading restraint. "You won't get far."

"That's for me to worry about."

I start pumping him at a steady pace. It's difficult through his jeans, but I manage. Our difference in height comes in handy. My arm doesn't have to stretch far as I increase the tempo. Tension radiates through him. His response is intoxicating. I find myself preening, ready to unleash the full impact of my talents.

And then Byron whimpers. It's such a vulnerable sound, one I doubt he realizes he even made. Maybe he'll regret it later.

I made him do that. My touch is making him weak. Me.

My confidence sips on his surrender, the soft pleas that encourage me to keep going. He wants this. Maybe even needs it. Badly. I'll never hear him say it, but I can feel it with every twitch of his muscles. My own desires feed on it.

This tough man is submitting to pleasure he's so clearly been lacking. The fact that it's provided under my command is an addictive feeling. I want to push him further. All the way over the edge until he's begging me for relief.

And that's when he gives it to me.

"Please," he whispers.

I stroke him faster. "Please what?"

"Please don't stop. Please go faster. Please make me come. Just… please."

"Since you asked so nicely," I purr.

My palm grips him harder as I increase my pace. I press our bodies even closer, granting him more friction. Tremors quake through him before he's thrusting into my grasp. His hands clench at his sides. A loud drum beats in his chest. Tendons and muscles flex to the point of snapping. If he grinds his teeth any harder, he's going to crack a molar. The desperation in those reflexive actions is an incentive. I'm in control, which probably drives him even crazier than what I'm doing to his cock. But it's not enough to stop me.

"Fuck," he grunts. "I'm close."

I contemplate edging him or leaving him hanging. Neither feels like a victory compared to making him come undone. "That's a good boy. Make a mess in your pants. I want to see it."

And that's all he needs. He shudders and jerks in my hold, bucking against me. It's hard to hang on, but he's almost there. Breathy sounds spill from him. The helpless pitch of his lust turns me on.

His wild motions suddenly still. A guttural groan rips

from him as he finds release. My eyes widen on the dark stain that instantly soaks the front of his jeans. It's a visual I'll never forget.

"Consider that a parting gift," I murmur while putting some much-needed space between us.

Byron scowls, but the expression lacks fire. His chest rises and falls quickly. An unmistakable pink dusts his cheeks. This disheveled version of him is too endearing.

Especially when he says, "I'm not letting you get away with that."

"You just did." I flick the brim of his hat. "It was nice seeing you, stud."

CHAPTER FIVE

Byron

A smirk crooks my lips when Doug's cruiser pulls into my driveway. The young cop is all too eager to make a name for himself in this town. I'm more than happy to oblige. Especially when it comes to rounding up a certain hellion.

As the squad car comes to a stop, Frankie's glare finds me through the backseat window. She's spitting nails and it gets me hard. I widen my stance while returning her spite. There's something very arousing about fighting with this woman. That's why I'm delving deeper into this disaster. It's only fair I drag her into the trenches with me.

Doug steps out, tipping his hat in my direction. "Byron."

"I see you found what I was lookin' for."

His grin rivals the sun for spotlight. "Francesca was pulled over for speeding. Thought she'd make me chase her, but must've thought better of it. At least until I explained that she was coming with me. Put up quite a fuss after that. Not a fan of handcuffs. We impounded the motorcycle as requested."

Laughter tickles my chest at the visual he paints. "Appreciate it, Doug. The chief will be hearing about your dedication to the badge."

"Just doin' my job." He struts around the cruiser's hood, stopping at the rear passenger side. "Ready for this?"

My stomach damn near flips. "Let her at me."

Doug opens the door and reaches down to haul Frankie out. She's quick to shrug off his offer, flipping her legs to get both feet on the ground. Her movements are practiced and smooth as she stands in a fluid motion. Even with her arms pinned behind her back, she manages to look capable of destruction.

"Not her first rodeo," I joke.

"Probably not her last either. Be careful with this one," Doug mumbles.

"Where's the fun in that?"

Most likely against his better judgment, the young officer removes Frankie's cuffs. She doesn't say anything, but her body language is screaming at me. Her muscles are flexed and prepared for battle. There's a green blaze in her eyes that roars louder. Black leather hugs her sinful curves like armor. I soak in the glory of her upset as the cop drops a bag at her feet. Doug reads the room and leaves without another word.

Tension expands between us until I can feel it trying to push me to my knees. I cross my arms, refusing to budge.

After what feels like an hour in a pressure cooker, Frankie breaks the silence.

"What the hell is wrong with you?" She straightens her posture, trying to stretch herself to my level. What she lacks in height she makes up for in attitude. "You can't just have me arrested."

"Not arrested. Restrained," I correct.

"Is that what you call getting shoved in the back of a cop car against my will? It's illegal."

I shake my head. "That fine officer just had a few questions for you. There's no law against him asking you to go down to the station."

"Then why didn't he drive me there?"

I need to get her under my roof where I can take the reins and regain control. "Slight detour."

"Awww," she croons. It almost sounds sweet. But then her teeth gnash like a rabid animal. "Could've just called if you missed me."

She's mad as a hornet, but I rule this hive. The sooner she realizes that, the easier her life with us will be.

"Had a hunch you wouldn't respond to that," I say.

"Bet your shady ass I wouldn't," she snarls. "You can't do this crooked shit to me. I have rights!"

"I think we both know I can, and already did. You're not the only one with loose morals. I'm my father's son after all. Don't test me more than you have."

Frankie rips her fury off me to glare in the direction of Doug's retreat. "Was going that far really necessary?"

"I could ask you the same thing."

"This"—she holds up her freed wrists—"was payback?"

"Absolutely. You embarrassed me."

Her cackle is sharp. "You embarrassed yourself."

Shame burns up my throat, which only fuels the gurgling frustration. "It's a mistake I won't make again."

"Is that why you had me hauled to your house?"

I shrug. "It proves a point."

"The cops are in your pocket," she deadpans. "Real shocker."

A squeak from the old windmill drowns out my chuckle. "You're admitting I'm in charge?"

Her fingers wrap around an imaginary pole, stroking seductively. "Until I get my hands on you, stud."

"That was a moment of weakness. Won't happen again." No matter how hard my cock is straining toward her right now.

The confident quirk of her lips pumps my arousal faster. "We'll see."

"In the meantime," I drawl and nod at the house. "Make yourself at home."

"I'm not staying here," she protests.

My focus drops to the single bag beside her. "We'll get the rest of your stuff later."

"This is everything. Just missing my bike." The prideful lift of her chin dares me to pity her.

"Minimal belongings. Even better." I sweep an arm toward the front door. "Let's go."

Frankie's boots remain rooted to the ground. "Didn't you hear me the first time?"

"This will go a lot smoother if you cooperate."

"Don't talk to me like I'm an unruly child."

"Maybe if you quit acting like one."

She pops out a hip. "Gonna toss me over your knee?"

The visual is more potent than any drug, filling me with a heat I'll never escape. I grip her chin lightly. "Keep tempting me, little menace. There's only so much sass I can take."

Resentment hardens her stare. "You're an ass."

I hum in agreement. No bother denying it. "And now your ass is mine."

Frankie bristles. "Your family might run this town, but you'll never have me."

"Not with that attitude."

"Are you planning to lock me in a cage?"

"Tempting, but I don't think it will come to that."

"There's not a chance I'll stay here willingly."

"No?" I tilt my head, studying how the sunlight reflects off her red hair. "Doesn't matter what you say. You're not going anywhere."

On cue, Ronnie bursts onto the scene like a welcome wagon at full speed. "Frankie! Oh. My. Gosh. You're gonna live with us. I'm soooo happy!"

Before my eyes, I watch the ice queen melt into a puddle. My daughter has that effect on most people, me included. She's impossible to deny, which is why Frankie and I stand motionless to watch her race across the yard.

Ronnie doesn't hesitate to fling herself at the reluctant nanny. "We're gonna have so much fun together!"

The redhead exhales and hangs her head. It's the sight

of being bested by a worthy opponent. If I squint just right, I can picture her obedience belonging to me. She makes surrender look damn sexy.

"Couldn't resist if I tried," Frankie admits on a mutter.

My little girl beams up at her. "I'm having a tea party in the barn. It's just me and my dogs. Wanna play too?"

"Ummm…"

"Or we can play hide and seek. You can be it. Come find us, m'kay?" Ronnie whirls on her heel and takes off without waiting for a response.

"Welcome home, menace," I chuckle.

"You won't get away with this."

"Looks like I already am."

Fury vibrates from every pore in her body. "I hate you."

"That's not very nice."

"You catch on quick."

"Are you going to behave?"

She spews contempt from her flared nostrils. "No."

A slow smile spreads across my lips. "Promise?"

"Quit gloating." Her heavy stomps pound the grass as she begins following after Ronnie.

"Why would I do that? This is cause for celebration. We're tied together."

Frankie tosses me a grin over her shoulder. "Good thing I packed scissors."

CHAPTER SIX

Frankie

A BALL OF ENERGY BURSTS INTO THE ROOM LIKE AN alarm clock cranked to max. "Wake up, wake up, wake up!"

I fling upright in bed. My fuzzy vision barely makes out the shape of Ronnie rushing at me. She's carrying a tray and a smile that could replace the rising sun.

"Such a sleepy head. Don't worry. I brought you breakfast." She places what now appears to be a large storage container lid on my lap.

I blink at the assortment of plastic items and clay blobs. "Um, I can't eat this."

She huffs. "It's just pretend. Like yesterday, remember? You have to use your imagination."

The disappointment in her tone hits my inexperience like a slap to the back of the head. I deserve it. Never did I ever think I'd be in a situation like this.

For whatever reason, this innocent kid believes I'm capable of being her nanny. I couldn't be less qualified if I tried. But her pretty green stare is full of anticipation.

A long sigh breezes from my lips. I might not be fit for the position, but I'm not a quitter either.

"This looks delicious." I grab the spoon and scoop some beads from a dish, bringing what I imagine to be rainbow soup to my mouth. "Yummy."

Ronnie leans forward. "Is it good?"

My nod is instant. "Mhmm, best breakfast I've ever had."

Her giggle is shrill and forgiving. I realize I'm smiling, which is startling. That's not enough for Ronnie. Before I can brace myself, she's launching herself into the empty space beside me and settling under the covers. Disbelief snorts out of me in an obnoxious noise. She just beams at me as if I'm the reason for her happiness. This girl has no boundaries with someone who's practically a stranger, but I applaud her tenacity.

I put the food tray aside and give her my full attention. "So… uh, now what?"

Ronnie scrunches her features. "We could watch a movie."

My gaze slides to the large screen hanging on the wall in front of us. It's one of the many comforts surrounding me. The room I've been put up in reminds me of a luxury suite. It's all expensive furnishings in complimentary tones. My fingers slide over the sheets that are a higher thread count than I've ever felt. Wouldn't expect anything less in a Benson house, even for the hired help.

"What movie?" I scan the numerous glossy surfaces in search of the remote.

Ronnie frees herself from the sheets, leaping to her feet like she just downed a shot of espresso. "*KPop Demon Hunters!*"

A dull throb strikes my temples as the springs creak from her nonstop motion. I need several sips of the energy tonic she's obviously guzzled. It takes my sluggish brain a moment to process the name of the movie she suggested.

"Are you allowed to watch that?"

She stops bouncing long enough to gawk at me. "Uh, duh. It's my most favorite everrrrr!"

"Right, of course."

I shouldn't be surprised. It's clear Ronnie rules the roost, which now includes me. I'm here to do her bidding, but she'll get tired of me soon enough. When that happens, her tyrannical father will let me go. Until then, I'll play the part she's cast for me.

That means I need to find the freaking remote. Maybe there isn't one. "Do you know how to turn on the TV?"

"Yep!" She tumbles off the mattress in an acrobatic move that would break my hip.

I wince at the phantom ache. "What time is it?"

Ronnie shrugs while grabbing a tablet from the nightstand drawer. "I dunno."

"Feels early," I mumble.

Especially with this mental gymnastics routine I'm performing before coffee. Ronnie is already dressed and ready for the day. Meanwhile, I'm barely functioning and a shag carpet has replaced my tongue.

"No more sleepin'. Get outta bed." She tugs at my arm.

"I thought we were watching the demon movie."

"Oh, yeah!"

The little girl stabs at the device in her hands, bringing the television to life. Her fingers glide over the tablet screen with practiced motions. It doesn't take longer than ten seconds for her favorite film to start playing. Kids and their technology.

A pressure in my bladder presents itself as the opening scene kicks things off. Ronnie's focus is glued to the TV. That allows me to creep over to the bathroom unnoticed. At least until the light turns on automatically.

Her head whips toward me. "Where are you going?"

"Nature calls," I explain.

She gives me a blank stare.

"Potty," I reiterate.

"Do you want privacy?"

Now it's my turn to gape at her. Would she actually watch me pee? "Yes, I need privacy."

"Close the door, but don't lock it." That statement sounds like one she's heard a time or two. "And don't forget to flush."

"Got it."

I go about my business, taking a few extra minutes to brush my teeth. A glance in the mirror is a mistake. The reflection staring back at me is a wreck. My hair is a tangle of red knots and dark circles sit heavy under my eyes.

"Rough night," I mutter.

A knock interrupts my musings. "What's taking so long?"

I can't help but laugh. "I'm trying to fix my face."

"Is it broken?" The muffled question sounds like she's pressing her mouth against the door.

My head hangs between my shoulders as I allow the humor of this situation to shake through me. "It's a real mess, kiddo. Just give me a few moments, okay?"

There's a pause as if she's weighing the options. "Hurry up."

"Yes, ma'am."

"What was that?"

I straighten out of habit. The reflex is extra ridiculous since she's a child and can't see me. "I'll be out soon."

Which ends up being entirely too long based on the defeated expression Ronnie is wearing. She's sitting on the floor, blocking my path, which forces me to see the upset I caused. But before I can soothe her hurt feelings, the little girl is up and on the move again.

"Finally," she huffs. "You were in there forever."

"That's a slight exaggeration."

Ronnie parks a hand on her hip. "Huh?"

My palm swats away the unnecessary vocab lesson. "I thought you were watching the movie."

She glances over her shoulder, but dismisses the film quickly. "I wanna do something else."

My thoughts whirl as her bottomless energy spins in fast twirls across the room. "Like what?"

"You pick."

My severe lack of skills makes another appearance. "Don't you have school?"

"It's a home day."

I've lost track, but it must be the weekend. "What do you like to do for fun?"

"Lotsa stuff," she chirps.

My empty stomach clenches. Gosh, this is awkward. But only for me. Ronnie seems fine with idle chit-chat. I mentally add that to her list of interests.

"How about we find your dad?"

Ronnie skips to the breakfast tray she brought me and picks up a clump of clay. "He's busy."

"With what?"

Her tongue pokes out as she works hard on molding a new creation. "Talkin' to Uncle Chance. He's mad at him again."

"Why?"

She shrugs at my misplaced curiosity. "He told me to stay put in the kitchen. I was still eating cereal, but then he walked away. My feet were so super quiet as I spied on him. Daddy's voice got really loud. Like a lion. Roar! Didn't you hear it? I think Uncle Chance is in big trouble."

I'm nodding along with her until she's done. "Do you ever get in trouble?"

"Why would I?"

"Maybe for not doing as you're told?"

Ronnie's lips squish to one side. "Nope."

What a childhood that would be. A pang of longing

spreads through my chest. It's a useless fantasy where I came from. But there's something even the likes of me can ask for.

"Well, I could use a cup of coffee."

"Oh, yay! I'll make it for you. C'mon!" The bubbly bundle of exuberance turns and takes off faster than I can follow.

"Let me help," I plead. "There's no fooling my caffeine addiction with pretend. It has to be the real deal."

Or else I'll be even more worthless while Ronnie runs circles around me.

CHAPTER SEVEN

Byron

IT'S MID-MORNING WHEN I STEP OUT ONTO THE PORCH in search of my daughter and her new sidekick. They've been busy doing who knows what while I've been handling Chance's latest fuck-up at the auction barn. I spy them under the large oak, the bare branches doing little to block the fierce wind. Frankie is sitting on the cold ground as Ronnie skips in a circle, pretending to pat invisible heads.

"Duck, duck, duck," my little girl chimes. Her bouncy gait continues until she reaches her nanny. "Gray duck!"

Ronnie takes off at a sprint, squealing her excitement. A low groan escapes from the other player. My lips roll between my teeth to trap a chuckle. The woman is in her early twenties and struggling to get up off the frozen grass. It's clear she's reaching her limit.

And not just from hours of keeping up with Ronnie. The pair is bundled up against the late November chill.

Frankie's cheeks are noticeably red and not in the bashful shade I'd prefer to see.

"Hey, Ronnie," I call across the yard. "Time to come in for a snack."

"Yipppppeeeeee!" my daughter cheers. She grabs Frankie's arm and practically drags her toward the house. "C'mon, Frannie. Daddy is gonna feed us."

Laughter bursts out of me at hearing her nickname for the surly ex-con. Except this isn't the same badass who swung herself out of the back of a squad car. There are no sharp edges to be found at the moment. She's been worn down into a flimsy shape from Ronnie running all over her.

My little girl ditches her exhausted nanny to run full speed at me. I bend and scoop her into my arms, swinging us around. Her carefree giggle is pure joy. My chest expands as I try to recall the last time I heard it.

"Are you having fun, cupcake?"

Her small but mighty arms squeeze me tighter. "Yes! This is the best day everrrrrrrr!"

Emotion burns my eyes and I bury my face in her jacket, soaking in this moment. "That's really great to hear."

"We found her, Daddy." There's awe in her voice. "Now she's taking my sadness away."

I get choked up, struggling to breathe normally over the lump in my throat. "My sweet girl. I love you so much."

"Love you too, Daddy. Gotta wash my hands!" And then she's pulling away to race through the front door.

While I compose myself, Frankie relies heavily on the railing to help her up the porch stairs. She's going to need something stronger than coffee and fruit when the working day is done.

I hitch a thumb in the direction Ronnie went. "You're receiving high praise, little menace."

"Better be. I can't feel my legs." The redhead trudges along as if there's concrete in her boots.

It's a challenge to smother my smirk. "Rough morning?"

Green flames threaten bodily harm when she glares at me. "You should be a detective."

"Somebody needs to take a load off." I guide her inside, swerving from the foyer to the kitchen.

Frankie drags the wool hat off her head, leaving her hair a mess. Her coat is unzipped next and gets carelessly tossed on the table. A pained groan wheezes from her chapped lips as she lowers herself onto a stool. She slumps across the granite island like it's a pillowy mattress.

"It can't be that bad."

"You're right. It's worse," she whines.

"How about that," I chuckle. "Didn't think a five-year-old had the power to take you out."

"She's superhuman."

And showing off her bottomless pit of energy by running down the hall, waving her hands wildly in the air. "All clean!"

Which prompts me to open the fridge. "Cheese and crackers?"

"Yummy in my tummy!" Ronnie leaps onto the seat beside Frankie. "Are you hungry?"

The reluctant nanny forces herself to sit upright. "I'm too tired to eat."

My daughter frowns. "Do you need more coffee?"

"Always," Frankie mumbles.

I pause the snack prep to pour her a fresh cup, sliding it across the counter. "Don't say I never did anything for you."

She curls her upper lip at the plain dark roast I brewed. "Thanks."

"Problem?"

"Nope." She sips from the mug, her swallow audible purely for my benefit. "Hits the spot like a cold sore."

Ronnie sighs. "This is boring. Oh, oh! Frannie, let's have a Barbie pool party."

The redhead blinks at her through bleary eyes. "How about a nap?"

"What? No." Her giggle mocks the suggestion. "That's silly."

"I'm not cut out for this," Frankie grumbles under her breath.

My smirk takes great pleasure in her misery. "Where are the scissors that'll snip you free?"

She glares at me, but it lacks her usual wrath. "I misplaced them somewhere between Ronnie's dentist office and the ball pit."

"Frannie," my little girl whines. "I wanna keep playing."

"She needs a break," I say gently. "And you have to eat."

Ronnie bounces off her stool. "M'kay."

Frankie's jaw drops when my daughter twirls to the table. She pulls out a chair, plopping down in her usual spot. Our typical routine has gone a bit sideways, but there's always time for snacks. I choke on a laugh while delivering her plate and a glass of milk. Ronnie doesn't hesitate to dig in, clearly ravenous after a morning full of activities.

"Thanks, Daddy." My little girl gives her approval with a double thumbs-up.

"You're welcome, cupcake." There's an added pep in my step as I return to the kitchen, facing the redhead who's busy stammering.

"How…? What…?" Frankie rubs her temples. "Did you arrange the cheese and crackers into a smiley face?"

"Ronnie appreciates the added effort I put into the presentation."

Her dazed stare is comical. "Who even are you?"

I scrub over my mouth, exhaling heavily. "We're not opening that box. My backstory isn't your business."

"If I'm taking this job, I want to know who I'm working for."

That gets a bullish snort from me. "Strong morals and dependable character traits are suddenly important to you?"

Frankie's temper rebounds with a snarl. "I'd rather be freed from this forced arrangement. What's it gonna take for you to let me go?"

"A trial period. Prove that you're as shit at the job as you keep claiming."

She flips a section of matted hair over her shoulder. "Easy enough."

I narrow my eyes. "Not on purpose."

"Believe it or not, I'm trying to be good for her. I just suck at this." The fight leaves her on a weary exhale.

It's not in my nature to compliment her, but this is unavoidable. "I haven't seen my daughter look this happy in months. That's all you."

Frankie sucks in a sharp breath, her gaze sliding to where Ronnie is playing with her food before eating it. "Really? She seems so… resilient. Like nothing could slow her down."

A sour gurgle roils in my gut while I reflect on the struggles my daughter has gone through recently. "We hit a rough patch. There were days she'd barely speak or leave her room. I wasn't sure what it would take to pull her out of it. Then you showed up like the missing piece to the puzzle. She clung to you and asked you to be her mommy for a reason. That little girl sees something special in you. I'd recommend you don't turn your back on it."

This tough woman suddenly looks terrified, which has nothing to do with Ronnie finishing her snack. "Ohhhh, no. No, no, no. Don't put that pressure on me. It was a matter of convenience."

I chuckle, but it's humorless. "Whatever you gotta tell yourself, menace."

"You're just trying to get me to stay."

My nod is automatic. "Her happiness is all that matters to me. You can't leave yet. Give it a chance."

"Won't that traumatize her even more? She'll get attached and then it will be worse when I leave. If I go now, it'll be a cleaner break."

I scoff. "It's obvious you don't know Ronnie well, but you're going to."

Her focus shifts to where my little girl is sprawled out on the living room floor, mimicking the motions for a snow angel. "I don't get much of a choice, huh?"

"If you really don't want to stay, that's fine. We'll figure it out. She might forget about you eventually. But the scar of your abandonment will last forever. Don't do that to her."

"Ouch," Frankie hisses. "You pack a mean punch."

"Trust me," I drawl. "I wish she idolized anyone else. But that's not the case. We're stuck in this together. Might as well try and get along."

She groans and thumps her forehead on the granite. "Quit trying to sweet talk me."

My lips twitch. "Wouldn't dare flirt with the nanny."

Her gaze searches mine, digging deeper than I prefer. "I can't believe you convinced me to be her nanny."

"You'll stay?"

"For now," she hedges.

A smirk slants my mouth. "Gotta say I'm surprised."

"About accepting my fate?"

"Didn't take you for a doormat. You're letting Ronnie run all over you. She'll take advantage as long as you let her."

"What's the alternative?"

"Tell her no. At the very least, you can compromise. She's not going to cry if you need a moment to breathe."

"Easy for you to say," she mutters. "I can't find it in my ice-cold heart to deny her."

"You'll find a happy medium."

Frankie sighs, glancing out the window as if still planning an escape. "We need to discuss my hours. I can't be on the clock twenty-four-seven."

"Wondering how long it would take." I grab a set of keys and slide them across the counter. "For the house and your car."

She glares at the fob. "I don't have a car."

"It's an employee perk."

"How thoughtful." Her cutting tone suggests the opposite.

I straighten to my full height. "You'll be driving Ronnie around. She isn't allowed on your motorcycle."

"Speaking of, where's my bike?"

"In the garage. One of the guys dropped it off earlier."

"One of the guys," Frankie repeats. "There better not be a scratch on her."

My features harden. "I'm not careless."

She wrinkles her nose. "But you're granting me access to the palace."

"It's not my finest decision, but Bianca and Colton vouched for you. Mostly. And again, it's for taking care of Ronnie."

"Of course."

I study her in silence for a moment. My gaze rakes over her disheveled appearance. Frankie could've taken off easily enough, but chose to stick around. That tells me more than her snarky retorts.

My head cocks to the side. "Can I trust you?"

"No."

Gruff laughter rumbles from me. "At least you're honest."

She inspects her chipped nails. "Wouldn't go that far."

"I'm not gonna keep you on a leash. Just do right by Ronnie. That's all I ask."

"Message received." She goes quiet again, skewering me with her laser focus. "Don't let this inflate your ego, but you're a really good dad." The pinch in her features makes it look like that's painful to admit.

"I'm just a dad."

Frankie shoots me a flat stare. "I've met my fair share of crappy ones—my own sperm donor very much included—which makes me somewhat of an expert. Take my word for it. You're a good dad."

Warmth spreads through me, but that's from the heat kicking on. "Now who's trying to be sweet?"

"Meh." She waves off my words. "It's just an act so you'll lower your guard. I'm crooked like that."

"You're not going anywhere," I say.

"So I've heard."

A thought occurs to me, growing roots meant to last. "Do you have plans for Thanksgiving?"

Frankie cackles, losing herself to a one-sided joke. "Very funny."

"How about Christmas?"

She wipes unshed tears from her lashes. "Just me, myself, and I singing carols that have lost their cheer."

"You've got us now. We'll celebrate together."

"Doesn't that cross a line?"

"As if you're concerned about boundaries."

"I'm worried about confusing your child," she retorts.

Which gets me thinking. "Has Ronnie asked you to be her mom?"

"Not today, but it's still early."

That's somewhat of a relief. "Well, you're already living with us. Ronnie will want you at our table for family meals. We just have to make your position clear. It might take time, but she'll learn to accept it."

A loud snort spews from her. "I'm still not intruding on your holiday traditions."

"Who says we have any?"

"There's no way you're convincing me the Benson clan doesn't go all out."

Memories rush over me in a cold wave. "It hasn't felt the same since my mom left. And after Marion's passing, I'm not sure what the rest of them are doing."

Frankie flinches at the mention of my aunt's death. It was a brain aneurysm. Killed her instantly. Her absence created a hole that the town and our family will never recover from. But we do our best to live each day like it's our last, the way she would've wanted.

Which involves creating new traditions.

"Nothing fancy," I mumble. "Hope that's okay with you."

The redhead rolls her eyes. "Nope. You've lost me. Caviar and champagne or I walk."

"I'll see what I can do."

Her smile almost appears genuine. "Let's circle back to my hours before you rope me into anything else."

As if I'm including her for my benefit. "Ronnie has

school from nine until four. I need you to drop her off in the morning. The bus brings her home in the afternoon, but you have to be at the road to get her or they won't let her off. Other than that, it's flexible. Jot down a schedule you can commit to."

"What about cooking and cleaning and"—Frankie cringes as if whatever comes next is appalling—"other household responsibilities?"

"I don't expect you to do any of that unless you want to go above and beyond." When she snorts, a chuckle puffs from my lips. "It's not like you're a normal nanny."

Her wary expression scrutinizes mine. "Am I getting paid?"

A slimy wriggle turns my stomach. "Assume what you will, but I don't expect you to work for free. How does a thousand a week sound?"

She sputters. "What?"

My palms lift to stave off her upset. "Didn't mean to offend you. Can we agree on two thousand?"

Frankie's mouth works silently for several seconds. "You must be joking."

"I won't go higher until you prove yourself."

She gapes at me. "It's too much already!"

"My daughter's safety and happiness are priceless. You're responsible for both."

"Uh-huh, sure. Let me get this straight." She pauses to gather her thoughts again. "You're giving me a place to stay, a car to drive, minimal tasks, and freedom to roam while also paying me two thousand dollars a week?"

"For taking care of Ronnie," I reiterate. "I'll shadow you for the first month or so to make sure you're comfortable."

"And until you're sure this isn't a mistake." Her tone is rolling its eyes.

"Like I've said, don't fuck it up."

She rubs her temples. "This sounds… too good to be true."

"I'm not trying to trick you."

"Says the man who had the cops deliver me to him personally."

"Still mad about that?"

She leans forward and lowers her voice. "Until I return the favor."

Flames lick down my spine, gathering in my groin. "That's how it's gonna be?"

Her nod is slow, but absolute. "I might be a sucker for your daughter, but don't mistake me for a fool. I'll never be anything other than the nanny."

"Says the woman who had her hands all over me."

"To prove a point," she grinds out through clenched teeth.

"Same here." I push away from counter, leaving her to it. "But you can't deny the truth."

Frankie quirks a brow. "And what might that be?"

"We're a match made in mayhem, menace."

CHAPTER EIGHT

EVEN THROUGH THE THICK PROTECTION OF MY helmet, the wind calls to me like an escape. If only it were real. Byron Benson has me trapped. I'm pissed at myself for allowing it, but my circumstances left me in a tight spot. Now doubt and loathing plague me at every turn.

My Harley roars as I crank the throttle for more speed. A thrill shoots up my spine. This is what I call therapy. Miles pass in a blur until the drop in temperature chases me back to town.

Lights along Main Street guide me to one of the only places still open at this hour. After dinner, Byron was gracious enough to let me leave the confines of his ranch. I'm staying out until exhaustion demands otherwise.

A swanky country song is playing as I park along the curb in front of The Paddock. Warmth welcomes me when I step inside the Western-themed bar. The stares and whispers aren't as friendly. I smirk at the Saturday evening crowd. The people of Cloverleaf Meadows aren't my biggest fans. These fine folks will just have to choke on their judgment.

It's dark enough to lurk in the shadows, but I'm not afraid to be the center of attention. I strut straight for an open stool with my confidence held high. Cold shoulders surround me like walls of ice. Unfortunately for them, I'm a born and raised Minnesotan who's built to handle a frigid atmosphere.

I'm also an expert at binge-scrolling Reels and TikTok to pass the time. My thumb swipes up at a steady pace as I wait for the bartender to acknowledge me. A clip from one of my favorite reality shows plays, stalling the mindless loop and brightening my mood.

"Hey, stranger."

I startle at the greeting and swivel to confront the voice. Recognition smoothes my features into a wary grin. "Paisley. Hi."

The blonde who helped me throw together an impromptu wedding for Bianca and Colton doesn't hesitate to plop herself on the stool next to mine. "Surprised to see me?"

"I'm surprised you're talking to me."

"Ooooh, why?" She leans in as if we're about to share a secret. "Did you do something bad?"

"Depends who you ask, but that's not my concern. You're putting your spotless reputation at risk just being near me."

She tips her head back and laughs. Several people glance

over at us, probably assuming I spiked her drink. Humor brightens Paisley's gaze when she refocuses on me.

"Don't you remember who I'm married to?" Her wedding ring catches the light and almost blinds me.

I shield my face. "Watch where you're pointing that thing. Gonna poke someone's eye out."

"It's a bit over the top," she muses.

"Brody is many things, but subtle isn't one of them." My gaze slides to where the man in question is causing a scene just by standing against the wall.

Paisley follows my focus and sighs, a dreamy smile curving her lips. "Can't take him anywhere."

I flinch when a bartender appears out of nowhere and sets two cocktails in front of us. "Umm…?"

"Thanks, Ty." Paisley wiggles her fingers at the man still hovering. "Glad to see my sparkly reputation remains intact, regardless of who I order for."

"Thank your husband for me." He knocks on the counter and wanders off.

I haven't had a sip of alcohol, but my mind is spinning. "What did Brody do?"

Paisley shrugs, lifting her glass in his direction. "Probably padded the guy's pockets to make sure our drinks are never empty."

"Only one way to find out," I mumble while lifting the cocktail for closer inspection. "What's in this?"

She blinks at me. "It's an espresso martini."

My mouth waters from the name alone. "Been meaning to try one."

Her jaw goes slack. "You've never had an espresso martini?"

"They're not on the menu at my typical dives. And if they were, I wouldn't order one there."

"Well, you came to the right place tonight. The Paddock makes the best I've ever had."

I take an undignified swig, making sure to lick some chocolate powder from the rim. The explosion of flavors almost makes me choke. Sweet, rich, creamy, and strong. It's everything I love about coffee with an added kick that makes me moan.

"Holy shit," I breathe.

"Told you." Paisley's smug tone is well deserved.

My finger twirls in the air. "Keep 'em comin.'"

She does a happy-dance on her seat. "We're gonna be besties in no time."

Espresso martini spews from my mouth in a terrible waste. "Never gonna happen," I croak.

The bubbly blonde rears back, looking wounded. "Brat."

I mop up the mess I made on my leather jacket. "No offense. We're just from very different worlds."

"So?" She rolls her eyes, settling on my phone. "What're you watching?"

I shift my gaze to where the same clip is still playing on repeat. "It's a scene from *The Challenge.*"

She takes a closer look. "I've seen this one."

"Really?"

"Don't sound so shocked. CT is my ultimate crush."

I gasp. "Same! I love him and his dad-bod."

"And the seasons with Diem," she sighs. "I'll never get over it."

"Me either." My nose burns and I sniff. "I've robbed people and threatened bodily harm without an ounce of remorse, but their tragic love story slays me."

She's nodding along as if we're cut from the same cloth. "See? We have more in common than you think."

That gets a smile out of me. "A mutual infatuation with CT is bonding material."

"Not to mention we're both living with Benson men." She nudges me and I stiffen.

"Not by choice."

"Byron can't keep you against your will."

"That's what you think." I scoop up my drink and take a healthy swallow.

Paisley scoots her stool toward me until our shoulders touch. "Do you want to talk about it?"

The weight of isolation slams down on me. I struggle to pull in a full breath. It's been a long damn time since I've confided in someone.

I'm not sure I can rely on her, but I could use an ally. Concern and understanding shine in her blue eyes. That type of inner compassion is hard to fake.

"Long story short, I feel forced into this nanny position."

She makes a sound low in her throat. "I know a thing or two about getting caught in a trap."

Which refers to the arrangement Brody proposed when he needed a wife to secure ownership of Benson Farmstead.

"But that worked out for you," I argue while tossing a

look at her devoted husband. The man can't take his eyes off her.

"Eventually. The beginning was rough."

"My shit-uation isn't like that. Byron is holding me hostage for his daughter. He'd never speak to me otherwise. I'd never stick around if it weren't for her either. It's painfully obvious I don't belong there. Whatever Ronnie sees in me is fleeting. I just have to wait it out."

Paisley purses her lips. "It's not that simple. Ronnie has been going through a lot lately. There's something about you specifically that's significant to her. I doubt she's going to get over it that easily."

"Which is why I've agreed to stick around."

"You don't sound too thrilled about it."

"I don't belong," I repeat and wave at our surroundings.

"Who told you that?"

"It's a known fact. I'm bad news and shouldn't be trusted to care for a child."

"Ronnie disagrees," Paisley is quick to reply.

"She's just a kid. Her opinion shouldn't hold that much power."

She shrugs. "He'd do anything to make her happy."

A heavy sigh hunches my shoulders. "Yeah, I'm aware."

A lull that's thick with conflicted emotions slides between us until Paisley speaks. "Do you want out?"

That gives me pause, which is terrifying. That little girl already has a tight hold on me. Just thinking about leaving her makes me feel queasy. But I also loathe Byron. For numerous reasons. Unfortunately, the combination of those aren't enough to send me packing.

"I'm gonna ride it out until Ronnie comes to her senses."

Paisley grins, clearly pleased with my decision. "Maybe this is your chance to take a new lease on life."

"Maybe." But my tone lacks conviction.

"Why not? If you're not going anywhere, you might as well make the most of it."

"We'll see," I hedge.

"Are you dating anyone?"

I choke on my martini for the third time. "Stuck in this town? Absolutely not. Besides, I have more trust issues than a psychologist would know what to do with."

"Single and not ready to mingle," she breathes a laugh. "You've been through a lot."

"That's putting it mildly." But those traumatic skeletons are part of me.

Paisley's smile is warm. "I'm serious about being friends. It isn't just because we happened to be at the same bar or that you're Colton's cousin. We can meet for coffee and gush about CT."

I'm already nodding. "Two of my favorite things."

"How do you feel about *Project Runway* and *Survivor*?"

"Oh, my gosh." I slap the bar. "Quit flirting with me, woman. You're married."

The gawking from our fellow patrons cranks up a notch as she giggles loudly. "Okay, fine. I'll cool it. But we're totally doing this."

My head bobs again while I warm up to the idea of having her in my corner. "All right, thanks."

Her brow furrows. "For what?"

"Just… whatever." I motion to my drink for starters. "This might come as a shock, but I haven't had many friends."

"Bianca can vouch that I'm a pretty good one."

"I believe it."

"Glad that's settled." She lifts her glass to mine.

A resounding clink follows, announcing my agreement. "Cheers."

We finish our cocktails just as the bartender drops off a fresh round. I snort while Paisley blows a kiss at her husband. Brody is still guarding her from a distance, plastered to the wall like it's his job.

The blonde who's weaseling her way under my defenses slides off her seat. "I have to pee. Will you be okay here alone?"

Disbelief sputters from my lips. "Um, yeah. I think I can manage."

Before I can reach for my phone to resume scrolling, a cagey voice crackles from right behind me. "Thought I recognized you."

My hackles rise as I peer over my shoulder. The man is probably middle-aged, but appears older. The glint in his eyes is too familiar, like a sharp edge received from a tough life.

"Can't say the same," I tell him.

"You were part of James Keller's group."

Old habits flow through me to harden my tone. "Not sure what you're talking about."

He wags a gnarled finger in my face. "Can't fool me. You stick out like a sore thumb."

That's when a large figure materializes from the shadows. "Is there a problem here?"

My spine snaps straight at the authority in Brody's appearance. "Nope."

But then I realize the grumpy cowboy's gaze is fixed on the man standing next to me. He must sense the danger closing in and shrinks back.

"Just having a word with Frankie," he mumbles.

My eyes widen. I never told him my name. The upset must reflect in my features because Brody's glower turns lethal.

"And now you're done," he tells the stranger. "I suggest you leave before I show you the door."

The guy doesn't need to be told twice. He tucks tail and weaves his way toward the exit like a pest about to get squashed.

Paisley chooses that moment to return, glancing from her husband to me. "What did I miss?"

"Nothing," I blurt.

Rather than call me out, Brody stays silent. An upward glance freezes me on the spot. I fight the urge to squirm under his scrutiny. He doesn't relent, forcing me to explain more than I usually would.

"It's just my past trying to catch up to me. Don't worry about it."

Her eyes narrow on me. "Are you worried about it?"

"No," I scoff. But that's a bigger lie than my qualifications as a nanny, not that I'd ever admit it.

"Okay…" Paisley doesn't sound convinced as she reclaims her stool.

Brody doesn't go back to his darkened post. The wall of muscle sticks close to his wife, wrapping a protective arm around her waist. Can't say I blame him.

Trouble still clings to me like a parasite.

CHAPTER NINE

Byron

I'M SCANNING OVER THE ENTRIES FOR OUR upcoming horse sale when there's a knock on my office door. Dennis strolls in without waiting for an invite. It's not as if my uncle needs one.

"Afternoon," I greet.

The older man tips his hat while ambling to the chair across from my desk. "Got a minute?"

"Absolutely." The papers in my hands are already pushed aside. My full attention is focused on him getting settled on his seat. "What can I do for you?"

Dennis takes a moment to look around, tugging at the persistent knot in my gut. "How are things going 'round here?"

My mind immediately goes to Chance and what he could've done to fuck things up now. "Can't complain. The stock for the final fall auction looks promising. It's already bigger than last year's and registration is still open until the end of next week."

"Good. That's real good." It's obvious from his distracted tone that he didn't come here to talk about the sale numbers.

I study his attempt at nonchalance for another second. "How's everything going with you?"

"Right as rain. Retirement has really cleared up my schedule. Not much to do with the snow starting to fly."

"Want me to put you to work?"

His laughter fills the entire room. "Nah, kid. I appreciate the offer, but I'd rather keep trying my luck at pull tabs and bingo. There's actually something I wanted to ask you."

I brace for the worst. "Shoot."

"Have you heard from your dad?"

Air whistles from between my clenched teeth. Try as I might to expect it, the stench of betrayal chokes me. My father's crimes against our family are vast and detrimental. A dark cloud has loomed over us since Dad ran off, too chickenshit to face his latest—and most ruthless—attack. If I ever see him again, it'll be too soon. I tell my uncle as much.

He bobs his head in agreement. "That's what I figured, but those incidents at our properties had me curious. He might've found a new organization to hide behind and they're coming after our business for a payout."

What he's referring to are a handful of sporadic hits,

such as stealing our grain storage and snatching the spare tires from our trailer lot. It's a nuisance more than anything. But now that I'm thinking about it, they could be related to what's happened here.

"Chance had a few strange hiccups recently, but I blamed it on his shitty work ethic," I drawl.

"What happened?"

"Minor snags. Mostly scheduling errors and missing documents. Nothing I couldn't fix. Chance and his lack of focus are probably responsible."

My uncle scratches at the whiskers coating his jaw. "Keep an eye on it, yeah?"

"Already am."

"That's what I like to hear." And with that subject covered, it might be time for him to leave. Dennis stays right where he is.

I clear my throat, ignoring the discomfort in my gut. "Something else on your mind?"

A suspicious gleam flickers in his gaze. "Rumor has it that Ronnie is doing better lately."

My eyes move to the framed picture of her on my desk. Warmth spreads through my veins at the sight. She's buried in sand at the beach, smiling wide for the camera. There wasn't a cloud in the sky or a worry in the world that day.

"You could say that," I hedge.

"Does it have anything to do with that nanny you hired?"

I study my uncle for a brief pause. That sparkle in his eyes is even brighter now. It warns me to tread carefully.

"Frankie seems to be having a positive impact," I admit.

"She's Colton's cousin, right?"

"That's right."

"Are you concerned that she was part of James Keller's crew?"

"Are you?" I counter.

Dennis chuckles and reclines deeper in his chair. "I'm not the one who invited her into my home."

"Ronnie was very insistent."

"I have a daughter who thinks she knows what's best too. Doesn't mean she actually does."

A casual shrug is my initial response. "Frankie is on somewhat of a probation period. I haven't left her alone at the house with Ronnie. What she does on her own time isn't as big of a concern. If she chooses to take my trust for granted and steals from me, I'll gladly hand her over to the cops."

"Wouldn't be the first time, hmm?"

"That served its purpose." And I smirk recalling Frankie's reaction.

Dennis grins too. "Don't blame ya for tryin' to fence her in. She's a beautiful woman."

My humor sobers. "Is she? I hadn't noticed."

He wags a knobby finger at me. "I'm old, but not blind. It'll be nice for you to have a feminine touch in the house again."

I scowl. "The nanny is for Ronnie. It's her job to make my daughter happy. Once Frankie no longer does that, she's free to go."

He leans forward and pats my fist. "I understand, son. My Marion just passed. I can't imagine ever moving on, but I'm near the end of my time. You've got decades left to live. No reason to spend them alone."

My heart clenches. Dennis shares the pain of grieving a spouse. It's been almost six years since I lost Nina. I haven't attempted to move on or fill the gaping hole she left behind. All of my effort went into being the best father I could be for our little girl.

Frankie put an end to my dry spell, but it was meaningless. Heat floods me and I curse her name. It's just the lack of sex, or physical contact in general. I went too long without intimacy. That's all. She's nothing special.

"My daughter is my sole priority," I state evenly.

"Sure, sure. Strictly professional with the nanny," Dennis concedes. "Will we see you at Thanksgiving?"

I shake my head. "Bianca invited us, but we're going to stay home this year. Hope that's okay."

He waves me off. "It's good to stay put and start your own traditions. You've got your hands full over there."

I pinch the bridge of my nose as he changes tactics. "Yeah, I've got a bit of a flight risk to deal with."

"Can I give you a piece of advice?"

"You're gonna tell me either way." My tone is a grumble, but there's no anger behind it.

"Smart man," he chuckles. "Choose to take it or not.

Frankie is a wild card and it shows. If she wants to run free, you gotta let her. She'll never be satisfied otherwise."

"Like I said, she won't be sticking around after Ronnie is done with her. Until then, I think we've reached an understanding."

My uncle stands, stretching his back. "Then you've got it taken care of. Keep up the good work, kid."

CHAPTER TEN

Frankie

Ronnie's voice startles me out of my creative headspace. "What're you doing?"

"Sweet Jeeee-pers!"

I drop the permanent marker onto the tile. It leaves a long black line that's probably not coming out. My lips curl into a grin. Works for me.

The little girl scoots closer, reminding me that her impromptu nap is over and she's waiting for an answer.

I reclaim the fallen Sharpie. "Just doing some… uh, coloring."

"On my daddy's boots?" She plops down beside me in the entryway.

"Yep." My limited artistic abilities get busy doodling a heart.

Ronnie leans over to inspect my design so far. "Why?"

"They're a bit boring." I hold up the left Tecovas that's still untouched. "Wanted to make them fancy."

But that's a lie. This is just a petty way to take a stab at Byron. These are the only boots I've seen him wear. I'm sure the leather is broken in just right. Now he'll have to walk around with my handiwork on his feet.

"Can I help?"

My hand pauses at the innocent question. "Ummm…"

"Pretty pleeeeaaaase? I'm gonna make Daddy's boots super prettiful. Promise!"

It's impossible to deny her, especially when she sticks out her bottom lip and whines. The wounded puppy look spreads to her eyes to secure my undoing.

I pass her a metallic silver marker. It's bright and extra obnoxious against the supple leather. If I'm going to land myself in hot water for this, we might as well make a big splash together. Ronnie snatches the unblemished left boot and settles in for destruction.

While putting a massive stick figure front and center, she glances over at the block letters I'm writing across the top of the other one. "What's that say?"

"Frankie wins," I chirp.

"Wins what?"

There's a brief hesitation from me, filled with plausible explanations. "I win bragging rights for coloring this boot."

"Oooooh," she croons. "Do I win too?"

"Of course, kiddo. Want me to write it for you?"

"Uh-huh. Put it here." She drags her finger along the side.

"Perfect spot. Everyone will see it." I grip onto the sole and get started. "The letters are just outlines. You can fill them in when I'm done."

Ronnie watches me write her name in huge font. "This is soooo cool. It's like tattoos for Daddy's boots."

"Let's hope our designs don't wash away."

The little girl frowns. "They gotta stay forever."

"I'm sure they will. If not, we can redo them."

Ronnie gasps and sits up straight. "Will you draw on me next?"

"Ummm…" I glance at her flawless skin. "I'm not sure that's a good idea."

"Why not?"

"We should ask your dad." Wrecking his boots is bad enough. I don't need to kick the hornet's nest.

Ronnie's gaze shifts to the ink decorating my arms. "Okay, fine. But I wanna be just like you when I grow up."

My stomach clenches and I almost drop my marker again. "No, sweetie. I'm a hot mess express. You don't want a seat on the train. Toot, toot." I laugh when she stares blankly at me. "But I'll take you wherever you want to go."

She sighs and it's a pleased sound. Her tongue pokes out from the corner of her mouth as she gets back to coloring Byron's boot. I'm about to do the same when her voice stops me cold.

"Is this what it's like to have a mommy? My heart is smiling."

Mine stutters as I gawk at her. My mouth opens and

closes uselessly. Words fail me for several seconds and then the truth spills free.

"I'm not sure, kiddo. My mom has never been around."

Her wide eyes lock onto me while she absorbs this similarity that's shared between us. Except… our situations couldn't be more different.

I'd bet the Benson fortune that Ronnie's mother would give anything to be here with her today. Mine abandoned me at her first opportunity. She ditched me at my sperm donor's doorstep. He wasn't much better. At least he had the decency to drop me off at his brother's compound. James Keller wasn't much of a father figure, but he kept me alive. That's where I met Walker and the rest of my dysfunctional family.

Ronnie is looking at me expectantly. That silent plea does something to me. I have the sudden urge to hug this precious child, to shield her from the ugliness that threatens to dull the brightest sparkle. She deserves nothing but sunshine and rainbows.

As I return her unwavering focus, I realize we're bonded at a depth I can't fully comprehend yet.

"We'll figure it out as we go, okay?"

Ronnie tips her head, mulling that over. Her tiny shoulders bounce after a moment. "Okay."

And then she resumes the task of decorating her dad's boot as if my foundation hasn't just been cracked to its core. If she wants to accept me into her inner circle, I'm not going to stop her. But my fingers shake while I try to act normal.

I'm not sure how long we've been drawing in

concentrated silence when heavy footsteps boom from down the hall. It's enough time to resurrect my initial purpose. Is it immature? Yes. Did that stop me? No. As I add the final touches, devious delight tugs my lips skyward until I resemble a clown.

"Ronnie?" Byron's voice echoes from where he's been holed up in his office.

"Over here, Daddy!" Her giggle should set off several alarm bells. But just in case, she adds, "We have a surprise for you."

Her father halts in his tracks once he gets a good look at what we've done.

His perfect angel launches to her feet, thrusting the doodled Tecovas at him like a proud artist. "Look, Daddy! We made your boots prettiful. Do you love it?"

Byron just stands there like a statue I can shamelessly admire. What can I say? The grumpy cowboy is hot, especially when he's not talking.

"Uhhh," he finally utters. "That's… really something."

"Try them on!" Ronnie grabs the other boot from me, putting them both in front of her dad.

When Byron comprehends what I wrote, his shock tightens into a glare aimed directly at my waiting grin. "Real cute."

I get on my feet to eliminate his power position, but he still towers over me. "The big bow stretching across the back might be my favorite part."

"Oh, oh!" Ronnie points at a pair of adorable blobs she

made. "That's Darla and Dottie. They're chasing squirrels. Such silly pups."

"Uh-huh, very silly." Byron slips on the boots like the devoted father he is. "Better than ever."

His little girl squeals and latches onto him for a giddy squeeze. Her tiny index finger traces a line down his nose, swooping off the tip and landing for a tap on his chin. Byron does the same to her in return. It appears to be a meaningful gesture I don't understand and now isn't the time to pry.

Ronnie claps her palms against her dad's cheeks, giving him an exuberant shake. "I knew you'd like them!"

"How could I not? You made them special for me." Byron hugs her until she wiggles free. "Was this your idea, cupcake?"

"Nope! Frankie was coloring while I was sleepin' on the couch and then I woke up and asked if I could help."

When Byron straightens, his wrath pins me in place. "Do you think this is funny?"

"Obviously," I deadpan.

"I didn't hire you to be a bad influence on my daughter."

"Shouldn't have hired me then."

When Ronnie twirls out of earshot, Byron dips down to growl at me. "You're gonna pay for this, little menace."

I arch a brow. "Take it out of my check. I'm still getting paid, right?"

He seethes, but straightens when his little girl is within listening range again. "Are you complaining about money?"

"Asks the person who's never had to worry about it," I mutter.

Byron slips a credit card from his wallet. "Use that for whatever you need."

I pluck the sleek plastic from between his fingers. "You trust me not to go over your limit?"

"I dare you to try reaching it."

The narrowing of my eyes accepts his challenge. "Careful, stud. If you mess with the viper, she'll bite."

"Do your worst," he taunts. His gaze drops to his boots and a smirk slants his lips. "It's adorable when you try."

"Daddy! Guess what?" Ronnie pulls at his sleeve, done being on the sidelines. "Frannie is gonna give me lotsa tattoos. Just like you and her. I'm gonna have pictures on my skin too!"

If looks could kill, Byron would bury me alive in the back forty.

But I ignore the death threat by inspecting the sharp points of my matte black nails. "Adorable, right?"

CHAPTER ELEVEN

MY SHARP GAZE SEARCHES THE DIMLY LIT INTERIOR of Sip in the Stacks. According to my bank notifications, a certain redhead just paid a ridiculous amount for what this place has to offer. That approved charge led me straight to her. It's almost like Frankie wants me to hunt her down.

When the first floor doesn't expose her location, I stalk to the second level. That's where she's curled up on an oversized leather chair in a semi-secluded nook. Tall bookshelves provide the illusion of an escape from the outside world.

Frankie is captivated by the paperback that's spread open on her lap. That allows me to watch her undetected for a minute. Auburn hair the shade of roaring flames cascades around her like a shield. She's beautiful in a way that's untouchable. If I dare to get too close, I'll immediately regret it.

That doesn't mean I can't admire her from a safe

distance. Tight denim and leather protects most of her from my stare. She wiggles a pen between her fingers while reading, completely unaware of her audience. This appears to be her element and I'm getting sucked in.

Rather than surrender to the pull, I force my attention to shift. There's a large drink on the table next to her with entirely too much whipped cream. A bag overflowing with craft supplies is on the floor. Several books are piled in a tote. I find myself contemplating how she'll get all this home on her bike. But she's nothing if not resourceful.

That thought gives me pause. It's only then I recall how little I actually know about her. Maybe it's time to change that. For Ronnie's sake, of course.

"Is that the best you can do, menace?"

Frankie startles at my voice in the otherwise quiet space. Her shocked expression smooths over almost instantly, replaced with her typical indifference. "Is that how you usually greet a woman? No wonder you're single."

I almost laugh. She always has a snarky comeback waiting for me. It's impressive.

Without being invited to sit, I take the empty chair that's angled toward hers. "What're you doing here?"

Frankie huffs. "Minding my own business, which is more than I can say for you."

There's no controlling my laughter now. It's loud and booming and gains the attention of a couple who are several hideouts away. "Call me curious, but I couldn't help wondering how someone spends four hundred dollars at a coffee shop."

"They sell a lot more than coffee," she retorts like the crack of a whip.

"And that makes it more reasonable?"

"Obviously." She suddenly goes still. "Where's Ronnie?"

"Took you long enough," I scold. "She's at a sleepover. I just dropped her off."

"Why didn't I hear about it?"

"You're a shit nanny."

Frankie's flinch is incredibly satisfying. "Gonna fire me?"

"Nah, but you're gonna tell me what you spent my money on."

"Thought I could use it for whatever I need?"

"Spit it out already." The underlying rumble in my tone reveals my growing irritation.

Her eyes roll hard enough to pop out of their sockets. "I bought a round for the whole place."

"You bought a round… at a coffee shop?"

She shrugs. "Figured it would earn some brownie points from the locals."

"At my expense."

"You offered," she reminds.

"Not what I had in mind."

"Should've thought of that before handing it over without limits. You're practically begging me to max out your card."

"I dare you to try."

"There you go again," she taunts.

"Dammit!" I bellow in return, frustration bubbling over in an uncontrolled wave. "Always got something to say."

"That's why you pay me the big bucks." She mimics rubbing cash between her thumb and first two fingers.

"I'm not paying you to ruin my boots."

Frankie doesn't so much as blink at my swerve in subject, keeping her neutral expression locked in. "More like improved them." Her fiery green gaze inspects the doodles branded into custom leather that can't be easily replaced. "Are you actually mad?"

"Would it matter either way?"

She makes a noncommittal noise. "If you're asking me, it looks like you're wearing them with pride. Ronnie worked hard and you're showing it off. Just one more symbol of ideal fatherhood."

I stare at the designs covering my boots, refusing to acknowledge her assumption. "Why'd you do it?"

"I'm a shit nanny," she quips.

"What does that have to do with purposely destroying my property?"

"Just delivered the next notch in our revenge plot."

"This"—I tap my heels together—"was to get back at me?"

"Sound familiar?" Her left shoulder hitches. "You made the rules, or lack thereof."

"Revenge," I mumble. "Such a fickle concept."

"It's your turn. Take it or leave it."

I scowl. "You're responsible for taking care of my daughter. This isn't a game."

"Could've fooled me."

Our salty bickering is going nowhere fast. My gaze

drifts, searching for even ground. I jut my chin at the book still in her lap.

"What're you reading?"

"Has anyone ever told you that you're nosy?" She tries to hide the cover, but I catch the title.

"*Art Projects for Kids*," I recite.

Her complexion blazes red-hot to match her hair. "Couldn't hurt to be better at my job. Just said so yourself."

My heart thuds, and then begins racing. So much for avoiding bumpy subjects. Dammit, I cannot get soft. This woman is a snake. She called herself one.

"I take it back," I mutter. "You're not a shit nanny."

"That means so much coming from you." The drip of sarcasm in her voice is worse than a leaky faucet.

"Believe it or not, I'm willing to admit when I'm wrong."

"Real nice." Once again, the jab in her tone betrays her.

"Can you say the same, menace?"

Her lips flatten into an irked line. "I'm rarely wrong."

"Is that attitude what landed you behind bars? Remind me," I drawl. "How many times have you been arrested?"

"Don't you have better things to do than bother me?"

"That doesn't answer my question," I volley.

"You didn't answer mine."

"Ladies first." I tip the brim of my cowboy hat.

Frankie snorts as if the concept of me being a gentleman is outrageous. "It's a bit late for a background check."

"I'm curious, remember?" Which serves to remind me that we're little more than strangers and I had a hankering to fix that. "We can take this opportunity to get to know each other. That being said, how familiar are you with the inside of a jail cell?"

"Three stints worth mentioning." She holds up as many fingers, but then lowers the outer two. The middle one is left to flip me off.

"What's the worst crime you've committed?"

"When do I get to ask the questions?"

"After you provide me with a satisfying answer."

Her gaze burns into mine and I'm sure she's picturing bodily harm. "Armed robbery and intimidation were my specialties. I got locked up for almost two years after a job went sideways. Haven't stolen shit since. Happy?"

"Nah, but I appreciate your honesty."

"My turn." She straightens, pinning me with too much intensity. "What do you do for fun?"

"Work."

"How do you unwind from that?"

"Spend time with my daughter. I don't need more."

She makes a thoughtful noise. "What would you be doing if you weren't here?"

Nothing worthwhile. Not that I'll tell her that.

For whatever reason, I was compelled to follow Frankie's trail after getting that notification. Going back to an empty house didn't appeal to me. My office at the auction barn would've been worse. This option isn't as daunting. Not sure what that says about me.

"I'd probably be out feeding the horses right about now." Not a complete lie.

But Frankie's squint doesn't appear satisfied. "Why don't you date?"

"Not interested in adding more complications to my schedule." That's also mostly true.

"Do you have any friends?"

I grunt, ready to put her on blast for being a brat. Talk about a bold assumption. But the question gives me pause. The truth is that most of them quit calling after Ronnie was born. A few stuck around to support me through the struggle of adapting to parenthood while simultaneously grieving my wife, but those connections are long gone now.

A weary sigh breezes from my lips. It's pathetic to admit that I don't have a social life to speak of beyond my daughter's activities. I'm only thirty-four, but most days I feel ancient. Disconnected. Irrelevant. Maybe the lack of adult interactions is finally getting to me.

Should I give her the power those truths will provide?

Frankie raises her brows, twisting the knife of her latest low blow.

"None that I like," I find myself admitting.

"What about Chance?"

"My brother?"

"Do you know another?"

I scoff. "We don't really get along."

"Why's that?" Her head tilts as if she really wants to know.

Which is why my guard lowers further. "He doesn't like me. I'm more of a parent than a sibling."

"Have you tried bridging the gap?"

"There's no point. I'm his boss too, which only makes things worse. Besides that, we're too different." And those clashes far exceed the nine years separating us.

Frankie nods slowly. "Walker is my polar opposite. Most of the time, I can't believe we're related."

My eyes narrow as I watch her from under the shadow of my hat. "Have you gone to visit him in prison?"

"Just once, shortly after that whole ordeal. He chose his path. I've made my peace with that." Her shrug appears too casual for the topic of conversation.

"Turning over a new leaf, huh?"

"Trying," she mumbles, lifting the crafting book for emphasis.

"She'll appreciate the effort."

"Do you?"

I almost laugh. "Are you that desperate for approval?"

Frankie's features harden into stone. "I thought we were mending fences. My mistake."

A gruff sound of disbelief scrapes from me. "You'll have to try harder than that to win me over, but it's a decent start."

"Listen," she exhales. "Believe what you want, but I care about Ronnie. She's proved to feel pretty strongly about me too. That's not something I've had before. Nobody has ever fought for me. I've never been wanted beyond selfish means." Another loud sigh. "Now that I've experienced a tiny taste, I don't know how I survived without. But I guess that's what I've been doing. Barely surviving. I won't jeopardize the gift she's giving me or take it for granted or do anything to hurt her. At least not on purpose. A girl could get used to such genuine kindness. You can trust me not to run from it."

There's an unmistakable clench in my chest. I avert my gaze, avoiding the unmasked vulnerability in hers. Something tells me Francesca Keller doesn't expose weakness often. That knowledge sparks emotions I haven't felt in years.

"Good speech," I mutter.

Frankie scoffs and crosses her arms, rebuilding the wall between us. "Are you done bothering me?"

"Hardly."

"I'm certain you have better things to do." The defensive hostility in her tone doesn't penetrate my thermal flannel or motivate me to leave.

"Why are you in such a hurry to get rid of me?"

"Aside from the fact we've been arguing since you sat down?" She mutters under her breath about stubborn cowboys who need to read the room.

That could be taken as an invitation. But fuck, I shouldn't tease this temptress. She's already proven how quickly she can unravel me. That doesn't stop the words from free-falling.

"Are you uncomfortable, menace?" It's not the first time I've asked.

"No," Frankie grinds out.

"Do I give you butterflies?"

"Get real," she guffaws. "Fuck butterflies."

"Never felt 'em?"

She slices across her neck. "I don't believe in that fluffy shit and I don't understand why you're still here."

The answer to that is too complicated, becoming more complex the longer I stay. It's almost painful to admit that talking to Frankie is a tolerable way to pass the time. Dare I say enjoyable? Heat gathers in my gut, preparing to travel below the belt. Nope, that's going too far again.

"Just keepin' tabs on you and your spending habits."

"Uh-huh, which we've discussed. I've been reprimanded and put in my place. Consider the task complete. You're free to leave."

I glance around the empty space. Everybody else is gone or moved to the first floor. "It's getting late."

"All the more reason to get gone."

"You're the only one left."

"That's how I prefer it." Her stern voice shuts down any attempt to linger.

"Okay, fine. Message received. I can tell when I'm not wanted."

"Hold on a damn minute." Frankie studies me under a punishing scope. The force of her scrutiny locks my limbs in place. "You're lonely."

I scoff. "Try again."

"No way," she breathes. "That's totally it. You want company, even if it's mine. Who's desperate now, big boy?"

"Careful," I warn.

But she doesn't listen. "Are you looking to add benefits to this… arrangement? After getting a feel in the alley, I could be easily convinced."

A throb fondles my cock and my face goes up in flames. I leap off the chair like my ass is burning too. If her intention is to rattle me, she's succeeding. There might be smoke wafting from my soles at the rate I'm tucking tail.

At the last second, ingrained charm gets the best of me and I tip my hat at her. "I'd say this was nice, but that'd be a lie."

Frankie's cackle chases me down the stairs. "Keep telling yourself that."

CHAPTER TWELVE

A BLEND OF SAVORY AROMAS PAMPERS MY NOSTRILS as I inhale deeply. It's mouthwatering and almost distracts me from the pressure brewing in my gut. Instead, the knot twists tighter until I struggle to breathe. My regular don't-give-a-shit mode abandoned me as the sun was rising over the pastured horizon.

Byron notices my knee bouncing under the table. "Problem?"

I bite my lip and force my muscles to relax. "Nope, just hungry."

Which is a big, fat, juicy lie. If we were eating turkey, my dishonesty would steal the spotlight from the main course. In truth, my nerves are cranked to the max as if I'm being questioned for murder charges. The jumble in my stomach suggests it's worse than that.

And the why doesn't make sense when I shift on the

cushioned seat, trying to get comfortable. The three of us have shared many meals together at this point. Thanksgiving is a holiday and special occasion, but Byron and Ronnie aren't treating it as such. Not that I have any clue what it looks like in a traditional format. But festive decorations didn't explode all over the house. There isn't a grand plan or five-course feast in sight.

The little girl hasn't acquired a taste for roasted meat. Lasagna and garlic bread are on the menu. Our place settings are the same as usual aside from autumn-themed napkin rings that Ronnie made at school. It's casual and chill, yet my heart is racing.

"There's a rumble in my tummy," Ronnie sings. "Gonna need somethin' yummy."

"Almost ready," Byron says from the kitchen.

Baked cheese and Italian spices waft toward me after he closes the oven. His movements are practiced and collected. I envy that calmness. This is his natural environment and he's strutting around like a proud peacock.

"Such a great dad," I mumble under my breath.

Ronnie abandons her dolls, giving me her full attention. "He's the bestest."

Byron pauses while putting bread in a basket. "What's that?"

Before his daughter can call me out, I reach for a distraction. "Want some salad?"

"Ooooh, yes! We worked super hard on it."

I almost laugh. "You're very good at mixing the ingredients together."

"That's 'cause you cut 'em up just right." Ronnie mimics the fine act of chopping vegetables.

The urge to preen drops the tension in my shoulders and I'm able to scoop the salad without trembling. What can I say? My knife skills are worthy of praise. Byron doesn't miss the opportunity to interject.

"Frankie is an expert at slicing and dicing. That's how she gets the bad guys."

The little girl stares at me like I invented sugar and puppies. "My superhero."

And cue a fresh wave of jitters. It's been a hot minute since she's put me on that lofty pedestal. I'm definitely not deserving. But the stars in her eyes are bold and bright. Lopping off my own hand would be less painful than dulling her sparkle.

"You're the sweetest," I croon. "I'm a better person because of you, kiddo."

"Really?"

"Yep." And I leave it at that. My past doesn't have a seat at this table.

"Okay," Byron says to get our attention. "The lasagna is ready."

Ronnie rushes to finish her salad. "Yippppeeee! I've got lotsa room."

"The pan is really hot. It'll be easier to serve on the stove."

"Message received." I collect our plates and bring them to where he's standing.

"Thank you."

I almost startle at his words. Between the dark severity in his stare and the deep notes of his timbre, it's obvious that he's not just talking about the dishes. I'm suspended in his magnetic hold for several rapid beats of my heart. We don't look away, somehow tethered together by this unknown gravity. A shiver races up my spine like an icy finger. It's enough to free me from his trance.

"It's nothing," I whisper.

"It's everything."

Now I'm stunned speechless. Meanwhile, Byron gives each of us a heaping portion as if he didn't just knock me sideways. Gratitude is such a simple, often overlooked concept. Most don't give it a second thought. It's monumental to me, especially coming from him.

There's a sudden burn along the bridge of my nose. The last thing I need is to cry in front of Byron. Just the other day, we were heckling each other. Tonight, I can barely look at him without fidgeting.

My jaded exterior is usually reliable, but right now, it's nowhere to be found. An onslaught of doubt pours over me like a fat storm cloud. What am I doing here, pretending to belong? It's a joke. I'm a fraud.

While ignoring the lump in my throat, I drop my gaze and snag the filled plates. I scurry back to the table as if in a hurry to stuff my face. In all honesty, my appetite shrivels with each passing moment.

"Someone's in a hurry to dig in," Byron jokes while following close behind.

Like so many times before, I'm mesmerized as he

swoops down to press a kiss on Ronnie's head. She snuggles into his side for a quick embrace. Tingles spread across my chest as I take it in from afar. Their affection is warm and effortless and awe-inspiring. It's also foreign to me. Just one more reminder that I'm an outsider.

But they chose to include me in their small circle, which is more significant than my intrusive thoughts.

Byron lifts his chin at my untouched food, interrupting my spiral. "Well?"

"I'm waiting for you to sit." And drag my gaze away from the tender scene he creates with his daughter.

"Considerate," he grunts, taking his seat at the head of the table. "But we aren't that formal. You should know that by now."

Heat crawls up my neck. I pin him with a glare and blindly load my fork with what smells like the best lasagna in creation. "Prepare to be judged on this recipe you've been bragging about. I'm not a kind critic."

My features flatline into a stony mask as I slap down some much needed snark and sass. That's more like it. I'm just off my game.

But that freshly reclaimed bravado vanishes the instant the food touches my tongue.

One bite is packed with more flavor than I can comprehend. I flutter my lashes while instantly surrendering. The layers mix together in a tasteful burst that's meant to render me senseless. It's saucy and melty and more decadent than lasagna has the right to be. That's my only excuse for what happens next.

"Ohhhhh. Myyyyy. Gahhhhh," I moan loudly.

Ronnie lunges toward me, ready to leap across the table to my rescue. "Are you okay, Frannie?"

"Uh, yep. It's just… um," I grapple for an excuse, but fail against the savory punch. "Gosh, you know what? This is soooo delicious."

The little girl bobs her head with enthusiasm. "Daddy's a super good cook. My tummy is happy. Yum, yum."

"Mhmm," I agree, my mouth packed full.

Byron smirks. His cocky expression is well earned. "It's my mother's famous lasagna. One of the few things she left behind before leaving."

That truth bomb hits far too close to home. I pause chewing. In most cases, the food might turn to ash in my mouth. This meal is just too damn good.

"At least she was good for something," I comment absently.

His smile twists into a much sadder version. "Got that right."

There I go, soiling the positive energy. I swallow hard. "Let's brighten the mood, hmm? Tell me about your favorite Thanksgiving memory, Ronnie."

"Being with you and Daddy," she answers quickly.

"But this one is still happening," I laugh.

"Still counts," she insists. "It's already my favorite 'cause you're here. There's three of us now. It's almost like I have a mommy, but I know you're just my nanny. You're gonna be my nanny forever, m'kay?"

Ah, shit. There goes my bottom lip. The wobble would

put a drunk girl to shame. I blink rapidly, trying to reel in the emotional mess that's consumed my mental state.

Byron gawks at me like I've sprouted horns. I don't blame him. This is very uncharacteristic for me.

And Ronnie isn't done. "I love you, Frannie. Like this." She leans toward her dad and traces a line down the straight slope of his nose, tapping his chin to end the symbolic gesture. "That's how we show our love."

I've seen them exchange the action on a few occasions, but didn't understand the meaning. "Oh, my. What a very special gesture. Did you come up with that?"

"Daddy did," Ronnie explains. "He started doing it when I was just a baby. Maybe I can do it to you someday." The hope in her voice is my undoing.

Just when I thought I'd contained my tears, a single drop sneaks out and paints my cheek. I clear my throat, but there's still a frog stuck in there. "I'm not sure what to say," I croak.

"Your acceptance is plenty," Byron utters almost gently.

I find myself nodding. "I'd really like that, kiddo. Thank you."

"Welcome," Ronnie chirps.

Her father and I might not get along, but this little girl is determined to steal my heart. I just might let her.

"I'm not sure anyone has really loved me before," I add, almost as an afterthought.

Her adorable face screws up into disappointment. "How's that possible?"

My shrug is casual, trying to play off the deep wounds

that have scarred me. "I didn't have a normal childhood. Not even close. Believe it or not, this is the first Thanksgiving I've ever celebrated."

Shock slackens their features in unison. It's tough for them to picture not having a tight-knit family. For me, that's just the way it was. I didn't know an alternative existed until I was much older. I'm still coming to terms with that.

This is what it's like to live in a home filled with compassion and warmth. I'm not sure I'll ever get used to it. I probably shouldn't. The moment I do, it'll get ripped away like everything else.

"Good thing you're ours now." The relief in Ronnie's tone has the power to make me sob.

"Yeah," I breathe, eager to grasp onto this reality with both arms while it embraces me. "It's a very good thing."

CHAPTER THIRTEEN

AFTER THANKSGIVING IS IN THE REAR VIEW, I'M ABLE to focus on the work straight ahead. The turnout for our December sale might be the largest to date. That's really saying something since most don't want another animal to feed in winter.

The Wyoming rancher I'm dealing with smooths his bushy mustache, flipping through the thick catalog. "You're tellin' me every single one of these horses are solid?"

"All two hundred," I assure the man. "Quality stock is tough to find at a decent price, but Benson Farmstead delivers."

"Your reputation piqued my interest. Had to see it with my own eyes." Which means more than he knows. He drove twelve-plus hours just for this event.

"Appreciate you making the trip."

"Lookin' forward to you proving it was worth it."

My gaze slides to the narrow fenced-in area that's used as our auction block. Metal panels are arranged in a long rectangle from one side of the bidding room to the other. It's just about time for number one to enter.

"Find me after and I'll tally your purchases myself."

His laughter booms around the domed shape of the building. "You're confident. I appreciate that."

"You're about to see why. If you'll excuse me."

And then I walk the length of the pen, taking a final sweep to make sure we're ready to go without a hitch. The first group is lined up in the alley that connects this section to the stall barn and indoor arena. Ring crew and callers are perched in their designated places. From what I can see, we're set to have a very lucrative day.

Dennis sends me an approving nod from where he's talking to the mayor. Others wave or tip their hats as I pass. They bump into each other in the cramped aisle just to make a path for me. It's just that packed.

Every chair has an ass planted in it, leaving many to stand in whatever space they can find. Three walls of stadium seating isn't enough, but at least it provides a good look at the action. Even those sitting up in the nosebleeds near the rafters can participate. The full house is a sense of pride expanding my chest.

There's a buzz in the air, but it's not loud. This is the calm before the chaos. The moments where this doesn't feel like a job. Anticipation thrums through my veins while I prepare for the shift.

It happens when the announcer begins his welcome

speech. "And now, we've got quite the prize to kick things off."

Silence descends in a ripple, quiet enough to hear the rolling door slide open. A palomino stud prances in as if he knows all eyes are on his exceptional bloodlines. Enough famous quarter horses are stacked from top to bottom on his pedigree to make any breeder see dollar signs. He's going to go for a pretty penny and the opening bid proves it.

The auctioneer starts his rapid rambling at ten-thousand, which is quickly raised. Paddles lift faster than the callers can track. The rider shows off the stallion's agility with sliding stops and fast pivots. Shouts erupt from the crowd, growing louder as the palomino performs more tricks. The scent of sawdust and competitive energy whip across the room. It's an addictive thrill. As the gavel strikes down, I slip free from the high stakes through a side door.

"*SOLD* to the lady in blue for one-hundred fifty thousand!" the auctioneer bellows.

And we're off.

I smirk and go in search of my girls.

Whoa! That thought grinds me to a halt. Frankie isn't my anything. I don't want her to be. It's best I remember that. But this past week took me by surprise. I almost feel drawn to her, which is a very slippery slope.

Attraction is one thing. My dick and brain can agree that she's appealing. Genuine interest beyond that requires treading across a loaded minefield that'll blow my balls off with one misstep. Even so, I can't help wondering about the benefits she offered when we were at Sip in the Stacks.

Maybe she was just fucking with me to get a reaction. Or there's a possibility we could agree on exchanging more than insults.

While I'm debating if entertaining the idea is worth the risk, I catch sight of Chance in front of the bleachers next to the indoor arena. His stare appears to be locked on a very specific target. He's solely focused on that spot, not hearing me approach.

I clap him on the shoulder. "Who's captured your eye?"

Chance rips his gaze away from the point of interest. "Uh, nothing. Just, um… hanging out."

The fact he can't look at me is extremely telling. I search the section he'd been watching. My visual scan lands on Gemma Keaton, which kicks my brows to the clouds. Paisley's younger sister hasn't been seen much on the scene since her accident last year. From what I'd heard last, she switched colleges and was headed in a very different direction.

"Is she getting back into the circuit?"

Chance is looking everywhere but at the raised portion of bench where Gemma sits. "Who?"

The urge to slap him upside the head twitches my palm. "Didn't you used to be friends? I thought you were close."

"Years ago," he grumbles.

"What happened?"

His upper lip curls in a sneer. "I could ask the same about your boots."

Amusement rumbles from me as I admire the sloppy designs from Ronnie and Frankie. The redhead was right.

This is an improvement. I might go as far as saying they're my most prized possession. Not that I'll admit it aloud.

"Nice deflection." I honestly couldn't care less about his personal life except he's slacking on the job. "Go figure out your shit and get back to work."

"Fuck off, boss."

I bristle at his angry retort. Damn, that girl must really have her hooks in deep. He's going to pay for that later, but not while our customers are an audience. The little prick turns and stalks off toward the gate where upcoming auction entries gather. That's where he's supposed to be getting horses lined up in order. Such a slacker.

I grumble under my breath about mixing blood and business. Benson Farmstead is built on family, but my brother is a weak link. He needs to get his shit together before I fire him, regardless of his last name.

Those concerns flee when I notice Frankie and Ronnie at the far end of the arena. My daughter and another little girl are twirling circles together while her nanny is unnaturally still. Her rigid body language is giving off all sorts of defensive vibes. One glance at the redhead's icy expression raises my guard higher. She's spooked and I want to know why.

"Where's the threat, little menace?"

Frankie's glare remains fixed straight ahead. "It's not your problem."

My exhale is worn thin. The attitude I'm receiving from left to right is tiring. "We're back to that?"

"We never left," she volleys.

I rock on my doodled boots, trying to ignore the ache in my chest. This isn't the same woman who began thawing for me on Thanksgiving. One step forward is quickly followed by ten in reverse. Her walls are back up and reinforced with steel. Our combative dynamic suggests I drop it. That's the easy way out.

But since she's important to Ronnie, I'm determined to squash the bug that's crawled up her ass. I hunt for the source of her distress, over rows of nameless faces. There are three men halfway up the bleachers with their eyes on Frankie. My glare strongly suggests their leers move elsewhere, not that they're paying a lick of attention to me.

"Friends of yours?" I ask the spitfire next to me.

She doesn't turn to confirm their identities. "They wish."

"What's that supposed to mean?"

As far as I know, her crew has fallen apart. Maybe not entirely. There could be a few stragglers.

Her reshaped edges threaten to maim me when she says, "My reputation haunts me."

I grunt. She's spouting to the spigot. The battle to shed accusations and assumptions is often lost. My father's crimes and bad decisions are stuck to me like a tattoo of an ex's name.

"Did they approach you?" I take a meaningful look at where Ronnie is playing three feet away.

"Not here."

"What aren't you telling me?"

Frankie huffs. "I've got it under control."

"That's not comforting."

Her shrug brushes off my concern. "That's your problem."

"No, you're my problem."

"Gonna fire me?" She flutters her lashes obnoxiously.

"If only."

"Mhmm." That's the only agreement I'll earn from her.

I glance between the men still watching her and the fierce determination set on her features. The stench of trouble floats across the artificially heated space like poison. What's with all the drama in the stands today?

My stance widens. "Want me to get rid of them?"

Frankie's sharp nails swat away the suggestion. "They're harmless. Just a local biker gang."

That's when it clicks. These guys were sent to recruit her. She might've rejected them at first, but they don't look like the type to take no for an answer. The one in the middle is older and has a cruel glint in his beady gaze.

Heat crawls up my neck, as if the past is hounding me rather than Frankie. I check to see that Frankie's focus is still firmly forward before signaling to security. Four of our best guards rush to where I discreetly directed, removing the bad news without making a scene. This trio is clearly making her uncomfortable. It could be temptation or fear. Either way, I'm the only one who gets to make her squirm.

"You're not working with them," I state plainly.

Her chin lifts. "That's not your decision."

"Fuck around and find out, menace."

The flicker in her green eyes is the swish of a blade in

darkness. It's obvious I'm toeing a very thin line. My cock twitches as I contemplate nudging her a bit further.

If Frankie wants to disappear, it would be easy to do in this crowd. But she won't abandon Ronnie. My gut tells me so. If it were just me holding her in Cloverleaf Meadows, I'd be left for dead weeks ago.

"Daddy!" Ronnie tugs on my flannel sleeve. "I gotta tell you a secret."

Talk about perfect timing. The nanny needs a reminder of why she's here.

My knees creak as I squat beside our distraction. "What's up, cupcake?"

She shields her mouth with a curved hand while whisper-shouting in my ear. "Frannie wants a horse."

The redhead in mention makes a choked noise. "Um, no. Frankie does not."

Ronnie scowls at her. "I'm telling Daddy a secret. It's rude to listen."

Frankie rolls her lips between her teeth, trapping what I imagine to be a throaty laugh. "Pardon me, prissy pants."

"What're prissy pants?"

"Look at your attitude and find out."

I smother a chuckle. Damn, this fiery woman is bickering with my kid like they're catty best friends. It appears the polite polish on their relationship is smoothing into a more comfortable shine.

My daughter scoffs, filling the role seamlessly. "I don't have an attitude."

Frankie buffs her manicure on her leather jacket. "Whatever you say."

Ronnie purses her lips. "Are you getting your period or something?"

Another strangled sound escapes the unqualified nanny. "Excuse you?"

"Brenna at school told me that her older sister said girls get crabby when they're on their period. Daddy,"—my little girl turns to me—"what's a period?"

"It's, uh. Uh…" My mouth opens and closes uselessly for too many seconds. A cold sweat breaks out across my forehead. It's too early for this discussion. I should have five more years, at the very least.

"It's lady business," Frankie fills in. "And for the record, I'm not due for it until the end of the month."

Relief whooshes from me in a noisy gust. I could kiss her. But I won't. That would be… inappropriate? It's unclear. My thoughts are jumbled into muddled confusion.

The redhead bends low to join me at Ronnie's level. She taps my little girl on the nose. "There's also a thing called girl code. You can't be calling me out like that, sis. We gotta stick together."

Ronnie tilts her head at an exaggerated angle. "Huh?"

"I don't want that horse," Frankie simplifies.

My daughter blinks at her. "But you said you did."

"That was in a dreamy sort of way. It's like when some-one wishes they could afford a fancy car or diamond neck-lace. That doesn't mean they're serious about it or, for that matter, will ever get it."

Ronnie thinks on that for a brief moment before returning her focus to me. "Can we buy Frannie the dreamy horse? She doesn't have any money."

I cough out a laugh as the redhead stammers on her shock. My gaze slides to the grulla mare in the arena. Her color alone will draw attention and raise the bid. The smoky gray shade is a rare variation, especially when paired with excellent conformation. Even from this distance, I can tell this quarter horse is put together well. Her muscular build and smooth gait speak highly of her performance too.

After another glance, I find myself grinning. "Sure, cupcake."

"What?" Outrage rings loudly in Frankie's voice.

"What?" I echo.

"You're not buying me a horse."

I rub a palm over my mouth to hide a growing grin. "We don't know each other well, menace. But you shouldn't try telling me what to do. It only makes me want to do it more."

"That's a terrible excuse and very unoriginal."

"Doesn't make it less true."

"I don't want a horse," she reiterates.

"You do," I counter. "Wouldn't have voiced it aloud otherwise. Especially with little ears listening."

"It was just an offhand comment. She's a beautiful animal." Frankie gestures at the grulla mare.

"Which is why she'll make a great addition to our herd."

"Don't buy her for me." But her long sigh reveals the truth of her inner desires.

"If it makes you feel better, she can be your Christmas bonus."

She frowns. "I definitely haven't earned that."

"Not your decision," I repeat her earlier phrase.

Frankie rolls her eyes. "I don't know the first thing about horses."

"Ronnie will teach you. She was on the back of a pony before she could walk."

My little girl nods eagerly. "Uh-huh, yep! I'm really super good. Daddy says I can compete in rodeos next year. We can go together!"

But Frankie is still stuck on my statement. A puzzled expression twists her elegant features. "Before she could walk? How is that possible?"

"Couldn't keep her away. It's in her blood. That passion is powerful. I'm sure you feel the same about motorcycles. You love the thrill of a ride."

She clucks her tongue. "Can't really compare the two. One has a mind of its own and isn't afraid to use it."

"I bet you're a natural in the saddle." My gaze feasts on her supple curves covered in snug denim.

Her snort calls bullshit. "We're not gonna find out."

"Prefer bareback? That can be arranged." I wink at her.

Frankie balks. "What's gotten into you?"

"Acts of service is my love language. You're in desperate need of a mount. I'm more than willing to provide one." Am I still referring to the horse? Maybe. For whatever reason, the thought of burning money on this woman gets me hard. "But you should know that mares can be... temperamental."

She quirks a brow at my choice in phrasing. "Guess that makes us kindred spirits."

"Giddy up, little menace." I tip the brim of my hat.

"Wow," she breathes. "You're acting wild."

My shrug is unbothered. "Ronnie approves."

We look to where my daughter is petting the horse's nose through the fence. The owner must've smelled my money from across the ring. I smirk at the cowboy and the dollar signs in his eyes.

"She's probably really expensive," Frankie warns, as if that'll dissuade me.

My gaze burns into hers, long enough to make her shiver. "Worth every penny."

CHAPTER FOURTEEN

Frankie

I**T'S BARELY SIX O'CLOCK WHEN** I **EASE MYSELF ONTO A** stool, propping my elbows onto the granite countertop. The kitchen is quiet and dark. Everyone is still asleep, including the sun. I was dragged out of hibernation by an aroma too tempting to resist.

Steam rises from the mug in front of me. I inhale deeply, my mouth watering for that first sip. It doesn't disappoint. A moan slips from me as the caffeinated decadence of fresh coffee bathes my taste buds. The light roast blend is enhanced with traces of hazelnut and vanilla. It's complex, but straightforward. There are layers to enjoy without too much fuss. Much like the man who made it.

I savor another sip. This is a real treat after weeks of choking down the dark, bitter sludge Byron prefers to drink. It would've been easy to buy a kind I prefer, but coffee is even more delicious when someone else does all the work.

This cup is further proof. Based on the silence in the house, he must've scheduled it to brew for me. An odd warmth spreads through my chest, which has little to do with my senses waking up.

He's been different lately. Not as prickly. Much more generous. His acts of service aren't strictly monetary, but I'm still processing how much the grulla mare cost him. He insists she's mine, which is difficult to accept. Gifts aren't given freely where I come from whether it's the holiday season or not.

My stomach sours at the reminder, threatening to ruin my peaceful morning. Byron doesn't seem to expect any-thing in return. It's equal parts confusing and thrilling.

I glance at the black void beyond the window, getting lost in my thoughts. That's when a throat clears behind me. Hot liquid splashes over the rim of my mug when I startle and whip around.

"The fuck?" I screech too loudly for the early hour.

My heart leaps into my throat. The grumpy cowboy is standing near the front door, dressed in his outdoor gear. His stare doesn't leave mine as he kicks off his doodled boots and strides from the shadows of the entryway.

"It's not polite to sneak up on someone," I mutter.

His shrug isn't bothered by the bite in my tone. "This is my house. I'll come and go as I please."

"Don't I know it."

With my pulse pounding a frantic rhythm, I study him closely. His cheeks are rosy, but definitely not from being jolly. The frosted tips in his beard make him appear more salty than the usual gray specks. It's not a good look for him if I want to remain nonchalant.

I force the strain in my expression to neutralize. "Where were you?"

"Horses don't feed themselves in winter," he drawls while stripping off his coat. "Your mare fits in as if she was born in the herd."

"My mare," I breathe. "Her name is Greta. Your daughter picked it. That way, when you come to your senses, you can give her to Ronnie."

His chuckle is gravel and rough sex. "Maybe you'll scrounge up the courage to ride her one of these days. That's a sight I'd pay to see."

I tap my pursed lips. "Like forty thousand dollars?"

A gleam slides over Byron's eyes when I recite the amount he paid for her. He approaches me at a leisurely pace as if he needs to think it over. "I'd go higher."

I watch him crossing the room before he leans against the dining table. The four feet separating us doesn't spare me from his woodsy pine scent. "How much?"

"Your ass and tits bouncing in the saddle are worth at least half a million."

I choke on my coffee. This is the first time he's been the suggestive one. "Damn, maybe I should start selling tickets."

His gaze hardens into steel. "It'd be a private show, menace. Nobody else is allowed."

"Does someone have a possessive streak? Interesting," I purr. "Is that why you were watching me just now?"

"You weren't combative for once. It was a nice change of pace."

I scoff. "Liar. How long were you lurking over there?"

"Long enough to know you like the coffee I chose."

Heat stings my cheeks and I'm hoping the kitchen is dark enough to mask my blush. "Why'd you make it for me?"

Byron stretches the tension until it's thicker than his dick. "Thought I'd be nice."

"That doesn't seem like your style, stud."

"Goes to prove how much you know about me."

My mind is too sluggish to form a snappy retort. It'll hit me eventually. Until then, it's my turn to make him squirm.

My robe not-so-accidentally parts lower in the front, exposing the tops of my breasts. "Maybe you want to cash in on some of those added benefits I mentioned."

"Fucking hell," he grumbles.

"Mhmm," I breathe. "I can take you there."

"We're not discussing this."

I pout. "Why not?"

"You're my employee." But his gaze feasts on the sliver of cleavage I've revealed.

"Didn't stop you from coming in your pants against me." My attention drifts downward, recalling how the wetness spread so quickly.

Red blooms on his cheeks again, but for a very different reason. "You weren't working here yet."

"Convenient excuse." A sharp smile cuts across my lips as I admire his flustered state. Getting him riled up is one of my favorite hobbies.

"My daughter loves you. I won't jeopardize that for a casual fuck."

"But you'd be willing if I offered more of a… commitment?" It's difficult for me to even force that word past my lips.

Byron's gulp is audible. "Maybe."

My gaze slides away. "I don't do attachments. Meaningless sex is all I can offer."

Which is unfortunate as I give his towering stature a hungry once-over. This is a burn-on-both-ends type of situation. Nobody wins when we reject each other. It's probably for the best.

A pinch of disappointment weasels its way in. His gigantic cock might be worth the risk, though. Gosh, I'd be feeling him for days after.

He straightens as if listening to the dead-end struggle of my dirty imagination. "I've got shit to do."

My sigh is seeped in defeat. "It doesn't involve taking our clothes off, huh?"

"No, that conversation is over." His heavy stride pounds the floor as he leaves me hanging. "Enjoy your coffee, menace."

My signature stamp demands retaliation, but the snark won't spill free. "Thank you," I whisper instead.

Byron's retreat slams to a halt. A purposeful inhale lifts his broad shoulders before they fall. "Don't mention it."

CHAPTER FIFTEEN

Byron

FRUSTRATION BUBBLES OVER, PRYING MY EYES OPEN to glare at the ceiling. Sleep continues to elude me. The digital clock on the wall is too bright, revealing what I already know. It's half-past midnight. I've been tossing and turning for almost an hour. That's only after I forced myself to lie down in the first place.

Images of Frankie bouncing in a Western saddle taunt me. It's my own damn fault. I shouldn't have voiced the visual. Now, my fantasies are manifesting it.

"Dammit!"

I kick off the covers and lurch out of bed. My bare feet begin pacing manically back and forth as my filthy mind conjures more material. Fire traces along my spine, pushing me to submit to the urges. I'd go weeks without before Frankie's irresistible ass arrived on the scene. That woman is reducing me to a mindless fiend.

There's an easy solution, but I can't travel down that twisted road. I don't want to fantasize about her. It's a lie, one of many I tell myself when it comes to Francesca Keller.

But the truth is that she's my daughter's nanny. I'm paying her for a service and it's not to get me off. Once I let those desires roam free, I won't be able to shove them back into the stable. But I won't get a decent night's sleep either.

"Fuck it," I growl and drop my boxers.

While one fist gathers the discarded fabric, I use the other to grasp my cock in a punishing chokehold. Air hisses from behind my clenched teeth. There's already a throb pulsing through my shaft, demanding more. The intensity of my arousal is almost concerning. I've been depriving myself. That won't be a problem anymore. The box is open and my thoughts run wild.

As I blindly reach for the lube in the nightstand drawer, I'm picturing Frankie astride her beloved mount. Only a black lace bra and matching thong conceal her. The bombshell's thighs are straddled wide over the saddle. It's obscene how far her legs are stretched apart. She moans and tosses her head, spilling silky hair down her delicate curves. A cluck of her tongue instructs the beast beneath her to move.

"That's it, menace. Go faster," I command.

With a squirt of lube in my palm, I grip my cock at the base. The first stroke is an electric spark zapping through my veins. I bow forward from the force while spots dance in my vision.

"Shit," I curse. "Gonna make me blow in three pumps."

Frankie smirks from the depravity of my imagination. My hand slides along my dick as I picture her beginning to trot. Her breasts sway from the jerky motion, spurring me to jerk faster. I'm thrusting into my fist while she turns to give me a peek at her ass. The supple flesh jiggles as if I'm spanking her. That sends a fresh wave of heat to fondle me.

"Such a tease," I croak and beat myself harder.

That's another lie. I have no doubt that Frankie would be on the bed with her legs splayed if I allowed it. But I won't be an empty fuck for her. If we cross that boundary, she'll be mine whether her commitment issues can handle it immediately or not.

"If I can't have you, nobody else can."

The threat spews from me while I tighten my grip. My muscles contract from the slick friction. An ache expands from my groin, demanding more. My palm glides up and down as I envision Frankie bouncing on my lap. Fuck the saddle. She's riding me from now on.

"Yes," I whimper.

The sound is embarrassing, even in the privacy of my own bedroom. It doesn't stop me. Pressure builds and spreads until it's shooting out. I barely manage to get the crumpled boxers over my tip before I'm erupting.

The pleasure is blinding to the point where I lose my footing and stagger. I'm suspended in its clutches while the lust pours out of me. My hips buck along to the spurts of release. On the fourth, I'm drained dry. Relief expels from me in a labored breath.

And then I'm collapsing onto the mattress. A lazy smirk displays the contentment thrumming through me. It takes less than five seconds for me to pass out, fading into a warped Christmas miracle where Frankie could actually be mine.

CHAPTER SIXTEEN

"GONNA FIGHT THESE GUMDROPS," I MUTTER under my breath. To further antagonize me, one of the sugary blobs slides off the gingerbread roof. It takes several marshmallows along for the fall. "Icing is a poor substitute for glue. It's not like I'm going to eat this. Just getting sticky for nothing."

Gruff laughter mocks my frustration. "What's got your tit in a twist, menace?"

I widen my eyes at the usually G-rated father, but then realize Ronnie is missing in action. That allows me to slouch in my chair for a quick reprieve. "Hush over there. You're not even trying."

"Creativity is your wheelhouse." He nods in the direction of his boots in the entryway.

"Never gonna live that down."

He shakes his head. "Which is why I'm allowing you to put in enough effort for both of us."

"Jeez, that's almost considerate. Excuse me for caring."

"Ronnie will appreciate it." That's his trusty escape clause.

"This is my first gingerbread house. It needs to be perfect." The pressure is on, blazing a path between my shoulder blades.

"That's a mansion," he corrects.

"Thanks for noticing."

"You didn't have to make it so big."

"Is someone jealous?" I stick out my bottom lip, deciding to use this opportunity to secure my position on the naughty list. "Does it bother you that I'm erecting such a large structure in your presence?"

Byron scrubs a palm over his mouth. "Brat."

"Mhmm," I purr. "These piles of candy get me hot. Whoops, what happened here?"

The grump watches in rapt fascination as I pick up a piece of licorice. I pinch it between two fingers, inspecting the shape closely. It flops like a limp dick when I give it a wiggle.

"Well, that won't do." I replace it with a candy cane. "This is better. Stiff and reliable. Skinny girth that'll fit just about anywhere. Long enough to gag on."

He coughs while adjusting in his seat. "You should put that down."

"My throat? Yes, that's the idea."

I open my mouth wide, giving him an unobstructed

view as I slide the candy cane in as far as it can go. With the hooked part wedged at my tonsils, I mewl just to prove I'm capable of swallowing much more. I remove the temptation slowly, making sure to hollow my cheeks for maximum impact.

"Francesca," he growls.

"Oooooh, full first name. Aren't you enjoying the show?"

"I don't tolerate teasing."

That gets stored in a secret spot for a later date. For now, I give him a coy grin and lick the tip of the candy cane. "Turns out my love language is receiving gifts. I've been feeling very grateful since you bought Greta and started making me coffee every morning."

He scowls at the mention of his recent acts. "You don't owe me anything."

"That horse cost you forty-thousand dollars. The least I can do is provide visual stimulation. Do with it what you wish." I bounce my shoulder, lowering the neckline of my green sweater.

Byron's gulp is audible. "You're gonna have to choke on a lot of candy canes."

"Maybe you'll give me a more substantial shaft to suck on and settle the debt faster."

The fire in his gaze snuffs out instantly. "Don't sell yourself short, menace. Not to me."

I hiss out my next breath. In my experience, men don't refuse an offer like mine. But I'm quickly realizing Byron isn't like the guys I'd been instructed to keep company back in my old life.

He's opened his home to me. I've had my first tastes of holiday cheer thanks to him and Ronnie. We're sitting at the table surrounded by supplies to make gingerbread houses on Christmas Day. And here I am, trying to seduce him.

An ugly sensation crawls through my gut. Gosh, I'm so far out of my element I can't see straight. Heat stings my vision and I look away, focusing on the tree we decorated together. The shatter of a fragile ornament beats against my eardrums. They brushed off my mistake like cookie crumbs, but guilt still plagues me.

I wasn't raised to be domestic. I'm a stray alley cat rescued from the streets, suddenly treated with nothing but kindness and compassion. The adjustment is steep.

Another sharp jab punches my stomach. I almost forgot to buy Ronnie a gift. Christmas customs and activities are foreign to me. At the last minute, I recognized the absence of wrapped boxes from me under the tree. The mini motorized bike is the only thing I've spent my own money on since Byron gave me his card.

I was feeling really satisfied with my choice until she opened it. She immediately wanted to go for a ride, as she should. The only problem with that is Minnesota winter and the massive heap of snow we just got this week. Byron saved the day like a real hero. He cleared out the oversized garage and let his little girl go wild.

I'm woman enough to admit I shed a few tears. But

then it was time to reveal what she got for me. My hands wrap around the ceramic mug that's warm from my morning coffee. The clay is lopsided, lumpy, and a bit leaky. In other words, it's pottery perfection. When I first saw it nestled in black tissue paper, the dam burst and I became a blubbering mess.

Ronnie had cuddled up against my shaking form. *"I made it for you, Frannie. Do you like it?"*

Never have I felt so inadequate. That child deserves much more than a small scooter. I sniffle while returning from that special moment. It's strong enough to chase away the shadows of my past. A lone droplet dares to escape my eye and I swipe at it absently. My unbalanced emotions have been misfiring, which blurs the gingerbread structure in front of me. I clutch onto the mug tighter as if that will stabilize me.

Byron shakes his head. "If you don't quit that, Ronnie is gonna fill your room with handmade crafts."

"Really?" There's no downplaying the hope in my voice.

His hum is contemplative. "You really care about her."

I roll my watery eyes. "Duh, stud. She's irresistible."

"Fair point."

As a final touch, my lack of construction skills attempts to attach a lemon drop as a doorknob. "I'm beginning to realize there's nothing I wouldn't do for her."

He nods slowly. "Good. That's the way it should be."

"Wowwwww," Ronnie breathes from right beside me. "Your gingerbread house is amazing!"

I startle at her sudden reappearance. "Just trying my best."

Her smile is full of pride. "You're really good at it."

"Thanks, kiddo. Where've you been?"

She glances at her dad and he offers an encouraging nod. It's only then I realize she's holding something behind her back. When she reveals the item, I'm not sure what to think.

"Every Christmas, we look at pictures of my mommy. Her memory lives within us always"—she taps her heart—"but this is our… umm…"

"Tradition," Byron fills in for her.

"Yeah! It's something we do lots, but especially on Christmas. It's almost like she's celebrating with us."

There's an undeniable quiver in my bottom lip. Ohhhhh, no. I'm too unhinged for this. A lump forms in my throat and I can't pull in a decent breath.

At my prolonged silence, Ronnie shuffles closer. "Will you look at the pictures with us?"

As if I could ever say no. Although, speaking is a challenge while I'm struggling to compose myself. "Of course, kiddo. Thanks for including me in your tradition."

She scoffs as if I'm ridiculous. "We want you here for all the things. You're part of our family now."

And I'm crying again. Tears trickle down my cheeks faster than I can wipe them away. The hormones are out of control.

"Don't be sad. She's always with us. Even if we can't see her. I'll show you, 'kay?"

My head bobs obediently. I accept her hand when she offers it, allowing her to lead me to the couch. The cushions absorb my collapse when the significance of this scenario bears down on me. It's personal and intimate and not meant for me.

But Ronnie's smile soothes my frayed edges. "Can I sit on your lap?"

I press my quivering lips into a firm line and pat my thighs. "Hop on."

She gets settled, reclining against me like this is a daily occurrence. The thick album creaks as she opens it. I can almost hear the whispers of memories seeping out.

Her tiny index finger taps the first picture. "This is when my mommy and daddy first met. They went to school together. Mommy didn't give Daddy the time of day until they were seventeen. He was so super excited when she finally let him take her out on a date. They went out to dinner and a movie. Isn't that romantic?"

"Mhmm," I croak.

Ronnie's grin spreads as she turns the page. "Look! It's their junior prom. Daddy rented a limo and bought Mommy flowers. They danced a lot. At the end of the night, Mommy told Daddy that she loves him. It was the first time she'd said it."

"Did he say it back?" I find myself asking, completely engrossed in her retelling.

"Uh-huh, Daddy loved Mommy before Mommy loved Daddy."

"That's the way it should be."

She hums in agreement before moving on. I can feel Byron's gaze burning into me, but I avoid his stare. If I look at him, I'll crack and the damage might be irreparable. This moment is too vulnerable.

Instead, I listen to Ronnie and get swept up by the past. Her delivery is beyond impressive. The way she describes each photo in vivid detail reveals how often Byron has explained them. She's memorized her parents' history as if she was there to witness it.

Each page highlights a major milestone, special occasion, or cherished moment. When Byron got down on one knee and Nina said yes. Their wedding. The day they bought their first house. Holidays and birthdays. Their horses and dogs. Byron's promotion at Benson Farmstead. Nina's round belly. Ronnie's nursery in phases.

I'm getting lost in the sea of memories. The torrential downpour of tears drowns me and I fight against the storm thrashing in my chest. Ronnie's gentle tone doesn't skip a beat as she treasures her mother's life. I can't be envious of a dead woman. That's low, even for me. But I've never seen a person loved so loudly. My heart clenches painfully at what Nina is missing. It's breathtaking and tragic and has me ripped apart. She should be here, wrapped in unconditional devotion. Not me.

"This is the last picture Daddy ever took of my mommy. It was right before I was born," the little girl chirps. There's not a hint of sorrow in her voice.

"She looks so happy," I murmur softly.

"Yep," Ronnie giggles. "That's 'cause she was about to meet her miracle."

I gasp and fling my weepy focus to Byron. His rapt attention is already on me. My eyes search his, pleading for the answer.

"Did she get to?"

His nod is a single dip.

Relief pours down my face in messy streaks. I must be puffy and splotchy beyond recognition. If ever there was a time to release the reins, it would be now. It's almost like my soul is being cleansed.

Ronnie sighs while closing the photo album. The sound is full and content. Like everything is the way it's meant to be. But I feel Nina's absence. There's a hole in this house that I didn't comprehend until today.

Silence follows, allowing us to trudge through our emotions separately. Mine are a disaster. I'm being pulled in conflicting directions. The seams are pulled taut, seconds from snapping. But Ronnie isn't sad or upset. There's a peaceful expression on her face. Byron created happiness where many others would only experience the devastation of loss. Nina's life is celebrated the way it should be.

He's kept her alive for their daughter. If he suffers with grief, he never lets it show. I'm in awe of this man.

"Who takes care of you?" It's not the first time I've asked him, but my purpose has changed.

Ronnie wiggles off my lap. "I do! Wanna help?"

I force the needles in my throat down with a long swallow. "You've got it handled, kiddo."

She pouts. "But Daddy likes you."

As expected, Byron snorts his disagreement. "Frankie is here for you, cupcake."

"For us," she insists. "We're family. Frannie wants to marry you and then she can be my new mommy."

Air is punched out of me and I fold in half, hacking up a lung. "No, that's not true."

Byron crosses his tattooed arms over his chest, the beginning of a smirk teasing his lips. "Am I that bad?"

My puffy eyes narrow at him. "Don't even start."

Ronnie groans. "But you gotta fall in love and have a big huge wedding and make babies and then ride off into the sunset."

A wave of dizziness crashes over me, spinning until I'm clutching at my throat. It's like my windpipe is being squeezed under a crushing force and I can't breathe. "Sorry, kiddo. That's just… no. It's not going to happen."

"Why?" There's a sharp whine in her voice that chips at my frozen heart.

A mountain of excuses stack on top of me. It's cruel to deny her after what she's shared. But I can't give Ronnie what she wants. Byron can't either.

There's no chance this man has room for another profound love in his life. Even if he did, the last thing I want is to be considered for the role. We'd ruin each other. Boundaries exist for a reason and I'm staring him right in his ruggedly handsome face.

I'm not sure where we stand, but it's not on equal ground. A few rolls in the hay could be acceptable. Our attraction is evident and mutual. Compatibility is a different thread I don't plan to tug on. But I'm not opposed to the idea of exploring our sexual chemistry. That'll be an impulsive decision, which is somewhat of a specialty. Maternal instincts are the opposite.

I gather Ronnie's hands in mine. "This might be tough to hear, but I'm not marriage or mommy material. You deserve so much more than I can give. When you least expect it, someone very special will appear to make all your dreams come true. Until then, I'll be your nanny and friend and whatever else I'm capable of providing. But I have limits, kiddo. I'm very sorry I can't be everything you need."

Her slim shoulders curl inward. "Okay."

Guilt stabs into me, leaving me weak and drained. This is too much. We're supposed to be celebrating. Leave it to me to spoil the festivities. That means it's my responsibility to fix this wreck.

I leap off the couch with enthusiasm I don't actually feel. "Why don't we play a game?"

Ronnie squints at me skeptically. "What kind of game?"

"Maybe a contest?" My gaze sweeps to the gingerbread house supplies. "How about who can fit the most gumdrops in their mouth?"

I'll make those gooey blobs my bitch yet.

The little girl perks up. "I wanna do that!"

"Heck yes."

"Best. Idea. Ever!" Ronnie wraps me in a tight hug before racing out of the room.

A challenging brow quirks at Byron. "What do you say?"

He motions toward the kitchen. "After you."

We reclaim our seats at the dining table and divide the gumdrops into piles. Ronnie is practically bouncing in her chair. Her father is sprawled out in all his man-spread glory, announcing that his attempt to win is zero. I'm just glad the mood has shifted to our usual comfort level.

My gaze swivels between them. "Any guesses how many you'll get?"

"A million!" Ronnie shouts.

"Wow, I can't beat that."

Victory already brightens her features. "Ready?"

I nod and snatch a sticky piece between my fingers. "Go!"

Ronnie immediately dives in. Her style is a rapid fire as she shoves the candy into her mouth. Byron's pace is lazy at best. Mine is fast enough to appear like I'm at least trying, but I never stood a chance.

The little girl squishes in one more and it's over. "Mer hawim!"

The handful in my mouth shoot out at her adorable declaration. Not to mention her cheeks puffed out like a chipmunk. "You won!"

Ronnie chews quickly, ingesting entirely too much sugar at once. "I did it!"

"Didn't doubt you for a second, cupcake." Byron beams at her as if this was a gold medal competition.

"How many fit in there?"

She shrugs. "I dunno. They're in my tummy."

"A million plus one," Byron says.

"That's soooo many!" Ronnie giggles loudly.

I exhale a laugh. We're back to fun and happy and light. It's our safe space. That's where we belong.

CHAPTER SEVENTEEN

Byron

AFTER STOMPING THROUGH THE HEAVY SNOWFALL of what might become a Christmas blizzard, I find Frankie in the barn with Greta. My stride is nearly silent as I approach the horse's stall where the redhead is hiding. She snuck out of the house after tucking Ronnie into bed. If privacy is what she's looking for, she's not going to get that from me.

"Need an escape?"

She shivers regardless of the heated interior. Her haunted green eyes latch onto mine. "Always."

My nod is slow but steady. "I thought we should talk."

"That's not ominous or anything."

An easy chuckle rumbles free. This version of Frankie is manageable. I was at a total loss while she was crying. Offering a sympathetic shoulder to lean on isn't our norm.

"You handled that well," I offer as a peace agreement.

"Are you surprised?"

I dip my chin. "It's unfamiliar territory. For both of us. Not sure how I would've responded."

"Probably wouldn't have gotten yourself in that position to begin with."

My grimace tries to be empathetic. "The holidays can be heavy."

Frankie's grin lacks its usual sass. "Especially for someone who never celebrates."

"Was that too much?"

I probably should've asked sooner, but I've trained myself to solely focus on Ronnie. It's a reflexive habit at this point. More so, this woman has proved to be fiercely independent. If she's not pleased, I'd be the first to know.

"It's strange to witness the power of love. The devotion and comfort and affection. I… envy you," she admits on a whisper.

My brows lift. "I can't imagine why."

"Is that hard to believe? There's so much warmth in your home, embedded in every fiber. The entire town is wrapped around your little finger. You're worshipped around here. That's the breeding ground of jealousy for a person like me."

The persistent ache in my chest makes an appearance, reminding me of everything I'm missing. "Don't be jealous of me."

"Easy for you to say." Frankie drops her gaze, drifting a palm across Greta's neck. "Tonight was another reminder of what I'll never have."

"Who says you can't have it?"

She shakes her head. "I'm not meant to be a kept woman trapped behind white picket fences. That's not a secret. But sometimes I forget how far apart we are."

The despondent note in her voice slashes at me. "Do you want a family?"

A sound of hollow amusement trickles from her. "Can't you see I'm having a bit of a pity party, stud? Nobody else is invited to attend."

"Is that your attempt to get rid of me?"

"Stubborn man," she mutters. "Can't take a hint if it was stamped on his forehead."

My boots remain firmly planted on the concrete floor. I smirk at the bold words she wrote in the worn leather. Frankie takes pride in winning and isn't the type to surrender, but her mood is off. That's really saying something, seeing as this woman has more sides than a decagon.

I squint at her rigid posture. "Planning to run?"

Her glare is a loaded weapon when she aims it at me over her shoulder. "As if I'd tell you."

"Didn't take you for a quitter, menace. Gonna prove me wrong?"

Her sigh is hardly an answer. "I won't get far in this snowstorm."

A sudden urgency pushes me three steps forward. "You said I could trust you. Don't abandon Ronnie."

"What will you give me to stay?"

"What do you want?"

She licks her lips. "A distraction."

I don't move or even breathe. "Such as?"

Frankie turns toward me, giving me the full impact of her dangerous appeal. "Why don't you date?"

"We've been over this."

"Have we?" She tips her head, studying me closely. "I might need a refresher. It's been nearly six years since Nina passed. That's a long time to go without."

My heart thumps to a hollow beat. "Are you trying to hurt me?"

"More like understand."

"I'm not interested in complications," I remind her. "Most women my age aren't dating for the fun of it. They want to get married eventually or at least have a serious commitment. I'm a dead end in that department."

"Are my ears deceiving me?" Frankie sways closer, walking two sharp fingernails up the zipper of my coat. "Or do you want a fuck buddy?"

The suggestion in her tone curdles my stomach. "That's not what I said."

"It's what you didn't say that I heard."

I scowl. "We're not sleeping together."

She blinks up at me, drawing attention to our height difference. "But you want to sleep with someone?"

"No," I snap.

"Are you sure? It doesn't have to mean anything. Just two consenting adults in need of an orgasmic release."

The thought of another woman's hands on me is worse than dozens of spiders crawling over my body. "I don't want anyone else."

Frankie cocks her head, a slow grin quirking her lips. "Does that mean you want me?"

My jaw clenches to the point of cracking a molar as I refuse to answer.

Her scoff smacks my denial to the peaked ceiling. "You may never have sex again at this rate."

In an impulsive move I'll probably regret, I cinch an arm around her waist and yank her body flush against mine. Warmth instantly engulfs me as if we're standing by a blazing fire. A soft groan slips from my pressed lips. I didn't know how starving I've been for touch until she's snug against me.

It's just a hug, but the significance goes far beyond a simple embrace. The close contact exchanges a comfort we both desperately crave. But Frankie is resistant to accept the relief while clutched tight in my arms.

She's stiffer than an oak board in my hold, but I don't let go. My palm smooths along her back in lazy strokes. After a few passes, she begins to relax. A shudder trembles through her limbs. In the next breath, she exhales raggedly and slumps into me. Based on her reaction, she hasn't been on the receiving end of a gentle caress in a long time. Maybe ever. My gut clenches just picturing what she's suffered.

Seconds stretch into minutes. Silence settles around us. For once, it's not hollow or tense. In the stillness of this moment, we've found each and met in the middle. It almost feels like the warmth of companionship.

But then Frankie shoves me away as if I've offended her. "Don't touch me," she hisses.

"Menace," I murmur and reach for her again.

"No!" She swats at her cheeks in frantic motions. Whether she's crying in anger or sadness remains to be seen.

But either way, I pushed her too far. It feels like the air has been snatched from my lungs. "Fuck, I didn't mean—"

Her laugh is brittle. "Liar. You've been forcing me to comply for weeks."

"Don't make it sound like that."

"It's exactly like that!" Frankie tosses her hands up. "I didn't want this job, but you made it impossible to leave."

"Shit," I wheeze. "I was just trying to make Ronnie happy."

"Which is admirable, but at the expense of my free will. Your daughter is incredible and deserves only the best. Why she insists on me being her nanny I'll never know. And to answer your earlier accusation, I won't abandon her. No matter what you do to piss me off. But that doesn't excuse your behavior or change the fact I didn't choose this. I'm stuck here one way or another."

"You're making me sound like the bad guy. A hug isn't some depraved act."

"It is to me," Frankie snarls. "Your pity is repulsive."

My grunt is loud. "I don't pity you."

"It doesn't matter." Frankie pushes past me, stomping down the barn aisle like a furious mare on a rampage. "I'm going to bed. Don't follow me."

"As if I'd dare," I call to her retreating form.

And in the quiet that follows, I realize I don't regret it.

CHAPTER EIGHTEEN

IT'S THE NEXT MORNING, BUT THE SUNNY SKY HASN'T offered clarity. If anything, my mood is full of storm clouds. The man to my left scooted his stool away the instant I barged into The Paddock. I must reek of a frigid chill and frustration. That's probably why Byron left a note on the fridge, telling me to take the day off. He couldn't even face me.

"The audacity of that man," I grumble into my mimosa.

Paisley lifts her glass in solidarity. "Screw him."

"Good for nothing but heartache," Gemma adds.

This is my first attempt at leaning on others. I've heard it can be therapeutic. As it turns out, I got a two-for-one special. The Keaton sisters arrived as a dynamic duo now that Gemma moved back to town. They're off to an impressive start, but we just sat down.

Paisley gives me a heavy dose of eye contact. "How did Byron fuck up this time?"

A long exhale delays the gratification. "He hugged me."

"He… hugged you," she repeats.

"After he shot me down."

Her lips part. "He *what?*"

"Can you believe that? Could've had a sure thing." I gesture at my goodies that are stuck on the shelf.

Paisley shakes her head as if to clear it. "Why did he hug you?"

"Beats the hell out of me."

"Was he trying to comfort you?"

"How should I know?"

"You spend a lot of time together."

"Doesn't matter. It's not like we really communicate openly. That's a foreign concept for me." One of many. But I'm not trying to tally my insecurities. "The point is he's not willing to give me what I want."

"Which is casual sex."

"Don't be so condescending. You make me sound like the wicked witch in this scenario."

"If the ruby slipper fits…" she mutters under her breath.

"Hey!" My palm slaps the wood bar top. "I didn't invite you to boozy brunch to criticize me. You need to blindly support me like a best friend. Aren't you in my corner?"

Her eyes are wide and unblinking. "Um, yes?"

I huff at her blatant uncertainty. "He crossed a line. We don't hug. It was too warm and fuzzy."

"You're just not comfortable with that level of intimacy," Paisley counters.

"I don't *need* that kind of intimacy."

Which is the lie I'm telling myself and anyone who will listen. In truth, I'd never felt more cherished. The tears were unexpected. It freaked me out and I overreacted. But damn, Byron shouldn't test me while I'm in such a vulnerable state.

His woodsy scent still burns in my lungs. I wonder if my perfume is clinging to him. My eyes squeeze shut. No, it doesn't matter. I'm just the nanny. Ronnie is the only commitment I can manage and that's already costing more than I can afford.

Paisley hasn't moved a muscle during my internal crisis. "Are you okay?"

"Yeah, of course. It's nothing I can't handle. Pissed me off more than anything." I roll my shoulders back. "Do you know what I need?"

She winces. "I'm honestly afraid to suggest anything."

"Why?"

"You're kinda scary," she mumbles.

"Really? Awww, I'm honored." And she hasn't even seen my knife collection.

Paisley snorts. "Because that's the correct response for a sane person."

"Oh, hush. I never claimed to be mentally stable."

"Is that on your resume?"

I lift my arms and spread them as if unrolling a banner. "I've got issues."

Gemma scoffs. "Don't we all?"

"Mine are toxic."

The sisters exchanged a weighted look. Paisley clears her throat. "Have you ever talked to someone about that?"

"What do you think I'm trying to do?" I motion between them.

She laughs. "We aren't professionals."

"I don't need a shrink to psychoanalyze me. The thought alone is fifty times worse than anything I've survived. Big shocker here: I'm fucked up. That's not going to change. I've learned to deal with it just fine." When they just stare at me, I roll my eyes. "Mostly."

"You're perfect just the way you are," Gemma croons.

"See? She gets it," I chastise Paisley. "As I was saying, I need to get laid."

Mimosa shoots from her mouth when she sputters. "Is that the best solution for your emotional state?"

I glare daggers at her, but she presses on.

"I'm just saying. If a hug set you off like this, something more… sensual could really trigger you."

"It depends on the type of contact. A hug from Byron is too personal. Sex with a stranger is strictly for pleasure. I don't do strings or attachments of any kind."

She makes another face. "Never?"

"That's it, you're fired. Swap seats with your sister." I make a weaving motion between the two blondes.

But Gemma is distracted. Her shrewd blue eyes sweep the interior of The Paddock like she's a security guard.

I quirk an eyebrow at her oh-so-subtle tactics. "Are you looking for someone in particular?"

"Me?" A bright scarlet blooms across her exquisite bone structure. "Ah, nope? Not at all."

Dry laughter flakes from me when she sucks down her drink to seal her lips from spilling the truth.

"Have fun with those evasive maneuvers." I slip off the stool and stretch my back. "Welp, you know what they say."

Paisley listens dutifully as my spine cracks in several places. "You'll catch more bees with honey?"

I give her a blank look. "Uh, good guess. But if you want someone done right, you gotta do them yourself."

Her features screw into utter confusion. "That's not how it goes."

"Which is why you're staying behind." I tap her on the nose and whirl to survey the weekend crowd.

My hunt begins with a scenic route to the bathroom. Several men glance at me, but quickly avert their stares. I'd be at risk of developing a complex, but my reflection in the mirror clearly reveals I'm in fuckable form.

On my second lap around, I spot a guy who's practically drooling at me. That's more like it. I plaster on a coy grin and add more swivel to my strut. He fidgets as I approach, which is endearing. Making people nervous is a guilty pleasure.

I blink at him from hooded eyes, adding a smoky rasp to my voice. "You look lonely."

He shifts his stance. "Is your name Frankie?"

The seductive pretense drains from my expression. "Have we met?"

"That's what I was afraid of," is his muttered reply.

He appears crestfallen, which doesn't make a lick of sense. I'm practically throwing myself on his lap.

My finger twirls around a curled section of hair. "Is there a problem?"

The guy gives me a lingering once-over. "When you're available, come find me." Before I can argue, his towering height disappears in the throng.

A similar pattern forms from that point forward. Whenever I get near someone, they skitter off in a hurry. It's as if there's a warning label stuck to my ass. That biker gang might be more problematic than I pegged them for.

The fifth rejection raises a red flag I can't deny. I tap the closest man on the shoulder. His blatant lust eye-fucks my curves, coasting along my snatched waist and boobs. But the hunger fizzles when his gaze reaches my face.

"Oh, shit. Sorry." He stumbles backward.

"Why are you sorry?" I park my hands on my hips.

"You're not mine to look at. I'm attached to my eyes."

"What's that supposed to mean?"

The guy takes another step away. "I've already done enough."

Such as test the possessive streak of a certain grumpy cowboy who has no right to make such a claim.

Before he can flee, I snatch his shirt sleeve. "Did Byron Benson tell you to leave me alone?"

His gulp is audible. "You're gonna get me in trouble."

I release him, getting the dirt I need. That traitor thinks he can put a chastity belt on me. If he believes that's wise for our revenge plot, he's got another thing coming.

My boots cut a direct path to where Paisley and Gemma are watching me strike out. "This place is a bust. Let's go to the next town over."

"Why?" But Paisley is already grabbing her stuff to dutifully follow my lead.

"I'm revved up and he's pressing all the wrong buttons."

Gemma tips her head at an angle that reminds me of Ronnie. "Huh?"

But now isn't the time to get distracted.

"Change of scenery. Fresh meat. Escape the rumor mill." And Byron's jurisdiction.

I keep that last one to myself. Don't need anyone else fleeing the scene. Not until the deed is done.

Soon enough, Byron will realize this bitch always gets her itch scratched.

CHAPTER NINETEEN

Byron

As I'm finishing evening chores, a furious cyclone whips into the barn. My smirk is ready to greet Frankie before I even turn around. A pair of green blades are narrowed and raised to strike me down where I stand.

I cross my arms, preparing for battle. "We need to quit meeting like this."

"You," she bellows while storming toward me.

My lips press in a firm line to contain my sheer glee. It's been the better part of a decade since I've felt this kind of thrill. "Something the matter?"

"Don't act innocent. What you did is irredeemable."

"Really? Wow. Thanks, little menace."

Frankie jerks to a halt within inches of crashing into me. Steam is practically rising from her fiery stance. "That wasn't a compliment!"

"No? Could've fooled me coming in all hot and bothered. You're much more flustered than when I had you tossed in the back of a squad car."

She looks seconds away from throttling me. "I hate you so much."

"Don't lie to yourself."

Hostility drips off her, but all I smell is guilty pleasure. "I'm so mad I could stab you."

My wince is exaggerated. "Please don't."

She pokes my chest with a pointy talon. "You deserve far worse."

"What'd I do?" But the jovial notes in my tone reveal foul play.

"Does the entire county think I'm off-limits?"

I scratch at my stubble while pretending to consider the distance. "Word travels fast 'round these parts."

"We went to six different bars. The response was always the same."

"Good to know that threats of bodily harm and lost wages still get the message across."

Her hands clench into dangerous fists. "You're a dick."

The latest insult gives me pause. She's taken the lead whenever the moment gets heated and lines are blurred. It's my turn to see how far we can push the limit.

I glance down at the rigid length bulging from the front of my jeans, done fighting the inevitable. "Would you like to get reacquainted?"

"Are you being serious right now?" she sputters.

My nod is genuine. "Might ease this unresolved tension."

"What happened to not sleeping together?"

Logic smacked me upside the head. I've deprived myself long enough. Our tension won't quit until we fuck it out of our systems. We owe it to ourselves at this point.

"Consider this a compromise." And my surrender. "This mutual attraction between us can't be avoided. We might as well explore it and see what happens. But there won't be any sleeping involved. At least not until you're thoroughly fucked and filled to the brim with my cum. At least not until you're thoroughly fucked and filled to the brim with my cum."

Frankie drops her jaw with an audible whoosh. Desire replaces the fury in her haze while a flush stains her flawless complexion. I might've just shocked her into silence. My cock twitches in victory.

While she's at a loss for words, I shamelessly gorge on the temptation her outfit serves. She's wearing black leggings that stick to her body like a bad habit. Her low-cut sweater is just as seductive.

I've controlled my urges without issue for years, but then Francesca Keller entered the scene. She makes me ache and yearn in ways I forgot existed. There's no chance in hell I'm walking away from her unscathed.

My heart pulses to the feverish beat of my lust. "Fair warning. I don't share."

She finds her voice. "Good for you?"

"You're mine, menace."

Frankie tips her head back and cackles. When her gaze

sears into mine again, there are sparks sizzling from those emerald depths. "I'm not a possession you can claim, stud."

My smirk spreads into a full grin. "Tell that to the men you tried to use after I denied you."

Her expression crashes into a scowl. "Are you trying to make this exclusive?"

"Yes."

"You're delusional."

"Keep flingin' those insults at me and my inflated ego won't fit out the barn door."

"That'd be a real shame, gramps."

My chuckle applauds her antics. "I've been called worse."

She taps her lips. "Such as cockblocker? There's plenty of me to go around."

The noise I spew is one of finality. "If you need to fuck, you fuck me. There's no other option."

"Nice try, but you're not trapping me in monogamy. You had your chance and blew it. Premature ejaculation suits you well." Frankie takes several steps back.

I immediately move to follow her. "Where are you going?"

"To bed. Alone." She fakes a yawn. "I'm tired of this conversation."

Frankie whirls on her towering stilettos and prepares to flee again. My humor bleeds out, allowing irrational impulses to consume me. I rope an arm around her waist and haul her against me. The shock factor is on my side, locking her limbs for several seconds.

"Not this time," I murmur close to her ear.

"You can't tell me what to do."

I lock my wrists across her stomach. "We've been over this. You're mine."

She thrashes in my hold that's loose enough for her to escape if she wishes. "I belong to no one."

"That's where you're wrong. I've got you in my town, under my roof, where I can monitor your every move. When you talk to someone, I hear about it. Try to run and I'll find you. Nothing gets past me."

A full-body shiver ripples through her. "Fuck."

"Mhmm," I inhale the sweet scent of her surrender. "You like the sound of that."

"Do not," she fires in response, but her resistance is melting.

I widen my stance to support her slouching weight. One of my hands drifts to clutch her hip. The other takes a more intimate path.

Frankie's gasp echoes to the beams above as my palm flattens and travels down the valley of her torso. "What're you doing?"

My hand cups the heat between her thighs. "This pussy is mine." I grind into her from behind. "This ass? Mine." My cheek presses into hers, our lips almost touching. "Your bratty mouth is mine, along with that forked tongue you constantly lash at me. I'll even claim your stubborn streak. The fierce determination to contradict everything I say. All mine."

"You're still fooling yourself."

"How do you figure? As I recall, you're the one who

suggested extra benefits. This is me accepting. You're right where I want you. The faster you surrender, the easier this will be."

Frankie's purr is a siren song to my neglected needs. "Do your worst, stud."

I bundle the crotch of her flimsy pants in a fist and yank. The material rips like tissue paper. Another tug shreds her sorry excuse for underwear, exposing her from clit to crack. Frankie expels a dreamy sigh at my show of strength.

A quick swipe along her center confirms what I already assumed. "Soaked for me."

"You're welcome."

"Unzip my jeans," I instruct.

Eyes hooded with lust find mine over her shoulder. "So bossy."

My nose traces a path to her ear and I smirk when she trembles. "Get my dick out. Now."

Without turning, her fingers find my belt and get to work. Cool air caresses my arousal as she releases me from the confines. She wraps a hand around my shaft, stroking from root to tip. A bead of precum applauds her method and she smears the moisture around with her thumb. Her lashes flutter shut while a smile curves her sinful lips.

"Rock solid for me," she breathes.

My dick jerks in her grasp, eager for more. Heat tingles along my spine in a familiar sensation. If she keeps jacking me off, this will be over before it begins.

I move us to the right and guide her hands to the bars on the stall door. "Hold on."

Frankie obeys with surprising speed. My belt buckle jangles as I situate myself behind her. A blinding urgency thrums through my veins, stealing all semblance of common sense. Her skin blazes against mine when I erase the last inch of space. But realization strikes at the last second.

"I don't have a condom."

Frankie presses against me in open invitation. "Don't need one unless you have something that hasn't cleared up after all these years."

I give her bare ass a gentle swat. "Brat."

Her laugh is meant to ridicule me, but I like hearing the carefree sound from her. "Gonna have to try harder than that to make me behave."

And I'll do so with pleasure.

I kick her heels apart, spreading her legs wide for me. My grip on her waist pulls her back until she's positioned at the optimal angle. Her slick arousal lubes my cock as I coast along her slit. When I repeat the motion, my dick nudges her entrance. That's all the warning she gets. I fill her pussy to capacity with a single, punishing thrust.

"Savage," she hisses.

"I'm your savage," I manage to croak from my strained vocal cords.

Her hips wiggle against my brutal onslaught. The squeeze from her inner muscles borders on uncomfortable. There's a pinch of pain when she flexes around me. I remain still for a moment, allowing us to gather our bearings.

She's a vise clamping me, cinched tight as if barely

broken in. But that can't be right. Ten years might separate us, but her bold assertiveness suggests plenty of experience.

My cock throbs, demanding movement. I withdraw an inch and immediately get sucked back in. It's a snug fit.

"How long has it been for you?"

She huffs. "None of your business."

My hands massage her lower back and hips to relax the strain. "Do I need to be gentle?"

"Only if you want me to fall asleep."

"Such a little shit." My flattened palm gives her another spank, harder this time.

Her shrug is unfazed. "You asked."

That insufferable attitude is in desperate need of adjustment. I pull out and quickly plunge forward, jostling her prideful stance. My grip on her ass clutches harder, sure to bruise. She lets a low moan slip free. That spurs me faster. But after no more than three strokes, the error in my madness speaks up.

I refuse to come before her, staving off the pressure with thoughts of spreadsheets and unanswered emails. But then Frankie clenches herself around me with purpose. My vision blurs into hues of pleasure.

"Fuuuuuuck," I groan.

It's been entirely too long since I've been buried in a wet pussy.

That knowledge sparkles in her gemstone eyes. "Not gonna last, big boy?"

I grit my teeth. Right then and there, I make it my mission to have her screaming my name before I erupt.

"Gonna last longer than you." And then I'm switching gears.

What I lack in stamina, I overcompensate with skill. While one hand reaches for stability from the stall bars, the other lifts Frankie's left leg and drapes it over mine. I accept her weight easily while never breaking stride. This allows me to get even deeper. Frankie notices the change instantly.

Her lips part on a ragged exhale. "Ohhhhhhhh."

The encouragement pushes me to a brutal pace. She jolts up and down from the force of my motions. I wrap an arm around her, pinning us together for the ride. My thumb stretches to work her clit in fluid circles. The added stimulation grants me a slew of praise.

"Yes, yes," she chants. "Right there."

I swoop down and lick a sloppy trail along the curve of her shoulder. She tastes erotic and dangerous, like trouble dipped in sugar. It's a tease more than anything. Now my mouth waters in anticipation of getting her pussy on my tongue.

Frankie blows out a rushed breath as if it had been blocked. Her chokehold on my cock slackens as she gets accustomed to my girth. That allows me to slide in and out with ease, heightening our joined pleasure. The connection crackles and binds us as one.

"This doesn't mean anything," she whines, feeling the same sparks as me.

I chuckle into the slope of her neck. Words are cheap. Frankie slings them at me like pennies in a wishing well.

But she can't hide what her body tells me. This combustible chemistry between us is priceless.

"You drive me insane," I rumble against her cheek. My beard scrapes a burning path along her skin to match the damage she's inflicted on me. "I was fine until you darkened my path."

"I'd apologize but I'm not sorry."

"At least you admit it."

Her nod is a jerky bounce. "Part of my appeal. I'll burden you like you've never been burdened before."

"Sounds sexy," I growl.

Frankie's giggle cuts off in a loud mewl. "That's the crazy talking."

"You know all about that."

"Such a charmer," she rasps.

My cock sinks to the hilt and I grind against her, putting an end to the discussion. She leans against me in complete submission. It's such an unguarded pose and deserves a reward.

I stimulate her clit with rapid swipes. My dick continues wrecking her cunt for any asshole who dared to believe he could follow this exhibition. She babbles nonsense and I'm here for every syllable.

"Too thick," she wheezes. "Almost hurts."

My motions falter. "Too much?"

"No!" Frankie squirms. "Don't stop."

Which only pushes me harder. The rhythmic slap of skin serenades us. Each stroke solidifies our sexual compatibility. This isn't an empty fuck we'll forget tomorrow.

It's a declaration: this woman belongs to me. Nobody else gets to touch her.

I pound my cock into her like it's a branding iron. "You're going to be feeling me for a week."

"Yes, please. Take out your anger on me, stud. Give it all to me," she pleads.

"Gonna leave my mark on you." My mouth suckles a blistering path along her throat.

She cries out. "More!"

I nip at her sensitive skin. "Whose cock is buried inside you?"

"Yours."

"Can any other dick give you this?"

Frankie whimpers, but doesn't respond otherwise.

I slow my motions, pulling out until just my tip kisses her entrance. "Do you think I'll allow other men to try what's mine?"

"No," she whispers.

My body stills completely, earning me a petulant whine. "Would you let another guy have you like this?" I jostle her limp form, proving how much trust she's placed in my grasp. "Bent to his will?"

"No," she repeats.

"Are you agreeing this pussy belongs to me? That I'm the only one who gets to fuck you?"

Her chest rises and falls with labored breaths. "Yes, you possessive jerk! Happy?"

My grin stretches wider than her thighs. "About to be."

I resume plunging deep, reigniting the friction burning

between us. It doesn't take long for the tingles across my lower back to return as well. My abs contract as I give her the best I've got. She responds with enthusiastic cries. We're headed toward a simultaneous finish that might be the end of me.

Frankie begins to quake, begging me to let her come. As if I'd stop her. Sweat prickles across the nape of my neck while I strum her clit to a silent beat.

"Almost there. Don't stop," she gasps. "So close. Oh, oh!"

I falter when she screams her release. Her sharp nails stab into my arm, most likely drawing blood. We're both too lost to notice.

The clench of her climax triggers my own. There's an unmistakable gush that drowns my cock. It's hot and erotic and unrelenting. A final thrust delivers me to the cusp. I explode with a guttural shout.

Waves of pleasure crash over me in a force that wobbles my knees. I'm barely aware of the pulse shooting through my dick or the stream that spurts out in convulsive bursts. White light streaks across my vision as I succumb to the release. Tremors twitch my muscles while I bask in the afterglow.

And I'm not the only one. Orgasmic bliss brightens Frankie's features. She's never looked so peaceful. The sight steals my breath and delivers another punch of relief.

We remain tangled in each other while the buzz wears off. It's long enough for a breeze to cool the slippery warmth between us. Frankie winces as I pull out.

My heart thuds. "Was I too rough?"

Any trace of pain wipes clean from her features. "Just the way I like it."

The urge to hug her rumbles through me, but I doubt the embrace will be well received. "You don't have to put on a brave act for me. I want you to be honest."

Her gaze avoids mine. "Uh-huh, sure."

"It's okay to let me in," I try again.

"Just did," she quips, but still won't look at me.

Shit, this is awkward. It's been ages since I've dealt with an adult woman's emotions. It's clear Frankie is shutting me out. I'm at a loss as to why after what we just shared.

"You know what I mean," I say gently.

"I really don't," she huffs. "It was just sex."

Which is true. I'm ashamed to admit I forgot to kiss her.

"Frankie," I murmur. "Tell me what you need. Please."

"That's a big ask, stud." She crosses her legs, reminding me that I destroyed her pants.

"Shit, let me grab something to clean you up."

Her arm shoots out to stop me. "Absolutely not. This is my mess now. Your part is done."

And then for the second time in as many days, Frankie leaves me guessing without a backward glance.

CHAPTER TWENTY

Frankie

"I REALLY DON'T THINK THIS IS A GOOD IDEA."

Ronnie sends me the same annoyed expression I've already received no less than seventeen times since trying to ditch my first riding lesson. Her small boot taps in the dirt, impatiently waiting for me to grow a pair. Greta would probably stamp her hoof if it wouldn't spook me. The horse has done nothing wrong except appear so tall. She's honestly better behaved than most humans. I'm beginning to think I'm overreacting.

But there's more to it than hoisting myself up into the saddle. "We should save this for tomorrow. It's supposed to be warmer."

Ronnie's lips squish into a more severe line. "The indoor arena is heated."

"Uh-huh, but it's dusty."

"We're just gonna walk."

This is how it's been for the last twenty minutes. Every lame excuse I toss out gets promptly swatted down. There's no proper way to explain that her daddy rearranged my internal organs with his monster cock last night and I'm still recovering.

I've never been pounded that hard. My vagina is throbbing, radiating an ache down my thighs. Don't even get me started on the chafing Byron's beard left behind. Good thing he didn't hoover my basement or I'd still be in bed. But I loved every filthy second of it.

And now, here I stand. Prepared to go for a totally different ride.

I attempt a squat and almost collapse. "Whoa, did you see that? I'm not sure my legs can handle this."

Her eyes narrow. "It's just like sitting on a motorcycle."

"How do you know?"

"You bought me a little one for Christmas," she deadpans.

I deserve her snark for that one. "Why are you so smart?"

"My brain is humongous."

"That's such a big word! I bet you get really good grades."

"Yep!" She beams with pride.

"Can you show me your report card?"

Her features scrunch. "Daddy has it. You gotta ask him."

"Pass," I mutter.

"Huh?"

"Never mind." I wave that unnecessary drama away. "As I was saying, let's go get ice cream. You've earned it."

"We just ate breakfast."

"There's always room for ice cream."

Ronnie doesn't appear convinced. "After lunch."

My mind whirls. "Gosh, your negotiating skills are top notch. Have you thought about becoming a lawyer?"

"What's a lawyer?"

"A person who can talk their way out of any problem."

She smiles wide. "That sounds fun!"

"Exactly. We should probably research the best schools to get you on the fast track."

Her head tips in that cute way. "But I'm only in kindergarten."

"It's never too early. Education is important." I almost snort at myself. It's only by some crooked miracle that I even managed to graduate high school. But that doesn't mean I don't care about Ronnie's future.

And she seems equally concerned about mine. "You need to learn how to ride a horse."

"Right now?"

"Yes." She stamps her foot again. "Greta needs exercise. You can't just let her sit around. That's a waste. Do you want Daddy to sell her?"

"No," I grumble. "I just really think—"

"Frannie," she states in a firm tone. "Put your boot in the stirrup."

She's beginning to sound like my gynecologist and we're not on speaking terms. That reminds me to find a replacement. But I digress. Again.

"Promise you won't let go?"

Ronnie smacks her forehead with both palms. I'm just that exhausting. But there's a more important matter at stake.

"You let go! She might run away." I point at where the lead rope is hanging limp from Greta's halter.

"She's not moving. Look." Ronnie waves her empty hands at Greta. The mare doesn't so much as swish her glossy tail. She's worthy of that outrageous price tag.

"But you dropped the rope. I'm not sure I can trust you once I'm up there," I retort.

"Don't be a chicken!"

I drop my jaw at her audacity. "Your prissy pants have no place here. This is my first time and I'm nervous."

She'd look sympathetic if it weren't for the exaggerated flare of her nostrils. "There's nothing to be afraid of. I warmed her up for you."

"I'm not sure what that means."

Ronnie huffs again. "Greta is a good girl. If a kid can ride her, so can you."

Well, when she puts it that way, I'm acting like a wimp.

I take a deep, calming breath. When that doesn't work, I flip my hair back and square my shoulders like the heartless criminal James Keller raised. It's just a horse. I've conquered much scarier challenges.

This dreamscape I'm caught in is about trying new things, such as letting the grumpy single dad dick me dirty in the barn after dark. My horizons are spreading like my thighs. A shiver zips down my spine at the reminder. Yes, that was delightful.

And there's no reason to limit myself now. I can pretend to be a cowgirl. It fits right in with my role as a nanny. No problem.

The little girl gasps. "Frannie! What happened?"

My head whips around, searching for the culprit. "Where?"

"On your neck!" She stabs her finger at me. "You've got boo-boos."

I lift my hand to the area, but don't feel anything. My fingers blindly reach for the knife holstered at my hip. The shiny blade gleams in the low light. It provides an adequate view of the hickeys decorating my delicate flesh. There are at least five of them.

This is why I should always check my reflection before going out in public. The rough patches on my cheek and jaw were obvious to the touch, but not very visible. There's no missing the red marks Byron gifted me like a brand.

"That son of a—"

Frannie makes another startled noise. "We're not supposed to play with knives. They're very sharp and can hurt us."

"Oh, I'm not playing." But I put the weapon away for her fragile mind's sake.

"Why do you have a knife?"

"For protection."

"Can I have one?"

I choke on my saliva. "No way, kiddo. You're too young."

"But you're young too."

My palm lifts to flatten against my chest. "Awww, thank you."

She stares at me expectantly.

"Oh, umm… you need to be a certain age."

"How many years old?"

"Uhh…" I stall again. Six is when I got my first knife, but that doesn't seem appropriate or safe. "Ten? Maybe twelve? You should ask your dad."

"M'kay." Ronnie spins on her heel, ready to do just that. "Wait!"

Shit, I need to think before I speak. This formerly innocent child already wants to cover her skin in tattoos thanks to me. Byron is going to kill me if she asks for a knife. Maybe we can call it even for the marks he left all over me. It's a small miracle Ronnie didn't press for the details of how those got there.

"You can't go now. I was about to get on Greta."

"Oh, yeah! Duh." She returns to her spot at the horse's head, gathering the lead rope in her tiny hand.

The moment has finally arrived. I gulp and test my footing on the step ladder. Ronnie was kind enough to drag it over to me. Usually I would've been offended at the assumption I needed it, but my current condition has humbled me.

My body trembles slightly as I secure my boot in the stirrup. A sharp ache radiates through my muscles when I reach for the saddle horn. I bite back a curse. That pain increases into stabbing cramps from the swinging motion needed to get my leg over. But then I'm astride Greta and the deep throb dulls into a manageable twinge.

"Phew, I did it." My fingers brush fake sweat off my forehead.

Ronnie beams at me like a proud teacher. "Okay, hold on."

I snort. That sounds familiar. The amusement vanishes when Greta begins to walk. Her gait is smooth, but I'm jostled to and fro faster than I prefer.

"Whoa! Why are we moving?"

She giggles. "That's the whole point, silly."

"Uh, can't I just… sit on her to start?"

"Nope."

"Go slow," I demand.

She rolls her eyes. "Yes, Mother."

Those words strike at the sensitive sliver she created in me. "Not funny. You shouldn't use that name as if I'm nagging you."

"Can I call you Mom to be nice?" That hopeful lilt in her voice will be my undoing.

Shit. I hang my head, once again stepping into a big pile of manure. Metaphorically or not, I'm really stinking it up this morning.

"Frannie is better. Stick to that," I murmur.

Her shoulders slump. "Fine."

We find a rhythm after that. It doesn't take long for me to realize riding is rather relaxing. I'm just going with the flow, rocking gently in the saddle. Ronnie seems happy to let silence rest between us. Greta's fuzzy ears are forward, which I take as a good sign. That allows me to sit and enjoy the rustic scenery.

But then there's a tingle across the nape of my neck, alerting me that we're no longer alone. A sideways glance reveals Byron darkening one of the many doorways. His arms are stretched overhead in an incredibly sexy, masculine pose that makes me thirsty. I swear he's standing like that on purpose. Even through the thick layer of his flannel jacket, I can envision the definition of muscle and control.

"Daddy!" Ronnie makes wild gestures with her arms when she should be focused on holding a horse. "Look, look! Frannie is riding."

A gruff chuckle rumbles from the cowboy. "I can't believe my eyes."

"What? You don't see her? She's right here." The little girl points at where I'm purposely avoiding Byron's stare.

I haven't been able to look at him since he double fucked me. My vagina was down to pound, but I didn't anticipate him screwing my mind too. After Byron shattered my orgasmic sexpectations, a familiar sense of panic rushed in and I needed to escape.

Sex isn't supposed to mean anything. It serves a purpose, such as giving a quick endorphin boost or dragging out secrets from an enemy. Byron made me feel too much and I'm not referring to the persistent ache between my legs.

That urgency to flee still pulses through me. My heart thunders like a herd of hoofbeats as his presence appears beside me and I'm no longer able to ignore him. A cloud of his crisp winter forest scent assaults me. He must've showered recently. Images of him drenched under the hot spray attempt to crack my composure. I keep my gaze firmly fixed ahead, trying not to breathe.

"Mornin', menace," he drawls.

Gosh, even his voice sounds like the best sex I've ever had. I barely suppress a shudder. My toes curl in my boots.

"Hey," I reply curtly.

Anything more than that might betray the calm I'm feigning. His exhale is disappointed. Serves him right after mounting me like a stallion while demanding commitment.

But Byron doesn't relent. I fight not to squirm as he remains rooted next to me. His determination to get a reaction rolls up the sleeves of his flannel as if it's that warm in the arena. My deprived eyeballs definitely notice every delicious inch of toned forearm he reveals.

Ronnie's loud yelp snaps me out of it. "You're hurt too! Just like Frannie."

I twist in the saddle to finally acknowledge him and see what the fuss is about. It's a mistake. His molten stare is burning into me, blazing a scorching path all over my face. Damn, the man can smolder. Sweat tickles my hairline while I choke on a staggered exhale.

"Where're you hurt?" Byron's gruff tone scrapes over me.

My throat is too dry. "Uhhh…"

"She's got spots on her neck," Ronnie announces.

His eyes lower to the mentioned area and heat like melted chocolate. "Not bad."

I scoff. "Admiring your work?"

"Can you blame me?"

My shrug is dismissive. "I didn't even notice. Ronnie had to point them out."

His expression hardens. "Looks serious to me. Like someone wanted to get a message across."

"Whatever you gotta tell yourself."

"I think Frannie got bitten by a monster, but she's a superhero and slayed the dragon with her knife," Ronnie cuts in.

"Let's go with that," I utter in agreement. My fingers discreetly cross in hopes she won't ask her dad for a blade.

Byron grunts. "Not how I would've described it."

"Were you there, Daddy? Is that why your arm's bleeding?"

That's when I remember he's raised her concern as well. There are four small gouges between his wrist and elbow. It's almost as if someone with very sharp nails grasped onto him with all their might while in the throes of passion. Satisfaction thrums through me—warm and potent and horribly misplaced. Shit.

"Just a scratch." His rasp is soft, but there's humor laced in the low notes.

"Did you wrangle a beast too?" I flutter my lashes in mock interest.

"She tried to buck me off, but I got the job done."

My cheeks go up in flames, probably putting his other marks on display. That will only encourage him. If there were reins on Greta's neck, I'd take my chances steering her away from this disaster.

Ronnie goes still suddenly, distracting me once again.

The little girl's eyes go wide and she crosses her legs. She clutches herself with an urgency we've all felt.

"I have to go potty! Daddy, you need to hold Greta."

As if she's going anywhere. I'm convinced this horse is part statue. But Byron dutifully takes his daughter's spot by the horse's head.

And then Ronnie is running off to the viewing spectator lounge built into the far end of the arena. The awareness that I'm alone with Byron clenches my inner muscles as if I haven't had enough. I hiss at the twinge spreading from the sensitive area.

His brow lifts "Problem?"

My shoulders straighten. "You branded me."

He tips the brim of his hat. "Ditto, darlin.'"

"Don't even start with that."

"How could I forget," he chuckles. "You're much more of a menace."

"Which is one of the first things you ever said to me," I recall absently.

"You remember?"

"My memory is still sharp at twenty-four. Don't make a big deal about it."

That smolder makes a captivating reappearance. The man can snatch the words straight from my mouth with that look alone. Maybe I didn't notice before now or he hadn't turned on the full force.

"But look how far we've come." That fiery gaze centers on the hickeys adorning my neck. "There's no question you're mine."

"Cool the obsession, stud. These are just hazards of hookups," I sigh. "We'll have to be more careful."

"You're saying there's a next time?"

"No!" I blurt.

"Do you regret it?"

The truth tumbles off my tongue before I can consider lying. "Not even a little bit."

He bites his bottom lip, dragging the plump flesh between his teeth. I almost whimper. My upper body most definitely leans forward, tipping me off balance. Greta doesn't twitch as I pinwheel in the saddle.

Byron steadies me easily. "Don't be reckless."

That's hilarious coming from the disturbance himself. "I'd like to get down."

"Why?" He smirks. "You look good up there."

"This isn't my idea of a safe space."

His sturdy grip is around my waist in the next second. Before I can question him, a seamless motion sweeps me off the seat. My boots land in the dirt while my chest presses entirely too close to his. I scurry back two steps before instinct gets the better of me.

"Uh, thanks."

Byron gives me another scorching look. "Did you enjoy the ride?"

My jaw drops. "We don't need to discuss it in detail. You were there."

"On Greta," he amends.

"Oh." If my face burns any hotter, I'll have to bury myself in the snow. "Yes, she's a very good girl."

"You two make a great team," he rumbles.

"Very funny. Are we done?"

"Somewhere else you need to be?"

My mind goes blank. I need at least an hour to decompress after this mental marathon. But admitting that is a weakness.

"Do I have to ask for permission?" I counter hotly.

He sighs, tugging at his hat almost in agitation. "I was thinking about taking Ronnie to visit Uncle Dennis. Want to join us?"

"Only if forced," I mutter.

Byron flinches. "Not planning to do more of that."

My nod appreciates that he's admitting fault in his actions, but the follow-through remains to be seen. "I think I'll spend the rest of the day testing the limits of this new-found freedom."

CHAPTER TWENTY-ONE

Byron

DENNIS HOOTS AND HOLLERS ALONG WITH THE rowdy celebration from the latest bingo winner. Luck hasn't been on his side tonight, but that doesn't stop him from joining in the ruckus. It's about community and moral support for him.

"Break time," he tells us. "We can stretch our legs."

"I'm busy." Ronnie's tongue is poking out as she covers her sheet in dots.

My grin approves of her rapid-fire method. "Looks like a winner."

"It's not, but that's okay. I'm gonna get all the numbers next time."

"That's the spirit!" Dennis shouts above the dull roar that's spreading through The Paddock like a victory lap.

This is the place to be in Cloverleaf Meadows for most notable social outings. Bingo is just one of many on their weekly event calendar. Not only is there a mega-jackpot coverall round, but they also provide a separate game for kids with a wide variety of prizes. The whole family can join in the fun and my little girl is taking advantage.

"B-I-N-G-O," she sings. "And soon they'll call my name-o!"

Dennis applauds her optimism. "Speaking of planning for the future, how are you ringing in the new year?"

"Same as usual," I drawl. Unless there's a kid-friendly event nearby that celebrates before bedtime, we're tucked safely at home for the occasion.

He scoffs. "That's not true. You've got a new member in your household. She's gotta account for a few changes 'round there."

My gut clenches at the mention of Frankie. Our situation is more complicated than she's willing to admit. If she thinks I'll be satisfied with a one-and-done, she's going to get another spanking. There's a noticeable twitch in my dick and I inhale a calming breath.

"Ronnie's nanny can spend the holiday however she pleases."

My daughter's hand pauses in midair, the dotting marker hanging in the balance. "Are you talkin' about Frannie?"

"The one and only." Dennis waggles his bushy eyebrows.

She discards the stamper as if it ran out of ink. Now we have her full attention. "I love her. She's gonna be my mommy someday."

My uncle chokes on his surprise. "Is that so?"

"Uh-huh, but not until she says so. I gotta be patient. It's so hard to wait."

"What's the holdup?" The force of his question rests on me.

"Aside from the truth?" I shoot the old man a scolding stare of my own. "You can't be serious."

"Why not? Seems legit."

My knee bounces under the table. "Frankie is Ronnie's nanny. We've decided that's all she'll be."

"For now," my daughter inserts.

"Forever," I correct.

She scowls. "Wanna bet?"

My exhale is ragged, much like this topic of conversation. "It's not a game, cupcake."

Dennis chuckles. "Your dad isn't much of a gambler."

"Not when the odds are stacked against me."

Ronnie's button nose crinkles. "What's that mean?"

"He doesn't think luck is on his side," my uncle explains.

An uncomfortable prickle crawls along the nape of my neck. "You know who raised me."

He dips his head. "I also know you're not him. Pretty sure you've spent the entirety of your adult life proving it."

"Which is why I don't take risks."

"Boring." My little girl pretends to snore before resuming her stamping project.

"Let's change the subject." But again, I'm on a losing streak and my uncle holds all the cards.

"I understand Ronnie is your whole world, as she should be," Dennis states in a tone that suggests there's more coming. "But you're more than a father. It's healthy to let the man out of the cage every once in a while."

I almost laugh. That's exactly what I did in the barn just yesterday. But there are limits, such as the one we're currently toeing.

The brim of my hat gets tugged down to hide any visible tells. "We're not discussing this."

"I believe we are. There are ample opportunities to let that part of you roam free. Don't deprive yourself, son."

"Are you speaking from experience?" This is beginning to sound like an exchange we already had recently.

"Absolutely," he booms. "What do you call this?"

The wide stretch of his arms refers to the commotion surrounding us. After his wife died, he spent several months locked away with his grief. But then Brody married Paisley and took ownership of Benson Farmstead. Retirement has rejuvenated him. He's got me cornered and the smirk lifting his wrinkled skin is smug.

"So," Dennis continues. "Be spontaneous for a change."

"I'll keep that in mind," I mutter.

He claps me on the shoulder. "You do that while I babysit Ronnie on New Year's Eve."

My daughter chooses that moment to pay attention, squealing at her grand-uncle's meddling. "Can we have a slumber party?"

"That's the idea. I'll be sure there are extra snacks and crafts to keep us busy. Bring the dogs along for the fun," Dennis says.

Ronnie cheers loudly, managing to steal the spotlight

over the crowd's noise. "Yay! We're gonna have the best-est time. Darla and Dottie looooove to stay up super late watching movies."

"With those two pups in charge, we might never go to bed."

My little girl giggles. "That's okay. Just don't tell Daddy."

"It'll be our secret." How this cheerful man is related to my surly father remains a mystery.

"I appreciate the offer, but it's not necessary." There I go, dumping a cold bucket of water on their excitement.

"Nonsense." Dennis swats my argument away. "This will allow you to let loose. Release your inhibitions. Dance the night away with a certain redhead. Whatever tickles your fancy."

"Oh, oh!" Ronnie leaps off her chair. "You can take Frannie on a date. Just like you used to do with Mommy. Make sure you buy her pretty flowers."

"What a great idea," Dennis praises as his primary focus takes shape.

Pressure settles on my shoulders. "I doubt Frankie likes flowers."

My little girl scoffs. "How do you know?"

"She's not the traditionally romantic type," I defend.

"Plan something more unexpected," Dennis suggests.

Ronnie gasps. "Get her a knife! She loooooves knives. Can I have a knife, Daddy? Frannie told me to ask you."

"Nobody is getting a knife," I state evenly. That woman is going to be the death of my sanity. "And I'm not going on a date with Frankie."

My daughter's broad grin wobbles at the edges. "Why not?"

"She's your nanny," I say as if that will settle this dispute.

Ronnie immediately dashes those strands of hope. "She's a superhero too! If you're nice, maybe she'll let you ride her motorcycle. It goes really fast. Like a rocket ship."

"I'll stick to horses. They're more my speed."

She blinks at me. "Horses can pull a sleigh in the snow."

"That's right," I agree with her random thought.

"Just like Sven in *Frozen*. Anna and Kristoff were together in his sled. You can do that with Frannie on a date!" The connection she makes is baffling.

I'd be more impressed if it wasn't at my expense. "How about I take you on a sleigh ride?"

"No, thanks."

A sharp snort flies free, offended by her brashness. "We could try—"

"I want you to go with Frannie." There's an edge of finality in her voice that dares me to argue.

"Cupcake," I sigh. "Frankie and I don't get along."

Her flat stare sees straight through me. "Yes, you do."

"We really don't," I reiterate.

"Then why do you get hearts in your eyeballs whenever you look at her?"

Dennis tries to muffle a bark of laughter behind his fist, but fails miserably. "Spit it out, son. We're all family."

I grind my molars until an ache spreads in my jaw. "You don't have to make this more difficult for me."

The devious twinkle in his eye is alarming. "This is for your own good."

There isn't much left to say, especially with these two teamed up against me. "I'm sure Frankie already has plans."

"Only one way to find out," Dennis croons.

"Ask her!" Ronnie applauds her correct answer.

"We'll see," I evade.

"What's she doing now?"

I glare at my uncle. "Does it matter?"

"Wouldn't hurt to send her a quick text. Just to get it out of the way."

"Yes, do that!" My seemingly innocent daughter points at where my phone sits on the table. "Tell her I miss her, m'kay?"

Before I can put an end to this spiral, the bingo caller turns on the microphone. Every voice in the room shuts off as if connected to a switch. "We'll begin round seven in two minutes. This will be a traditional bingo. Winner gets two hundred dollars or their choice of prize from the table." She sends a collective wink to the children spread around the large area.

"Yippppeee! I'm gonna pick the bedazzling kit. We need it to make our crafts sparkle." Ronnie claps in optimistic glee.

My smile returns easily. "You'll have to show me how it works."

"Frannie can teach you. She's got a whole book about it."

Warmth spreads through my chest. "Of course she does."

"Shhhhhh," she shushes me and presses a finger to my lips. "We gotta listen."

But my mind is elsewhere. The more I think about it, another night with Frankie is a fantasy I'm eager to explore. I glance down at the punctures she left on my arm. The wounds are healing, but my memory is infected with our explosive fuckery. She might need convincing. I could leave that up to Ronnie. Dennis would gladly join in the bombarding.

"Bingo! I got bingo!" Ronnie is jumping up and down, waving her paper in the air.

The caller laughs into the microphone. "Congratulations, cutie. Come on up here and get your winnings. For those playing for money, the game is still live."

My little girl wraps me in a tight squeeze. When she straightens from the hug, her tiny index finger races down the slope of my nose and taps my chin. I repeat the gesture instantly.

"Guess what?" she whispers.

"You love me?"

"Duh," she giggles and rolls her eyes. "That's not what I was gonna say."

"Tell me," I urge.

Ronnie twirls away, the widest smile plastered on her face. "I'm gonna make Frannie something really super pretty for your date!"

CHAPTER TWENTY-TWO

"Y OU LOOK SO BEAUTIFUL!" RONNIE STANDS OVER my right shoulder while I finish applying my lipstick. "That color matches your hair. It's really pretty."

I blow a kiss at her reflection the mirror. "You're too sweet, kiddo. Thanks for the confidence boost."

Her head cocks sideways at that adorably confused angle. "What's confidence?"

My leather-clad butt spins on the bench, putting us face-to-face. "I'm not quite sure how to describe it, but think of it as a bright light inside of you. That shine makes you feel strong and powerful. Certain things will make the light even brighter like compliments or good deeds. Others might try to dull your sparkle. Most of the time that's because their own confidence is weak. Just be a good person and let your light brighten each day."

"Um, okay. I get it." But her forehead is creased.

"Don't believe anyone who says you're not perfect just the way you are. If people are mean and talk down at you, don't listen. Or come find me. I'll deal with them. Remember it's what's in here that counts." I tap the center of her chest.

"I'm gonna keep my light shining super bright so I can be just like you when I grow up."

My wince is almost painful. "You can aim higher than that."

Ronnie's green eyes go round as she gasps. "Oh, I've got gifts for you. It will give you more confidence."

"Gifts? As in multiple?"

She giggles behind her hands. "You're gonna be so surprised!"

"But I didn't get you anything."

Her smile is a genuine burst of happiness that I feel in my dark soul. "You're staying here with me for always and that's the bestest present of all."

Emotion forms a lump in my throat. It spreads to my smokey-shadowed eyes in a fiery stint. I fan at my face rapidly, cursing the flood of tears that never plagued me until this little girl appeared in my life.

"Why are you crying?" Her soft voice only makes the pressure swell.

My shrug is helpless. "I'm not sure. It's something that happens now."

"M'kay!" She twirls out of the room.

I'm left alone with my inability to cope for no more than one minute. It's a blessing until I see what she's holding. The amount of rhinestones and glitter is blinding. My blurry vision struggles to identify the items she's holding.

"Wow," I breathe.

Ronnie rushes toward me. "I made these for you!"

Two dangling objects are thrust entirely too close to my face. The earrings are heart-shaped, as big as her palm, and covered in pink gems. My mouth works soundlessly for several seconds.

"These are… unlike anything I own," I manage to mumble.

"Put them on!" She gives them a jiggle, showing off their disco-ball quality.

After removing the small black hoops I usually wear in my first holes, I put in the much larger pair. They're made of plastic and thankfully don't tug too hard on my lobes.

I turn back to the mirror to inspect them. "Well, look at that," I croon. "They fit."

She appears behind me. "There's a ring too. It matches."

"That's too much. How did I get so lucky?" I stick out my index finger for her to put it on.

"I won a bedazzling kit at bingo. We can use it for our crafts!"

"Such a great idea." I stand and do a slow spin, gesturing at the full ensemble. "What do you think?"

Approval gleams in Ronnie's expression. "Your confidence is shining super bright."

"Thanks to you, kiddo."

"Are you gonna wear your jacket?"

"I was planning on it. Why?"

She giggles and I mentally brace myself. "There are sparkles all over it."

"The gems stick to leather?"

"Yep!"

"That's an unexpected twist." I force a smile while mourning the innocence of my oldest companion. "What time is Uncle Dennis taking you to dinner?"

"I dunno."

"Where's your dad?"

Ronnie glances over at the window where the sun finishes its evening descent. "In the barn."

My pulse leaps and takes off in a gallop. "I have to go. Can you go find Uncle Dennis? He's downstairs in the den."

She blinks at me. "No."

I silently scold myself. Not sure why I asked. "Your dad will be done soon. It's important that I leave before him."

"Why?"

"I don't want to ruin the surprise."

She narrows her eyes. "What surprise?"

"Umm…" The flashy bling is muddling my mind. "We're playing a game."

Suspicion deepens the groove between her brows. "What kind of game?"

If I'm being honest, it's where I disappear into the night without a trace to avoid another awkward exchange. We haven't spoken much since that morning in the arena and that was days ago. I'd rather spend New Year's Eve forgetting my troubles than inviting them to haunt me.

"Hide and seek," I blurt.

"Daddy has to find you?" The little girl doesn't sound convinced.

"Uh, yeah. That's how it works."

"Was it his idea?"

"Sure," I mumble.

"That's kinda romantic, I guess."

My head is already rejecting that term with a stern shake. "It's not meant to be."

"Yes-huh, silly. You're going on a date."

It feels like all the blood drains from my face. "Did he tell you that?"

Ronnie's face pinches. "I think so? But Uncle Dennis said it first. That's why he's babysitting me."

Urgency kicks me into motion. I don't know if she's telling the truth, but I'm not sticking around to find out. Ronnie is seconds away from calling me out for lying. After shoving my phone in my purse, I'm ready to flee.

I drop a kiss on her forehead, leaving a red stain behind. "Be good, okay?"

"M'kay!" She wraps her little arms around me for a quick hug.

"See ya next year, kiddo."

Her features crumple into a stricken mess. "No! That's super far away."

"It's tomorrow," I assure her. "That's just a phrase people use. It's supposed to be funny."

"Oh! 'Cause it's the end of the year." Her smile reignites. "I get it."

"Smart cookie." I boop the end of her nose.

She takes that as a sign to swoop down the bridge of mine, ending with a tap to my chin. Warmth injects into my icy veins and I almost repeat the motions. It's such a foreign comfort to be loved.

"Did you give Daddy a clue?"

My grin is still caught in the clouds. "For what?"

"Your hiding spot," she giggles.

That snaps me out of it and I straighten. "Nope."

"How will he find you?"

If all goes well, he won't. But that's not what she wants to hear. Adrenaline floods through me. My heart is suddenly racing too hard. It's probably visible through my tight shirt. The clock on the wall ticks loudly to mock me.

"Whose side are you on, hmm? Don't you want me to win?"

Ronnie shoos me toward the hallway. "Better hurry or Daddy's gonna get you."

A collection of water stains on the ceiling captures my attention while I fight a losing battle against sheer boredom. It's been a struggle since I arrived at Inn Kahoots. What I expected was a lost sense of nostalgia. The reality is much more bleak.

My lack of interest gives the packed biker bar another glance for old time's sake. That's what's kept me here this long. The dingy atmosphere is my scene. These are my scrappy people. But it feels stale and flat.

Honestly, the only bright spots are the rhinestones stuck on me. I got more than a few curious looks, but my reputation is louder than the unfamiliar sparkle. A few still needed a reminder. The dumbass who tried his luck by smacking my ass is still nursing his sprained wrist at the opposite end of the rail.

"We're planning to ride all the way to Montana without stopping," the shaggy dude beside me drones on, tugging my focus from the damage above.

"Thrilling," I murmur absently.

"The rally will be sick. You should join us."

"I'll think about it." Which is code for giving less than half a shit.

"Cool." He bobs his head loosely, feeling the alcohol and heavy beat pounding through the speakers. "Want another?"

My spirit is exhausted from feigning enthusiasm. I'm not even sure what he's talking about. That forces me to actually look at him. It doesn't do him any favors.

Rather than a rugged cowboy with a dirty mouth, there's a threadbare biker who could use a shower. A defeated sigh emphasizes the letdown. Another follows when I catch his beady stare bouncing between my drained glass and my rack.

"Sure," I mutter. "Why not."

He flags down the bartender and then returns his focus to my tits. "Tough day?"

I can't muster enough energy to shrug. "Not really."

His grunt is drowned by a sip of Bud Light. "Then what's with the long face?"

It's a decent question. It's also one I don't want to answer.

"Been spending a lot of time around horses," I kick back.

"Deflection at its best. I'll drink to that." He lifts his beer. "But I'd rather hear the truth."

My lips curl in pure condescendence. "I couldn't care less about what you want."

Interest sparks in his muddy eyes. They're the wrong shade of brown. "You'll say otherwise after I turn that frown upside down."

Nausea flips my stomach, churning faster when he grins at me with yellowed teeth. I want to cringe, but scoff at myself instead. When did I become so particular? He seems like a decent enough guy. We could probably exchange a few orgasms. But there's absolutely zero heat flowing to the basement region.

I allow my sights to wander again, as if I'll find anything more appealing between the ruined pool tables and broken jukebox. A hollow ache pierces my chest. I hate to admit it, but I'm disappointed Byron didn't find me.

That's when the front door bangs open. The entire bar falls silent as if the cops or a rival gang just strode in. But it's worse. Very much so. I whip around to get a better view, not believing my eyes.

Clogging the entrance like a character from a Wild West film is none other than Byron Benson. Everyone is dressed in leather and a criminal record while he wears his Stetson with pride. His shadowed stare searches the crowd, just waiting for someone to challenge him to a duel. The famous whistled tune from *The Good, the Bad and the Ugly* plays in my head.

Rather than a theme song, the hush around me turns into aggressive murmurs. This is biker territory and Byron just crossed a line. I consider running, but this is the most exciting thing that's happened since I stepped foot in this dive.

My boots stay glued to the sticky floor. It's not my responsibility to teach him the rules. If he's old enough to have gray in his beard, he should be wise enough to know better.

When his gaze meets mine, an electric charge surges between us. I swallow a gasp as his glare melts into a smolder. There's a glint of humor buried in there. The expression ignites my veins and I'm engulfed in his blatant desire. Fuck, I should've ditched this shit hole when I had the chance.

The angry mob parts, allowing him to walk the plank toward me. I keep my chin held high as many turn the scope of their fury. It appears we'll go down together for his mistake.

My jaw is clenched and about to snap in half when he reaches me. "Do you have a death wish?" I hiss.

Byron has the audacity to smirk. "I've got you to protect me, little menace. You don't look all that homicidal this evening, though. What's with the rhinestones?"

After a scathing roll of my eyes, I grasp his arm and drag him to the nearest corner for some semblance of privacy. I whirl on him and stab a finger into his chest. "What in the ever-loving hell are you doing here?"

"Finding you. That's the point of the game, right?"

My belly doesn't swoop. Definitely not. "Ronnie told you?"

"Of course," he grunts. "She was thrilled at the illusion of you being trapped in a tower and I arrive just in time to rescue you. It's 'romantical'. Her words, not mine."

I quirk a brow. "And what's all this nonsense about you taking me out on a date?"

The lighting in here is piss poor, but I swear he blushes. "Dennis and Ronnie were behind that. I just went along with it to get them off my back."

"We're not going on a date."

He lifts his hands. "Fine by me."

I huff at his easy surrender. "How did you know where I was?"

"Your phone's location is shared with mine," he states casually.

Meanwhile, it feels like I'm imploding. My muscles vibrate, coiling tight in preparation to launch an attack. "That's a massive invasion of my privacy! What the fuck is wrong with you?"

His eyes widen as if I'm overreacting. "It's a precaution for Ronnie. I need to be able to track you when you're not at the house."

"And you couldn't have told me that?"

"My fault. I was under the assumption you'd blow it out of proportion. I can see now that it would've been a rational conversation." The sarcasm dripping from his voice isn't appreciated.

"You're diabolical. I haven't taken Ronnie anywhere by

myself yet. Someone is still chaperoning as if I'm capable of hurting her." The thought alone makes me sick.

Byron's wince does little to soothe me. "Wasn't sure you were ready."

"Could've asked!" I toss my arms up. "About all of it."

"I'd apologize, but I'm not sorry." His eyes gleam as he recycles my phrase. "As I said, it's a precaution."

"I'm going to take that word and shove it—"

"Can we discuss the glitter and sparkles yet?"

My nostrils breathe fire. "Gifts from your daughter."

"Gotta be honest," he chuckles. "I'm shocked you kept them on."

"Goes to show how little you think of me," I fire in return.

"If only you thought of me at all," he rumbles.

The selfish insinuation makes me want to scream. Fury rises in me like an uncontrollable storm. "But I do! Constantly. That's the problem. You've tainted me."

"In what ways?" Byron towers over my shorter height, blocking out the mayhem around us.

At this distance, his woodsy cologne completely masks the stench of damp carpet and uncivilized savagery. I could almost pretend we're somewhere else. His stare anchors mine, beckoning me to delve in. To get lost in this darkened escape. But then a beer bottle breaks and shatters the fantasy.

My eyes clench shut, refusing to face the reality of our situation. "I used to be perfectly content in a place like this.

It's where I fit in. But now? I can't see past the rot and cracks and ruin."

"There's nothing wrong with wanting more," he murmurs.

"Easy for you to say. You live in that world. I'm just visiting."

Byron's thumb traces the upturned shape of my jawline. "There's no going back, menace."

"That's what I'm afraid of." And the misery in my voice proves it.

His smirk is obnoxious. It makes me want to punch him. "You missed me."

That deserves a jab to the arm, which I deliver automatically. "I most certainly did not."

"No? Should I leave?"

"Yes."

"Okay." Byron tips his hat and begins backing away.

This strange, reckless abandon bubbles up from my gut. It tries to strangle me. I struggle against the force, refusing to surrender. But the rush of desperation is crippling.

"Wait!"

He pauses. "Change your mind?"

My bottom lip is tortured between my teeth. "You shouldn't be driving right now. There are a lot of irresponsible idiots on the road."

"Are you concerned for my safety?"

I glance around the bar. Many are still glaring in our direction, likely to inflict pain. A smart person would read the room and seek shelter elsewhere. Based on the cowboy cooties wafting over me, I'm not in my most intelligent mindset.

"This doesn't mean I'm kissing you at midnight," I mutter.

Byron's grin isn't dissuaded in the least. "What if my tongue is in your pussy?"

My body goes unnaturally still. The air seems to freeze. Static crackles as I try to process his request.

Many months ago, a random guy who crossed my path was in a generous mood and begged to go down on me. He was hot and I was curious. Nobody had ever done that to me before. But just as he was about to get after it, I shoved him away. Something about it didn't feel right. Most likely accepting that level of intimacy.

"Hey," Byron whispers. "What's going on up here?"

My temples are throbbing to an erratic beat. "I'm having entirely too many intrusive thoughts at once."

"Tell me a few."

A tremble rolls through me from tit to toe. "I have the urge to threaten you with bodily harm while simultaneously riding your face."

Lust darkens his gaze. "That can be arranged."

I lick at my suddenly dry lips, trying to drag in a full breath. "Deal."

And then we're on the move. My hand latches onto his for the sole purpose of dragging him to the opposite end of the bar. Byron doesn't question me. The devious plotting reflected in my expression is frightening enough to remove innocent bystanders out of my way. But our path is suddenly blocked.

"Is this man bothering you, babe?"

I lurch to a halt when met by a burly chest the size of a barrel. My gaze climbs a long, gravelly path to the rough planes of a weathered face. The man's scowl looks more deadly than a loaded weapon.

A breezy laugh wisps from me. "He's the one you should be worried about. I'm taking him to the office."

A chorus of mock fear erupts from our audience. The guy still acting like a noble speed bump assesses me coldly. I treat him to the same offense. We're locked in a standoff that he'll lose. After ten more dreadfully long seconds, he decides to not let the gaudy bling fool him and steps aside.

My punishing glare slices across the captivated gawkers. "Don't even think about following us."

I yank on Byron's hand and set us in motion again. He's quiet, but I can feel the question burning into my back. We turn into the short hallway that brings us to a soundproof door.

"What's in there?"

I smile while grabbing a particular pin from my hair. "You'll see."

Byron coughs on his surprise when I pick all three locks in under a minute. "Tight security."

My shrug is casual as I push into the dark room. "If you can't get yourself in, you don't have permission to use it."

I walk a line forged from memory. A single lightbulb dangles in the middle, flickering on from a pull of the string.

The windowless room looks the same. Beer kegs and other random crap are piled against one wall. The other three hold an assortment of weapons. There's a chair bolted into the floor. Chains and ropes wait at the ready beside it. Nothing else is worth notice. My pulse skips a beat while I give every surface a second glance. It's a mixture between torture chamber and storage closet.

Byron spins in a slow circle. "What the fuck?"

A flash of movement slams us together. My knife is pressed against his throat in the next second. One wrong move and his jugular is at risk of severing. I'm volatile and unapologetic. If he didn't like it, he wouldn't tolerate me.

"I'll be the one asking questions," I seethe.

He gulps, but his body language is calm otherwise. "Whatever you say, menace."

"Who's in charge?"

"You."

"Will you let me carve my name in your chest?"

He blindly rips at the top buttons of his western shirt. "Do it."

I cluck my tongue. "You have to earn it. Are you going to behave?"

There's a naughty curve on his mouth. "Yes."

"Can I trust you?"

"Yes," he repeats.

"Don't make me regret this."

"I won't."

My sharp blade lifts from his skin. There's a small cut left in its wake, beading with a few drops of blood. A burst of satisfaction fills me. He looks even sexier with a fresh mark from me on him.

I back myself into the narrow gap framed by shelves of ammunition and racks of guns. A motion from my knife instructs him to follow. Byron obeys instantly.

"Get down on your knees." The tip of my blade points to the spot.

He lowers without hesitation, looking at me for the next command.

"Good boy," I praise.

But now I'm at a loss. This is when I enter uncharted territory. Stagnant heat spits from the vent in a rattle, calling out the awkward lapse. My bravado quivers for a moment too long. Byron notices and slowly lifts his hands toward my waist.

"May I?"

It seems like a requirement. The man might be built of brawn and arrogance, but even he will struggle to rip leather apart at the seams. I nod for him to proceed.

Byron opens my pants and peels the supple material down my legs, stripping off the scrap of my thong in one fell swoop. I assume he's going to undo my boots to finish the job.

"Brace yourself."

That's the only warning I get. He lifts my caged ankles off the ground, which hoists me higher on the wooden wall. A fluid ducking maneuver wedges his head into the split between my thighs as if it was created for him. It's stunning how quickly he pulled that off, but then my mind blanks out.

His exhales puff against my exposed center. A shiver ripples through me and I moan. In this position, we're locked together. I'm apprehended. It's vulnerable and requires trust—two things I avoid. But I decide to see where this goes.

I relax and allow my knees to hang over his shoulders. My ass kisses the cool panels behind me, chasing off some of the fire in my veins. Byron's palms are suddenly there to cradle my butt like a seat. He's holding me as if I weigh no more than a feather. I feel fragile and precious. It's not entirely unpleasant.

"Ready?" The question caresses my arousal.

I haven't dared to move during this readjustment other than where he's placed me. My nod is barely recognizable.

"Need to hear you," he rasps.

The embers of my stubborn pride burn through me, keeping my attention fixed straight ahead. "Go ahead."

But he doesn't listen. "Look at me."

That's the opposite of what instinct dictates. The thought of gazing longingly at someone induces nausea. I've never exchanged eye contact with my partners during sexual acts. It's too intimate and sensual. But this is Byron. He's not a faceless identity I get to walk away from.

My glare lowers to his. "I'm tempted to stab you."

There's entirely too much emotion swelling in those warm brown depths. "If that's what you need to stay suspended in this moment."

"Aren't I restrained enough?" I buck against him and get nowhere.

He tightens his grip. "Be here with me. I've got you."

That traitorous burn attacks my eyes and I blink quickly. "Okay."

I'm helpless to watch as his tongue tastes what nobody else has. The first swipe is gentle, almost like a tease. I squirm in impatience. His chuckle scolds me. Before I can discipline him with my knife, he opens wide and buries his face in my pussy.

It's a shock to my system. I jolt from the unexpected intensity. A hit of pleasure injects directly into my bloodstream, instantly drugging me. My muscles go lax as Byron eats like a starved man. The wet noises would probably embarrass me if I could focus. I'm mindless under his influence.

And then he zeroes in on my clit. A surge of tingles detonates, spreading in a throbbing wave. The impact seizes me and I drop the knife. It clatters to the ground as I knock Byron's hat off his head. My fingers tunnel into his hair to get a grip. I use that as an anchor while he aims to destroy me.

"Fuck," I choke out. "It feels too good."

But that's a massive understatement. My entire body feels plugged in and cranked to the max. Even the skin covering my elbows thrums to the tempo of his unrelenting onslaught. He licks me faster, swerving around my clit at a speed that makes me dizzy.

"You're so smooth." He pauses to explore the intimate

area like a treasure hunter without a map. "Did you shave for me again? I didn't get to ask last time."

My snort tapers off into a whine. "I wax, and don't kid yourself. My pubic hair has been routinely ripped from its roots long before I met you."

"But this silky pussy is mine now."

"Only if you quit with the social hour."

"Apologies."

There's humor in his voice, but I don't get the chance to reprimand him. He resumes his dedication with several devastating swipes across my clit before tugging it between his teeth. The suction he adds next might do me in.

I curl my toes as tension overwhelms me. The rasp of his beard strokes my hunger. That friction isn't enough. My grasp on his hair yanks harder and I begin grinding against him. Pressure expands with every jerky motion. I'm stimulated to the extreme. Almost there.

"If you stop, I'll kill you," I croak.

Muffled laughter tempts me. "Never gonna happen."

"Less talking. More eating."

His moan is rich and decadent. "My mouth is full of your pussy. I'd love nothing more than to drown in you."

Byron rolls his tongue in a certain way, shooting stars across my vision. When he slides a finger inside me, I'm thrown over the edge. The release isn't quiet or kind. I thrash against the climatic burst. Spasms quake my limbs as liquid fire rushes through my veins. A shriek wrenches free while I surrender to sensation. All the while, Byron continues working me over to drain every drop.

This is more than an orgasm. It's an awakening. There are tremors in places I can't name. I'll never be the same again. The broody cowboy has tainted me worse than before.

"Damn," I wheeze. My throat is a sandy beach after gasping uncontrollably.

I can't see straight. I'm strung out on his tongue. That's my only excuse for allowing another piece of my guard to crumble and remain present.

A cautious glance at the man responsible steals what little composure I was able to gather. My arousal coats Byron's lips in a natural gloss. It looks like he's fresh from the feast and I love it.

A pleased sound rumbles from him. He kisses my inner thigh, peering up at me with fierce possession. I'd think he was in the mood to eat me up if he didn't already.

"Happy New Year, little menace."

"Right back at ya, stud."

Byron breathes a laugh. "Can I take you home?"

I'd agree to just about anything right now, but my reputation is hanging on by a thread. "Do that again and I'll consider it."

CHAPTER TWENTY-THREE

OVER THE NEXT TWO WEEKS, WE DEVELOP SOMEWHAT of a balanced routine. Frankie dotes on my daughter and refines her skills as a nanny. I work around the clock while pretending not to track the redhead wherever she goes. After dark, we meet somewhere in the middle to fuck. If I catch her in a generous mood, she'll ride my face until the sun is set to rise. That's how I'm hoping to find her tonight.

There's a light on in the den, luring me down the stairs. Frankie is sprawled on the couch in front of the television. On the screen, a commercial advertises a quick fix for erectile disfunction. I almost snort. That'll never be an issue with this woman living in my house.

She hasn't noticed my intrusion, which allows me to watch her. The gleam of polished metal stabs at my retinas when she holds up a knife as if inspecting it. After approving the spotless shine, she moves to the next one. Her seamless process buffs six more before I announce myself.

"That's quite a collection, little menace."

Frankie startles at the sound of my voice, jolting in place as if electrocuted. "Holy shit!"

I should've considered the fact that she has a dozen blades within reach before sneaking up on her. But to my surprise, she doesn't launch an attack. Rather than worry about the unsheathed weapons, she lunges for the remote and punches the power button in rapid succession. Once that's done, she whips around to serve me her wrath.

"Do you want me to hurt you?"

"Kinky," I rasp. "Are we talking about just pain or is pleasure included?"

Her scowl deepens and she slices a blade through the space between us. "I could've chopped your balls off."

"That'd be a shame for both of us."

"There are many dicks in the sea, stud."

My sigh is exaggerated. "You know just what to say to make a man feel special."

Frankie drifts her thumb along the lethal points of a serrated blade. "It's a gift."

I take a meaningful glance across her impressive arsenal. "And here I thought we were getting somewhere."

"We were until you crept in behind me like a stalker."

"Got something to hide?"

The truth widens her eyes before she can smother the reaction. "Just a few dead bodies. Nothing out of the ordinary."

"What were you watching?" I didn't notice what show came on after the ads.

"Nothing," she blurts.

"A true crime documentary giving advice on how to get away with murder?"

She scoffs and flips a section of red hair over her shoulder. "As if I need any pointers."

Which is freakishly accurate. I should probably leave her to it and back away slowly. Instead, my curiosity spurs me forward.

I round the end of the sofa at a normal pace to avoid suspicion. "Plotting my demise?"

Frankie calculates my every step like a sniper with her finger on the trigger. "Unless you've got a better idea."

"This oughta do it." A single tap to my phone turns on the television.

"Noooooooooo!" Her screech might wake the neighbors miles down the road. The ear-splitting racket rattles the windows as she lunges for the remote again, but it's too late.

"*Perfect Match*," I read the logo in the corner of the screen.

"It's not what it looks like." Frankie's usually fair complexion resembles a stop sign, but I'm not obeying the law.

"Hot damn," I hoot. Dry laughter is shaking my entire frame. "You're watching a cheesy dating show."

She hides her face in the safety of her palms. "Paisley got me hooked. I know it's bad for me, but I can't stop. It's gotten out of control."

My giddy amusement is thoroughly entertained as a

couple sits on a picturesque beach while feeding each other strawberries. "Wow, I didn't expect this from you. I honestly thought you were watching porn."

Her glare snaps to mine. "While cleaning my knives? What kind of sex fiend do you take me for?"

I scrub at my beard. "That's a loaded question."

"My imagination is stocked to the brim thanks to you."

"I'll take that as a compliment."

Her eyes heat. "You should, big boy."

An insistent pulse begins to twitch my dick and I spread my stance. "That still doesn't explain the fluffy shit you're watching. Thought you didn't like that sort of thing?"

"Fine, make jokes. It's hilarious and ridiculous. I have an unhealthy addiction to trashy reality shows. You've officially seen the worst of me." It's as if she's admitting to a heinous crime.

"Don't be too hard on yourself." I try to roll my lips between my teeth to sober up, but it's just too outrageous. "We've all got guilty pleasures."

"Oh, really?" Her exhale isn't impressed with my failed efforts. "What's yours?"

"You."

A pretty pink streaks across her cheekbones and she dips her chin. "Those added benefits are stacking up lately."

"Won't hear me complain."

"Is that what you came for?"

"More or less," I drawl. "Is a blowjob too much to ask for?"

Frankie glowers. "I'd think that request through if I were you. I have a tendency to bite."

"Noted," I chuckle. "There's actually something I wanted to ask you."

She flops back against the couch cushions and folds her arms across her chest. "This ought to be rich."

"Ronnie got invited to a birthday party. It's on Saturday when I have a large load of horses arriving at the auction barn. Would you be willing to bring her?"

Stunned green eyes blink at me. "Alone?"

I grip the nape of my neck. "There's gonna be a lot of kids. It's at one of those indoor playground deals. If you're not up for that, I totally understand."

It might be my imagination, but there are unshed tears glittering at me. "You trust me to take her there by myself?"

My feet get restless and I shuffle in place. "It's about time. You've proven to be more than capable of caring for her. Besides, if anything happens, you'll punish yourself worse than I ever could. Ronnie also knows to call me in case of an emergency."

"Um, okay." She slips off the sofa to kneel where I'm standing. Her deft fingers begin working on my belt buckle.

I freeze as lust quickly hardens my cock. "What're you doing?"

"Gonna suck your dick," she says while lowering my zipper.

"You don't have to do this. I wasn't serious about the blowjob." Why I'm trying to dissuade her doesn't make a lick of sense.

"Hush," she purrs and wraps her hands around my shaft. "Don't overthink it. I need to keep my mouth busy so I don't say anything stupid."

"Whatever you gotta do," I croak as her tongue laps at the precum on my tip.

"Good boy." Frankie seals her lips around me, sucking hard enough to drain every ounce of logic.

My eyes roll shut. "Fuck, that's it."

And she's just getting started. While her fingers grip me at the base, she starts bobbing on my cock. I stagger and my knees almost buckle. Without surrendering my dick, Frankie guides me to sit on the sofa. My legs collapse when a deep throb pulses through me. She's a warm, wet dream playing in real time. The sensations fondle me in an unforgiving grasp, but the curtain of red shrouds my visual.

I gather her hair in my fist. It gives me a clear shot at the action. Frankie hollows her cheeks and pushes lower. My tip nudges the back of her throat, signaling her to retreat slowly. An upward stroke from her hand follows. The extra stimulation spreads tingles through my balls.

Almost immediately, she's sinking back down until meeting resistance. I'm not an average-sized man. There are a solid four or five inches that she hasn't conquered. Frankie accepts the challenge, forcing more of my length in her throat. Dark spots speckle my vision when she swallows.

A whimper trips out of me. It's such a pitiful noise. This woman has reduced me to a simpering fool again. Only she has this power over me.

Her moan jerks my hips off the cushion. Another inch

slips inside and the pressure triples. My molars clack when I clench against the force. It's too soon. Frankie isn't done, wedging the last of me beyond her gag reflex. I'm breathing heavily to match her labored exhales. This is a first and it compels me.

"Damn, menace." Awe tinges my voice as I cradle her stretched jaw. My touch is a gentle praise. "You're so fucking sexy."

While adjusting to the deep-throat intrusion, she blindly grabs my wrist and flattens my palm against the front of her neck. There's an unmistakable bulge underneath. I gulp at the implied fullness. Before I can spew more compliments, Frankie hums loudly. It sends vibrations through my entire pelvic region.

I'm thrusting before recognition can slap me. Tremors seize my muscles and jerk me to release. Frankie doesn't falter, taking the spurts in stride. White streaks blind me while relief pours in. I submit to the pleasure, getting swept away in a ripple of heat. It goes on for long enough that I lose feeling in my limbs.

Awareness seeps in when Frankie pops off my cock. "Dammit, I didn't get to warn you."

Her watery eyes narrow. "Not a quitter, stud. Don't insult me."

I chuckle, but it's mostly a wheeze. "My mistake."

As I give myself permission to bask in the afterglow, Frankie sits back on her heels. She wipes at the corner of her puffy lips and rises to park her fine ass next to me. After snagging the remote, she rewinds the show and resumes cleaning her knives. This seductress is completely unbothered while I'm caught in a daze with my dick still hanging out.

"Gonna make it?" Her attention doesn't waver from the blade in her grip.

By some miracle, I manage to unglue my tongue from the roof of my mouth. "Not sure what I did to deserve that."

Frankie is quiet for a moment that's thick with inner conflict. "Beats me. Maybe we'll figure it out together someday."

CHAPTER TWENTY-FOUR

SLICK CITY IS MY WORST NIGHTMARE. THE INDOOR slide park is loud, crowded, and smells like a sweaty gym sock. Unmonitored children whiz past me from every which way without a care where they're going. There are so many obstacles crammed in here, I can't see straight. It's nothing short of a cesspool.

My resting bitch face is in full bloom and spreading faster than dandelion fluff.

Ronnie notices, slamming to a halt rather than finishing another spastic lap around the climbing equipment. "What's wrong, Frannie?"

"I don't like kids."

She blinks, chomping on my answer for a moment. "But I'm a kid."

My sharp edges soften at the concern in her meek voice. "You're the only exception."

"What's an exception?"

I exhale a heated breath, some of my frustrations flowing out with it. "It means you're special. You've conquered impossible odds. My little loophole."

Her head tips sideways. "What's a loophole?"

"It's a good thing, babes. I don't like kids, but I like you."

"You like me?"

"Very much so. Wouldn't be here otherwise." I find myself smiling despite this horrific place. "Consider yourself lucky."

She tips her chin up. "I'm special."

"The best," I croon.

Ronnie bounces on the balls of her feet. "Can I go play?"

"That's what we're here for. I won't go anywhere." Besides, my butt is stuck to this seat with gum or something equally as offensive.

After she's left me in a cloud of sugar fumes, I spread my arms on the back of the bench and wait for this to be over. Whispers tickle my ears, insulting enough to pique my interest. I turn slightly to give the trio of women attention they don't deserve. My fingers wiggle at them as if I'm friendly. Animosity must be bleeding from my pores because they scurry off like cockroaches.

"Excuse me," a haughty voice chirps from my other side.

I swivel my head toward the brunette who's busy glaring down her upturned nose at me. "Yes?"

"Your outfit is making people uncomfortable. Could you put on a jacket or something?"

A catty giggle titters from me. My leather corset is chic as fuck and snatches my waist like a pinup doll. This housewife is jealous that I'm flaunting my cleavage. If I'm going to be tortured, I can at least look hot. Screw anybody who claims otherwise.

With a palm shielding my eyes, I make the effort to scan the surrounding area. "Where are these people? All I see is that guy and he hasn't taken his eyes off my tits since I arrived."

"That's my husband," she hisses.

"Sounds like a you problem then." I glance at her buttoned-up cardigan, offering an exaggerated pout. "Maybe show some skin and he wouldn't have to look elsewhere."

She makes an indignant squeak. "How dare you insult me."

"If that ain't calling the kettle black, I don't know what is."

Another unladylike noise scrapes out of her flat personality. "I can't believe Byron Benson hired you."

Well, it appears introductions aren't necessary. Shucks.

"You'd almost think someone got forced into it," I quip.

The brunette balks as if she can't believe I'd admit it. "You're actually a nanny?"

"That's what it says on my name tag." My middle finger taps at the empty space above my left breast.

"Not sure what he sees in you."

The condescending grin I deliver is bored of this conversation. "My pussy is tighter than a virgin's asshole."

She sputters on her most recent upset. "You're unfit to be around children."

"I agree but unfortunately, that's not your decision. Run along now, Karen. And tell the others to fuck off."

The brunette storms off in a tizzy I don't get to fully

appreciate. Ronnie is racing toward me with tears in her eyes. My knees meet the rubber floor as I open my arms to embrace her.

Once she's cradled against me, I search her for injuries. "Are you hurt?"

She shakes her head. "No, not really. Will you dry my tears?"

"Of course, babes." I wipe at her wet cheeks. "Why are you crying?"

"Jimmy pulled my hair and called me ugly."

My fingers pause mid-swipe. Some punk ass is trying to belittle my sweet loophole? Hell fucking no.

Several things happen at once. I see red. There's a pit of fury cracking open in my gut, spreading fire through my veins. Some dormant instinct kicks in and demands retaliation.

"Where is Jimmy now?" My voice is calm and collected, at total odds with the anger bubbling to a boil.

Her pointer finger seals the kid's fate. "Over there."

"Listen to me, kiddo. That boy is trying to shake your confidence. We're not going to let him. You don't cry over a man, okay? He'll get on his knees and crawl to you, begging for forgiveness."

"Ummm…"

"Just trust me." I stand and pin a target on the bully's forehead. "Be right back."

Ronnie grabs my hand. "Where are you going?"

"To teach him a lesson he won't learn in school." And then I'm marching over to the scrawny little shit, stooping to his level. "Heard you got a problem with my girl, Jimmy. That's a bad mistake. Really bad."

The mop head wrinkles his nose. "Who're are you?"

I bark out a laugh. "What scares you the most?"

He puffs out his puny chest. "Nothin'."

"Awwww, such a tough guy. You can tell me. Is it zombies? Snakes? Heights? The thought of your daddy leaving and never coming back? Whatever it is would feel like paradise compared to me. I'm the horror movie you'll never escape. Be afraid to check under your bed, Jimmy. That's where evil spirts wait until you're sleeping."

Am I being unnecessarily cruel? Absolutely. Should I back off? Probably. Am I going to? Not a chance.

His bottom lip wobbles. "You're mean."

"That's what you get for picking on Ronnie. If you ever bother her again, I'll find you. Got it?" I jerk forward as if I'm about to grab him.

He screams and stumbles back. The stench of urine fills the air. And my job here is done.

I rise to my feet, backing away to avoid any puddles. "Ohhhh, did somebody have an accident? What a baby."

Jimmy begins to wail, alerting his mother to the villain in their midst. She flutters in like an overpaid actress who doesn't do her own stunts. Not a hair on her perfectly coiffed head is out of place.

"What's the matter?" Even her tone is uppity.

Jimmy's stubby finger jabs at me. "She's a monster!"

I inspect my nails. "At your service."

The mom peers over at me for the first time, not bothering to rein in her sneer. "Why is he crying?"

My shoulders bounce casually. "I scared him. Bit of a chicken shit if you ask me."

Her jaw drops. "What's wrong with you?"

"We don't have time to get into all that. Just know that if Jimmy bothers Ronnie again, you and me are gonna have big problems." I point between us to avoid any confusion.

"I'm getting security." She waves her arms as if she's directing traffic. "Help! Someone help us!"

My stomach clenches. I know where this road leads. "Or we could go out back and handle this like real women."

Her face pales. "You're crazy."

I cackle like the best of 'em. "Thanks for noticing."

Two guards appear, boxing me in without asking a single question. Typical. The one with a substantial beer gut gives me a lewd once-over. His partner looks ready to whip out the taser that still has a factory sticker.

"Take it easy, buddy. This is just a misunderstanding," I say.

"Don't listen to her!" The mom blubbers, really pulling at the heartstrings. "She traumatized my son."

My sigh is heavy with surrender. I motion Ronnie over and give her my phone. "Call your daddy, okay? Just like we practiced."

Her wide eyes stray to the wannabe cops. "Are you in trouble, Frannie?"

I boop her nose. "Always, but this is the first time it was worth it."

CHAPTER TWENTY-FIVE

Byron

MY BOOTS TRUDGE THROUGH THE SLUSH AS I STOMP toward the entrance of Slick City. I actually laughed when Ronnie called to tell me the news. Those poor souls don't know who they're dealing with. But then I realized just how serious this is.

Leave it to Francesca Keller to get corralled by security for intimidating a child. I've got to give her credit. Even I didn't think she could pull off such an offense.

When I wrench open the door, a wall of noise smacks me in the face. This slide park was built in a repurposed warehouse and uncontrolled energy bounces from floor to ceiling. I let out a low whistle. Well, damn. It's no wonder she lost her shit.

A young guy smiles at me from behind the greeter's desk. "Welcome to—"

"Where is she?" My icy tone strongly suggests he doesn't fuck with me.

He visibly shrinks back. "The woman who caused a scene?"

"That's the one," I rumble.

Ronnie is still whizzing around with her friends. One of their parents volunteered to keep an eye on her while I handle this problem.

The employee gestures to a far corner. "They have her blocked—"

I storm off before he can finish blabbering on. Those standing in my path wisely remove themselves. My pulse drums in my ears with each furious step. It's too damn bright in here.

Two uniformed men are standing guard near an open room. That must be the place. I shoulder past them and slam the door behind me.

At the boom of my arrival, Frankie whirls to face me. Her wince has the decency to appear sincere. "I can explain."

I cross my arms. "You sure as shit better."

She drags her sharp, black talons through her hair. "That kid had it coming."

"He's a *kid*." This situation calls for emphasis on that word.

"Still should know better," she mutters. "If I yanked on a girl's pigtail and called her ugly, I would've gotten my bare ass whipped with the belt. Probably would've given me the buckled part too."

My frustration slams to a halt, swerving in a different direction. "What did he do?"

"I just told you." Frankie studies my stupefied expression. "You didn't know?"

I shake my head dumbly. "Figured he looked at you wrong or bumped into you on accident."

"Oh, fuck off. I'm not that unhinged."

My dry scoff claims otherwise. "You called him a baby after he peed his pants, which he only did because you scared the piss out of him."

"Hey," she snaps. "Jimmy got what he deserved. Nobody bullies my girl and gets away with it."

"Wait," I growl. "Jimmy Carlson?"

"How the fuck should I know?"

"He's a little shit."

She throws her hands up. "That's what I said!"

I'm stalking across the room in the next second. Whatever's burning in my stare has Frankie backing up until she's flat against the wall. There's no escape as I cage her upturned jaw in my palms, allowing me to crash our lips together.

An explosion of warmth rushes through me. It's like basking in the sunshine after spending years buried in the cold of winter. My groan is desperate, bordering on a plea. An equally relieved sound spills from her before she breaks free.

"What's happening?" she breathes across my mouth.

"Fuck," I groan. "I've been thinking about kissing you

senseless since you first mouthed off to me. It's my new favorite way to shut you up."

"Why didn't you do it sooner?"

"I prefer to keep my balls attached." And then I dive back in.

Frankie gasps, granting me deeper access. My tongue glides along hers in a sensual caress. She tastes like cinnamon and reckless abandon. It's addictive, much like her soft mewls. Another guttural noise rips from me as I push against her, needing to get closer. She fists my shirt and hooks a leg around my hip as if there's still space to eliminate. Our shared hunger burns hot between us.

Time lapses while we explore this new contact. It's more intimate than just sex. We're delving into emotional territory where two halves become a whole. I forget where we are. All I feel is Frankie's desire stroking mine.

But then she pulls away again. "Why are you kissing me?"

"Want to." I lean in, but she stops me.

"But I did something bad."

My forehead rests on hers. "Nah, you followed your gut and defended Ronnie."

Her eyelids are still hooded with seduction. "Would you have done the same?"

"Maybe in a slightly less volatile manner."

A throat clears loudly and Frankie peers over my shoulder. "The guards are watching."

"Good. Let 'em see what they'll never have." But the

frantic urge to maul her has been satisfied. For now. "Wanna get out of here?"

"Yes, please."

"Hmmm, so polite. Getting locked up at a kid's play place has humbled you."

She shudders. "I'm never coming back."

"Glad you feel that way," I chuckle. "You're banned from the premises, menace."

"You should've seen her, Daddy." Ronnie punches at the air with short jabs. "Frannie came to my rescue. She's a real superhero."

Frankie cringes. "Depends who you ask, kiddo. Jimmy's mom wants to see me behind bars."

My little girl scrunches her face. "Like in jail?"

"Exactly," the redhead mutters.

Ronnie gasps. "You can't go to jail!"

"She won't," I rush to say. "So long as she doesn't go near Jimmy or his mother."

"If I ever see that kid's pasty mug again, it'll be too soon." Frankie lifts her glass of iced tea.

I raise mine to clink against hers. "Cheers to that."

After fleeing the scene of the crime, we found our way to The Paddock. It's no Inn Kahoots, but the casual vibe and half price appetizers reignited Frankie's spark. She's sprawled in her chair like a regular local. I wonder if she knows about the mechanical bull. Only time will tell.

Ronnie sighs to a tune that concerns me. "You two love each other."

Frankie chokes on her drink. "No, no. Definitely not."

"Yes-huh! Brenna's mom saw Daddy kiss you at Slick City." She makes sloppy sound effects in case the message isn't received. "That means you're gonna get married."

My chest gets tight as a suffocating pressure sinks in. At the same time, a stroke of satisfaction boosts my ego. It's an odd combination.

Rather than read into it, I glance at Frankie. There's a wildfire spreading across her face. She flaps her mouth open and closed uselessly. All that reclaimed bravado falters from a few simple statements.

"It didn't mean anything," she finally stammers.

I ignore the strike to my pride. "Mhmm, just showing my gratitude after she defended you."

My daughter narrows her eyes. "You never kiss people."

"Not that you know about," I mutter.

The redhead's brows fling halfway up her forehead. "Wouldn't have pegged you for a kissing king, stud."

"Jealous?"

She scoffs. "In your dreams."

"How's it going over here?" Our server appears out of thin air like a magician.

Ronnie waves at the familiar face. "Guess what?"

Christa taps a pen to her lips. "Am I allowed to say chicken butt or is that cancelled?"

That gets a giggle from my little girl. "You're silly."

"Phew, still got it."

"This is our first date as a family!" My little girl looks happier than a pig rolling in spring mud.

I scrub a palm over my mouth to hide a grin. Christa has been working here since I can remember and is extremely well connected in town. This news is going to spread faster than if I posted it on the message board myself.

"Awww," the server coos. "That's so special. I didn't know your daddy was dating your nanny."

Ronnie bobs her head. "Frannie hid on New Year's Eve and Daddy had to find her and I think they've been kissing lots. That means they're getting married, right? It's what happens in the movies."

Christa slides a look my way and whatever she finds has her smiling wide. "Uh-huh, I think love is in the air."

My daughter inhales deeply. "Oh, I smell it! Frannie and Daddy are in love." She tugs on the redhead's jacket sleeve, which knocks her from the stupor she's caught in. "Are you gonna be my mommy now?"

Frankie's gulp is audible. She looks seconds away from either bolting or ordering a shot of tequila. "Ummm…"

Christa rolls her lips between her teeth. "I'm gonna bring you an order of mini tacos on the house to celebrate."

"Those are my favorite!" Ronnie shouts. "This is the best day ever."

"And the meat raffle hasn't even started yet," Christa says before wandering off.

Before we get the chance to recover, a dark cloud looms over our table. An upward glance reveals the three assholes whose ill intentions tried to drag Frankie down at the auction.

My mood sours with a scowl. "I suggest you take several steps back before I make you."

"Not here for you, Benson." The man talking is probably in his mid-forties, but a tough road has aged him well beyond that. "If you insist on gettin' in our way, we'll do more than mess with your business."

I stand to tower over the lot of them. "Explain."

"We both know that's not necessary."

"Those were all you?"

Dennis is going to lose his shit when he finds out someone was targeting us on purpose. The vandalism and petty theft add up to a giant pain in the ass.

The one clearly in charge smirks. "Small inconveniences for our entertainment. You'd know if we actually wanted your attention. Isn't that right, Francesca?"

"Can't catch a break today." Frankie's meek lapse in appearance is long gone, replaced by her signature death glare. "Buzz off, buddies. You've got the wrong girl."

"That ain't true. You just haven't come 'round to the idea yet, but I reckon you will."

"If that's supposed to be a threat, just spit it out." She fakes a yawn.

"We've got a job for you," the leader says.

"Not interested."

"You'll want to hear what I've got to say."

"Frannie said no," my daughter yells loud enough to

hush every other voice in this establishment. "No means no! Get on your knees and beg for forgiveness."

"All right, little lady. Didn't mean to get on your bad side." The man chuckles and tips his hat. "Been a pleasure. We'll be seeing you, Frankie."

They casually stride to the exit as if nobody will bother to chase them. The urge to follow has me stalking forward. Three against one aren't the worst odds I've had.

"Hey." A yank on my arm draws my attention back to what matters. Frankie nudges my empty chair. "Forget about them."

I grumble about a triple knockout, but drop my ass on the seat. "Where did they come from?"

"Who knows and who cares. They're all talk."

"Not entirely." A swig of iced tea makes me wish for something stronger. "Random instances have been happening on our properties over the last several months. A manufacturing error at one of our feed suppliers, scheduling mix-ups, trailer tires have gone missing, minor vandalizing at a few properties. Nothing too serious, but enough to notice."

Frankie shrugs. "Call the cops."

"I'd rather find their hideout and level it to the ground."

A recognizable spark flickers in her gaze and she leans toward me. "It's sexy when you talk bad boy to me."

That pulls a grin from the depths of my fading upset. "Go on a date with me."

Ronnie gasps, that word triggering her to rejoin our conversation. "Yes! Frannie really wants to do that."

But Frankie rolls her eyes. "Pass."

"C'mon, menace. What's something you've always wanted to do, but haven't had the chance?"

The question gives her pause. "Sturgis would be cool."

A grunt escapes me at her mention of the famous motorcycle rally. "I'll keep that in mind as August approaches. How about in the meantime?"

She sighs as if I'm hassling her. "I dunno. It's the middle of winter."

"You could visit an ice castle!" Ronnie's suggestion bursts out of her.

"We could visit an ice castle," Frankie repeats with feigned enthusiasm.

"I think we can find something more to your liking."

Her low hum isn't impressed. "Best of luck, stud."

"I gotta go potty!" Ronnie suddenly bounces in her chair like she's been holding it for hours.

Frankie is about to get up and take her, but then Christa swoops in from seemingly nowhere.

"I'm headed that way, cutie. Your daddy and future mommy can have a moment alone." She winks at us before escorting Ronnie to the bathroom.

The redhead watches them go, confusion creasing her brow. I use that to my advantage. My boot hooks the nearest leg of her chair and pulls, allowing me to catch her off guard. The momentum delivers Frankie into my clutches and I don't hesitate to fuse our lips together. She's stiff in my arms for a second, but melts as my tongue traces the seam of her mouth. My grin is a stamp of approval against her willingness to display affection.

I groan as our mutual desire rekindles. Frankie's lashes flutter shut when I deepen the kiss. With her distracted, I lift the cowboy hat off my head and drop it onto hers. The public claim spreads a round of hoots and hollers across The Paddock.

I'm the one to pull away, relishing the dazed gleam in her eyes. "Still didn't mean anything, little menace?"

Frankie's heavy-lidded stare openly admires me. "Uhhh…"

My chuckle is louder than the shocked whispers swarming around the scene we just made. "Your lies taste sweet, but your surrender is my drug of choice. I'm shamelessly addicted."

CHAPTER TWENTY-SIX

U NANNOUNCED TO ME, OUR ELUSIVE DATE ARRIVES on the following Saturday. We've been driving for almost an hour and I still don't know where Byron is taking me. The unease I've been pretending doesn't exist is getting harder to ignore. It doesn't help that he's been quiet behind the wheel, giving my thoughts too much space to roam. This is some sort of warped trust exercise I didn't sign up for.

When Byron exits the freeway at an unfamiliar town, my knee begins to jiggle. It's a heavily populated commercial area, which leads to countless destination options. My gaze scans from left to right without really seeing. I'm seconds away from slipping into a full-blown spiral.

"Are we almost there?"

Byron's chuckle grates on my frazzled patience. "You're worse than Ronnie."

"I've never been on a date," I whisper under my breath.

His palm lands on my jumpy thigh, giving me a gentle squeeze. "Honored to be your first. I hope this exceeds your expectations."

My gaze narrows in on where he's touching me like an anchored focal point. "I don't like surprises."

"You'll like this one." And then he pulls into a hotel parking lot.

But this isn't just any hotel. It looks more like a mountain resort plopped in the middle of suburbia. With multiple buildings and a water park, this place is over the top. Even the name is pretentious.

My nerves evaporate while I let out a wolf whistle. "Grand View Highlands? Damn, stud. This place is ritzy. If you wanted to whisk me away for a fuck-fest, I would've settled for a Red Roof Inn."

His chuckle tries to chastise me. "Gotta get a closer look before you jump to conclusions."

"If you insist," I murmur.

"But I won't say no to renting a room if you're interested," he adds.

A snort rips from me. "I doubt they have hourly rates."

"We can put the bed to use for a full night. You know I'm good for it."

When I clench my legs, Byron throws me a smirk oozing with appropriate smugness. He parks near the domed convention center, which does little to clue me in. All that's left to do is get out of the truck and begin the long hike to the entrance. It takes iron-clad resistance to stop myself from peppering him with questions the entire way.

My stride falters as I catch sight of a banner displayed over the bank of double doors. "Is this…?"

He dips his head, understanding what I'm asking. "It's a special weekend event."

"You brought me to a guns and knives show?"

The heat of Byron's smolder burns into me. "Figured you might find a new toy to taunt me with."

I'm still gaping at the bold letters of the sign. There's no chance of misinterpreting it. "This is… considerate."

"Considerate? Wow." He chuckles and rubs at the back of his neck. "Careful with the compliments."

My huff pairs well with a scowl. "Give me a break. You sprung this on me."

"And I'd do it again to catch that look on your face."

"Nobody's ever bothered to catch it before," I mumble.

"What's that?" There's an edge of humor in his voice.

"Nothing!" I'm quick to blurt.

"I'll shock your panties off at every available opportunity." Byron threads my fingers through his, giving me an encouraging tug. "C'mon, menace. Let's see what kind of trouble we can find."

But my boots are rooted to the snowy pavement. I'm staring at our interlocked palms, unable to take my eyes off the connection. A rush of warmth spreads from the point of contact. That foreign thrill stuns me further.

"What's happening?"

"We're going into the event." He gives me another yank.

"You're holding my hand." There's a rightful note of horror in my tone.

"Is that a problem?"

"Why are you holding my hand?" It occurs to me that I haven't pulled away, but that's beside the point.

Byron releases me and I'm struck by a loss I don't understand. "Was that too much for you? Guess I should've asked before doing it."

"I dunno." My gaze is fastened onto the empty space where his fingers fit snugly against mine. "It's very… normal."

There's a sudden semi-sweet kindness in his chocolate-colored eyes. "You don't like to be touched."

"I don't," I confirm. That soft spot in his stare has me admitting more. "But I like it when you touch me."

He stills, giving me a slow once-over that feels like hot wax dripping on my skin. "Are you warming up to me?"

My mouth drops. "Absolutely not."

His lips curl into a devastating grin. "I think you are."

"Well, you better think again," I fire back.

Byron laughs, loud and carefree. The corners of his eyes crinkle as he allows the amusement to spread. Even his teeth seem to sparkle. Damn, he's such a sexy man.

I grant myself permission to devour the visual, which unleashes a reckless heat in my lower belly. But rather than traveling south, the pooling desire rushes north. There's a swooping sensation doing an acrobatic routine in my gut. It steals my breath for a minute.

"Something strange is going on," I mutter and rest a palm flat over the attacked area.

A naughty gleam sparks in his gaze. "Am I giving you butterflies, menace?"

I snort. "Not a chance. Fuck butterflies and all that fluffy shit, remember?"

He rubs his bearded chin. "That was before we got to know each other. Now you're swooning over me."

"Get real. I don't…" But that weird dip takes another nosedive in my stomach. "No way."

Unharnessed joy brightens his expression until it's nearly blinding. "I'm growing on you."

"Like black mold."

Byron shakes his head. "You're glad we're on a date."

"I'm not."

"You like me."

"No, I don't."

"Yes, you do," he croons. He's clearly getting a kick out of this. "Some parts more than others, but the whole package is crushin' on me."

The traitorous swarm buzzes in my belly again. "I'll admit to twat flutters. She's easy to please."

His unwavering stare isn't letting me wriggle free. "Nah, it's more than that. Your heart and mind want in on the fun."

My pulse leaps in agreement. Thoughts of us in a committed relationship quickly follow. I don't even know what that looks like. It's all wonky and jagged, but there's an image forming in the uncertainty.

"This isn't supposed to happen to me. It's unsettling," I groan. "Ugh, make it stop. I feel sick."

"Quit fighting it. You might enjoy the ride." His dedication to my misery smacks me upside the head.

"Hold on a second." I narrow my eyes on his pleased smile. "You like me."

"Thought that was obvious." When he bites his bottom lip, I almost whimper and suggest we ditch the confessions for something simpler.

But dammit, we're expressing our feelings. I shouldn't shy away from that. "Nobody has ever liked me before."

"I find that hard to believe." When I scowl, he grunts and fights a grin. "Yeah, okay. You can be a real pain in the ass."

"Which is my standard setting. Why do you find that appealing?"

"I just do."

"There has to be a reason. Humor me." From my perspective, I haven't done much that would leave a favorable impression.

Byron sighs and squints off into the distance. "That's a bit more complicated to explain."

Much like the conflicting emotions wreaking havoc on my sanity. "It doesn't make sense. I'm jaded beyond redemption."

"Trust me, you're not."

"I've got a mountain of issues."

"Doesn't bother me."

My stomach somersaults, which spurs me onward. "I'm not a traditional girlie. You're not going to trap me at home, barefoot and pregnant."

He gives me a flat stare. "Do I look like the kind of guy who wants that?"

"Maybe."

"Rest assured that I'm not. At least not in the way you're thinking. I forced you to live with me for a different reason and that's where you're gonna stay."

"But—"

"Frankie," he rasps. "Quit trying to convince me you're not worthy. It won't stop me from liking you. If you need proof, just look down. I'm still wearing the boots you ruined, for crying out loud."

Some of the fight leaves me, hunching my shoulders. "I just don't get it."

"You don't have to." He takes off his cowboy hat to drag a hand through his hair, releasing a long exhale. After a brief moment, he puts himself back together into a picture of composure. "I haven't been with a woman since my wife died because I didn't see the point. I'm a simple man, but I'm very particular. I didn't believe someone who agreed to my limitations could also keep me satisfied existed. Not to mention dealing with me set in my ways. But here you are."

Oh, no. A familiar tightness clings to my throat when I swallow. My heart is beating too fast. There's a hot sting blurring my vision. I bite the tremble in my lip before it reveals what's impossible to deny.

But the truth is right there, blooming in the depths of my broken soul for him to nurture. He's already blown me away orgasmically. I guess it's only fair for him to destroy me in every other aspect.

"Fuck," I grumble. "Fine, you can hold my hand."

"That's okay," he chuckles. "We don't need to do shit that makes you uncomfortable."

I grind my molars and snatch his wrist, smashing our palms together. "If I didn't want to, I wouldn't offer."

"All right then."

"Glad that's settled." I clear the remaining dryness from my throat while ignoring the tingles between my fingers. "No more pussyfootin' around. Let's haul ass. I need a knife big enough to slice through your sex appeal."

"There she is." His smile is effortless and endearing and I can't pull my gaze off him.

Byron doesn't say anything else, just accepts my hand and leads me inside. We enter what has to be the largest ballroom in existence. My focus finally shifts off him to take it all in.

The space is split in two: guns and knives. Of course, I naturally gravitate toward the side that has the ladder. There's a stand in the center aisle that's practically gleaming at me. The vendor has a large variety of blades in every shape and size.

"Howdy, folks," the older man drawls. "Lookin' for something specific?"

My gaze scans the weapons on display. "Once I see it, I'll know."

He gives me a long look. "I've got just the thing to tickle your fancy."

The guy bends to retrieve something out of sight. When he straightens, there's a leather knife roll in his grip. In a practiced motion, he undoes the tie and opens it for my viewing pleasure. And what a sight it is to see.

My entire body convulses as the ten beauties wink at me. Each flawless, handmade blade is attached to an ivory handle that's polished to a shine. I've heard tales of knives like these, but I never imagined seeing them in front of me. This collection must cost a fortune.

"Ohhhhh, that's pretty."

Byron balks beside me, roving his gaze over my twitching muscles. "Did you just have an orgasm?"

I roll my lips between my teeth to stifle a moan. "Mhmm, yep. Couldn't control it if I tried."

He glances at the vendor. "We'll take two sets."

"What?" I think my brain just exploded, and I'm not the only one.

The man's overgrown eyebrows fling upward to meet his receding hairline. "This is the only one of its kind."

My delulu date isn't dissuaded. "Do you have anything else of a similar quality?"

The guy's jowls jiggle as he nods frantically. "Yes, sir."

"See this dazed expression?" Byron gestures to my blissed-out features. "I'll buy whatever keeps it in place."

As the vendor scrambles to gather his finest stock, I collect enough wits to gape at the man next to me. "You can't spend that much on me."

Byron smirks, bending to brush a feather-light kiss on my parted lips. "I'm gonna shock those panties off until there's nothing left."

CHAPTER TWENTY-SEVEN

"**Y**OU'RE INCREDIBLE," FRANKIE PURRS.

I'd be grinning like a fool if she were talking to me. Unfortunately, that's not how the evening is playing out. This smitten woman is whispering sweet nothings to her new arsenal. It's been much of the same for going on two hours. At first, it was fun to watch her drool over them. But now? I'm beginning to get jealous.

We're spending the rest of the night in the penthouse suite. That expense gifted me another shell-shocked expression. At least until Frankie remembered the treasures in her grasp.

All four knife sets are spread out on the table in front of her. I would've bought more, but she snapped herself from the stupor before I could spend a hundred grand. It's not a secret that I love blowing money on her. Frankie needs to get better about accepting it.

The chair creaks as I straighten, roaming my gaze over the best view in the resort. "Do you have a favorite yet?"

A sharp noise scolds me. "That's not a fair question."

"Pick one."

With a peek over her shoulder, green eyes find mine staring straight at her. "Why?"

"We're gonna christen it."

The beginning of a smile curves her lips. "And how might we do that?"

"Choose one and find out."

Frankie's hand hovers over the entire collection. "I don't even want to touch them."

Meanwhile, my fingers get busy popping open the pearl snaps on my flannel shirt. The fabric hangs open as I stand and walk to where she sits. I swoop the red curtain of hair aside to drop a trail of kisses along her neck. The sweet scent of temptation fills my lungs when I inhale. She tilts her head to give me better access, which I reward with a gentle bite. A long, slow lick eases the sting.

Frankie sighs and sags in the seat. I grin against her skin, pleased that my touch does the trick. Her knives are temporarily forgotten. That allows me to grab whichever one I want. After attaching the leather protective guard, I lift a double-edged fixed dagger from the holder. Its thick, bulbous handle is probably meant to ensure a steady grip while repeatedly stabbing into someone. My plans have a more pleasurable outcome.

"Careful, stud." Frankie breathes. "It's sharp."

"Take off your clothes or I'll do it for you," I command.

"Want to try that again?" She motions to the twenty-nine blades within her reach.

I flip the knife in my hand, catching it by the covered tip. "Only need one to get the job done."

She rises from the chair with a lethal grace I should take as a warning. Her gaze carves a path along the exposed muscles of my abdomen. I flex under her appraisal, arching my hips forward to reveal how hard she gets me. A recognizable hunger snarls from her hooded stare, jacking mine into a frenzy.

"You're lucky you're hot," she says while unzipping her black corset.

Arousal surges through me when her perky tits bounce into view. "Or you'd chop my balls off?"

"Something like that." Her pointy nails dip beneath the waistband of her skin-tight pants, dragging the stretchy material down her toned legs.

My gulp is audible as she stands buck naked. "No panties?"

Frankie's laugh is husky. "They disintegrated after all your surprises today. Saved me the trouble of removing them. Thanks for that."

I beckon to her with the dagger. "C'mere, menace."

She lifts a foot onto the chair, putting her bare pussy on display. "No."

That sass sets me in motion. I put the sheathed knife between my teeth while bending low. In the next breath, she's hoisted over my shoulder as I turn for the bed. She bucks in my grasp and screeches like a rabid raccoon. My palm smacks her ass, which drops a match on her fiery attitude.

"Savage," she hisses. Her body wriggles against me with the force of a hurricane. "I'm gonna kill you."

"Nah," I chuckle. "You'd miss me too much."

"Give me that knife and find out."

"I'd rather fuck some obedience into you."

When I drop her onto the mattress, she immediately flings upright. Tattoos and unbridled fury blanket her vibrating form. Her glare demands retribution. She's the spitting image of an unruly mare I need to tame.

I smirk around the knife still in my bite while shrugging out of my shirt. Quick, jerky motions undo my belt and shuck my jeans, leaving me in a tented pair of boxers. My thumb hooks the elastic band as I free the blade from the sleeve. It slices into the top of the fabric like melted butter.

A breathy moan spills from Frankie's parted lips. "Careful with that dick, big boy. It's too nice to maim."

"Maybe you should rip the rest."

She eyes the dagger in my hand, but her ass scoots forward. Her fingers tug at the cut I started, splitting the cotton straight down until it falls to the floor. A soft moan flutters from her as my hard cock bobs in the open. I caress the flat of the steel along her jaw. Our roles are reversed for a change. One wrong move and it's a disaster.

Before Frankie can reach for me, I kneel on the carpet and yank her to the edge of the bed. She yelps while collapsing onto her back, squirming in a weak attempt at escape. With minimal effort, her knees are draped over my shoulders and her pussy is a breath away from my tongue. I inhale her addictive scent, my mouth watering for a taste. But first,

I sheathe the blade and drift the protected tip along her arousal. Moisture soaks the leather guard instantly.

I swipe through her slick center again. "Does this turn you on, menace?"

Her hips shift restlessly. "Mhmm."

"Ever been fucked by a knife?"

"No," she wheezes.

"About to be," I warn.

And then I turn the dagger in my grip, sinking the bulbous end into her snug cunt. There's resistance, and I start with shallow thrusts. Frankie whimpers as her pussy struggles to accept the handle. That won't do.

"C'mon, menace. You can take it."

She thrashes against invisible bonds. "Too much."

"Relax," I coax.

Frankie does, or tries to. I lean in and lap at her clit. A gush of her tangy flavor bathes my tongue when I seal my lips around her sensitive nerves. My first pull is long and deep. The craving kicks in, demanding more. Gulps flood my throat with her taste. I'm struck by another shot of desperation.

My tongue works her faster as I push the handle in and out. She takes the whole length easily now. Soft cries praise me. Those noises grow louder as I increase the pace again. Lust wraps a fist around my dick, stroking harder with each drop of her that drenches me. Precum drips from my tip. I stave off the desire to chase relief.

Just as trembles begin to quake Frankie's limbs, she shoves away from me. A grip that's stronger than I'd give her credit for pulls me off the floor. In a swift maneuver, I'm flat on my back and she's straddling my lap. She hovers over me on her knees, canting her hips forward. It gives me a clear view of where the knife is still sunk to the hilt. While staring at me, she draws the handle out of her pussy and rests it above my dick. She's not empty for long.

"Your turn to be fucked, stud."

A yearning like I've never felt chokes me as she gets into position. Frankie feeds herself my cock, lowering slowly until we're locked together at the core. The dagger is wedged between us as she begins to rock. Pleasure is quick to clutch me in an unforgiving hold. My teeth clack and crunch into dust. Dammit, I'm not going to last.

Especially not with this woman on top of me. She rides my dick while grinding against the knife like a rodeo star. It's a damn fine sight to behold. I'll cherish the sheer bliss contorting her features until my last breath.

"Almost," she murmurs. "Close. So, so close."

I grab the leather sheath and take control of the knife. In response, Frankie's pace turns frantic. She bounces on my cock while I strum her clit. A clamp from her inner muscles shoves me to the edge. I can't go over without her.

My free hand lifts to cup her breast. She cries out, thrusting her chest into my grasp. A steady throb begins to pulse through me. I pinch her peaked nipple between my thumb and forefinger. That's what does it. Her climax hits with a full-body jolt. Tingles fondle what remains of my stamina. Relief swoops in, drowning me in a rush of warmth. It's nearly blinding.

"Just like that," Frankie mumbles while floating through her orgasm.

I watch through bleary eyes, victim to my own release. Heat spreads between us until I'm numb to it. All I sense is her squeezing my dick through the haze. My palms manage to find her hips and anchor me to the moment.

We arrive on the other side in a burst of labored breaths. Frankie lies on top of me, pressing her rapid heartbeat to mine. I trace the delicate column of her spine with two fingers and bask in the glow. Her hips lift slightly and she peels the blade from my skin. Its handle is soaked, glistening in the low lighting.

"Good call on the knife play," she rasps. "That was… fun."

"Glad we're on the same page." I chuckle, jostling our joined position. "Figured you were gonna carve your initials into my flesh."

Frankie props herself up on a wobbly elbow. "This is our first date, stud. Give a girl time to fully commit."

"We're not in a hurry." I roll her under me and gently pull out. "But you're not going anywhere. Get used to being mine."

She blinks at me as I sit on the edge of the mattress. "Where are you going?"

"This"—my palm rests between her thighs—"is our mess. I'm going to clean you up. Don't move."

"Ummm…" Her legs cross, trapping my hand. "I'd rather you didn't."

"Don't freak out, but I want to take care of you." My lips meet hers in a chaste kiss. "Please let me, menace."

Frankie's smile is almost shy. "If you insist."

CHAPTER TWENTY-EIGHT

Frankie

WINTER IN MINNESOTA IS A FRIGID BITCH. January's windchills are just plain mean. Twenty below zero isn't even that bad in the grand scheme, but it still feels like a million needles are stabbing into my exposed flesh. I tuck my chin tighter to my chest as the school bus takes its sweet-ass time arriving.

Finally, after my fingers and toes begin to lose feeling, those yellow flashing lights appear around the bend. I shuffle closer to the road as the brakes squeal and the door folds open. A burst of sunshine hops down the stairs to warm my soul.

"Frannie! Why is it soooo cold?" Ronnie's teeth chatter as she races toward me.

I cuddle her against me, bend low, and make a run for the house. "It's that time of year, kiddo. Spring will be here before we know it."

A shiver racks her whole body. "That's soooo far away! The snow is never gonna melt."

"Not with that attitude, prissy pants." I hustle faster to where the chimney is smoking with the promise of heat.

"My pants aren't prissy," Ronnie mutters from under the layers between us.

"We'll change into fleece pajamas and fix the problem." My palms hold her small frame steady against a fierce gust while we climb the porch stairs.

Just as we're about to step inside, a broken meow stops me in my tracks. I push Ronnie over the threshold before going in search of the poor animal stuck out in this weather. Huddled on the frozen ground beneath the steps is a black kitten. Its tiny body is curled in a tight ball to block the elements. Snow and debris cling to its matted fur like a dirty blanket. When it senses my approach, bright green eyes peek out at me.

My hardened heart lurches. "If that isn't like looking in the mirror, I don't know what is."

Another soft meow greets me. Better than a hiss.

Ronnie is still in the open doorway, waiting for me. "What're you doing, Frannie? It's freezing!"

"Don't I know it," I say through a tremble. "There's a kitten out here."

"A kitten? Is it lost?"

Abandoned or born as a stray is more likely. Although, it seems more friendly than feral. Desperation might be kicking in.

I tug off my glove and extend frozen fingers toward the little thing. "C'mere, cutie. I won't hurt you."

White whiskers tickle me as it gives me a cursory sniff test. Whatever the kitten senses has he or she creeping toward me. When they're close enough to scoop, I do just that and dash for the comfort of home.

"Phew," I breathe and rest my back against the closed door.

Ronnie is bouncing in place, barely able to contain her excitement. "Can I see?"

After unzipping my jacket, pointy ears on a much smaller head poke out. A quiet meow squeaks from its shaking form. The barely-audible noise alerts Darla and Dottie that there's a newcomer in their midst. Nails scrape on the hardwood floor as the pair rush toward me.

"Crap," I mutter.

The kitten puffs up to triple its size when the dogs swarm me. Wet noses poke and prod at the feline. In return, the tiny creature bats at them with its paw. I brace myself for a fight, unclear about the protocol in these situations. My misguided, scantily-clad maternal instincts suggest I shield the much smaller animal. Darla and Dottie make the decision for me, quickly losing interest. An exhale whooshes out of me as my muscles relax.

"Oh. My. Gosh. He's soooo super cute." Ronnie claps her cheeks while her mouth drops open. "What're we gonna name him?"

"Well, first of all, we don't even know if he's a boy." I

turn the scrawny thing in my grip and lift its tail. "You were right. He's a boy."

The little girl moves in for a closer look. "How can you tell?"

"Ummm…" I bite my lip to trap the truth about balls from spilling out. "I just can."

"Are you a vet?"

I laugh. "Not even close. We used to get a lot of random cats in the compound. They'd come and go as they pleased."

She tilts her head in that certain way. "Is that where you used to live?"

A knot forms in my belly at the reminder of where I came from. "Yep, but it's not there anymore. Everyone left."

Her forehead creases. "Are you sad?"

That uncomfortable ache loosens while staring at the face of genuine concern. "No, not really. I miss some of the people. We were like a family, you know? But they're gone and I'm okay with that."

"I'm really happy you're part of our family," she says. "Are you happy too?"

"Very." I crouch to wrap her in a hug, careful not to squish the cat. "Thanks for believing in me, babes."

"I knew you were meant for us." Her tone is gentle, just like her finger coasting along the bridge of my nose. She swoops off the end to land with a tap on my chin. "Gonna love you for always, Frannie."

There's a recognizable clench in my chest. "It's the same for me." Even if I can't actually say the words yet.

"And now we have a kitty!" Ronnie pets the little fella behind his ears. "What should we call him?"

I give his scruffy fur a thorough inspection, discovering a white spot at the base of his throat. "How about Tux? It kinda looks like he's wearing a tuxedo and this"—I point to the only splash on his black body—"is his bow tie."

She's already nodding. "That's perfect! Daddy wouldn't let me have a cat. I can't wait to show him. Thanks for getting Tux for us."

Which drops a rock into my stomach. But that's a fight for later. I smooth any trace of worry from my features.

"Do you want to hold him?"

"Yes!" She holds out her arms for me to pass him over and immediately clutches him against her. "Wow! He's light as a feather."

"Probably needs food," I muse. "And a bath."

Concerned eyes search mine. Tux might be glaring too. "But cats don't like water."

"Let's start with dinner. I bet there's a can of tuna in the pantry. He'd probably love some milk too."

Her smile is blinding. "Uh-huh! I bet he's super hungry."

"Maybe he'll let us clean him up a bit once his tummy is full."

"Maybe." But the little girl doesn't sound convinced.

I lead us to the kitchen. Ronnie cradles Tux to her chest like he's her most precious baby doll. An unmistakable purr rumbles from the tiny kitten. The sight chips away at my charred soul. That cat is going to be fat, spoiled, and lazy within days. My lips twitch into a grin. As he should be.

After gathering the supplies, we get settled on the tile floor. Tux immediately chows down on the tuna. Ronnie hums and it's a peppy tune. A cozy buzz fills my veins. This feels right. Settled. It's home.

That's how Byron finds us. Brown eyes the color of toasted chocolate are blown wide while scanning the scene we've created. I wince and prepare for battle. Damn, I didn't even hear him come in.

"What's this?"

Ronnie isn't bothered by his clipped tone. Her pearly-white teeth are on sparkly display when she gives him a megawatt grin. "Hi, Daddy! We found a kitten. Isn't he cu-uuuute? We named him Tux like a tuxedo with a white tie. Dottie and Darla don't mind him. We're all family!"

"You already named him?" Like the good father Byron is, he knows what that means.

I wink. "Sure did."

His frustration shifts to me. "You brought in a stray?"

In a fluid, graceful motion, I rise to my feet. "You're one to talk."

"Wasn't my idea," he grumbles.

I park a hand on my hip. "Are you complaining about the outcome?"

His glare loses its sharp edge as he gives me a leisurely once-over. "Nah, it's working in my favor. That cat is another story."

Tux understands the assignment. After licking his chops, he stretches and stalks his target. His lithe body twines around Byron's legs like they're long-lost buddies. The grump scowls at the feline trying to make friends.

"Smart pussy," I mutter under my breath. "Catch more fools with flirting."

But his grimace isn't impressed. "I don't like this."

"What's all the fuss about?" Dennis appears out of nowhere, much like his nephew. Must run in their genes.

"Uncle Dennis!" Ronnie launches off the floor to drag him into the kitchen. "You gotta meet Tux. He's our kitty."

The Benson patriarch ambles to where the cat is still trying to win Byron's affection. "Isn't he precious? Just a bundle of joy."

The grump grunts. "Mhmm, probably has fleas."

"There's a pill for that." As if I'm an expert in pet health.

Dennis glances at me, a twinkle gleaming in his kind gaze. "Ah, my fellow menace."

"That's… me?"

"We'll get along just fine. I've been known to cause plenty of trouble and mischief myself." Gruff laughter shakes his arthritic joints. "Why haven't we talked since the wedding?"

My mouth flaps open and closed, unsure how to navigate this scrutiny. "Been busy?"

"Yes, I've heard." His focus travels a path to Ronnie and Byron before returning to me. "Figured we were due for another chat."

"Um, okay?" Why I'm speaking in questions is beyond my scope. This entire situation is making me itchy.

He leans close and drops his voice. "That biker gang won't be bothering you anymore."

"Did you scare 'em off?" Try as I might to avoid them, snark and sarcasm pump through my veins.

Dennis pats my hand in that grandfatherly way I've only heard about. "We take care of our own."

Shock stuns me silent for a moment. My blind faith in this man is equal parts baffling and warranted. He's not the type to blow smoke. There's no doubt.

"You…" I begin on a stammer. "You consider me one of yours?"

His keen awareness strips away my defensive layers until the urge to cry tickles my throat. "Don't you, Frankie?"

My gulp is thick. "I'm not sure what to say."

He squeezes my shoulder gently. "Just keep doing what you're doing."

And that's the end of that.

Dennis straightens, wiping any trace of malicious actions from his expression. A charming grin is there to soothe my stunned astonishment.

It spreads an unfamiliar calm over me. "Are you sticking around for a bit?"

Dennis shrugs. "Depends what you're planning."

"I'll make supper." My legs are already in motion when I realize how natural that sounded. Damn, look how far I've come. It's almost scary.

Ronnie is hot on my heels. "Can I help?"

"Of course, kiddo. Couldn't do it without you." And that's the truth.

As I glance over my shoulder, acceptance reflects back at me from Byron's gaze. It's intimate, but I don't recoil. Maybe that's because I'm fighting to keep a straight face while he tries to sneak a peek at my ass.

There's something different in the air, and then it hits me. A deep-rooted sense of belonging rushes under my skin as if I'm wrapped in a comforting embrace. Thanks to this family, I know what that feels like.

CHAPTER TWENTY-NINE

"**S**UCH A SOFTIE." FRANKIE'S VOICE TEASES ME before she comes into view at the living room entrance.

I couldn't care less what she calls me when her tits are swaying in my direction. But then sharp claws dig into my leg, reminding me of the trouble I'm in. "Damn thing won't leave me alone."

She leans against the arched doorway while eyeing the kitten on my lap. "He's making biscuits."

"The fuck?"

Her giggle is mocking. "That's the kneading motion he's doing with his paws. Cats do that when they're comfortable and in their element."

The urge to shove him away again flexes my muscles. "For what it's worth, I'm not in my element."

Her eyebrow quirks. "Doesn't look like you're fighting too hard."

"Pushed him off at least ten times. He's stubborn."

"That's how you like 'em."

My hand absently strokes Tux's freshly washed fur. "I think he's someone's pet. No cat I've met lets a kid dunk him under water."

Frankie laughs, but it's brittle at the edges. "He knows what it takes to survive."

"Speaking from experience," I murmur.

She dips her chin. "We're kindred spirits. That's probably why Ronnie is so obsessed with him. You're lucky she wants you two to bond or he'd be making biscuits on her lap instead."

"What if he has an owner?"

"That cared enough to drop him at the side of the road in this weather? Finders keepers," she scoffs. "He belongs to this family now."

"As if I'd survive giving him the boot."

She clucks her tongue in agreement. "Your daughter would never forgive you."

My chuckle is low, which has nothing to do with not jostling the kitten. "Is she all tucked in?"

"Snug as a bug in a rug or whatever she taught me." She swats at the famous rhyme as if it's a pest.

"You're great with her."

Frankie avoids my stare. "Wouldn't go that far."

I shake my head. "Those are your own insecurities trying to break you. Deep down, you're made for this. It just took a brave little girl to prove it and give you a chance. Now, there's no going back." My exhale is thick as I admire her strength. "This isn't just a job for you, menace. It never was."

"Okay, Dr. Phil. Didn't realize this was a therapy session." Her green eyes sparkle like gemstones in the lamp's dim glow. "Mind if I take a load off?"

"Not sure what's stopping you. This pussy won't bite." When I scratch behind Tux's ears, a loud purr rewards my efforts.

"That makes one of us," Frankie quips while situating herself on the couch next to me.

Her floral perfume and a slew of untapped fantasies float in the air. Arousal is quick to surge through me. I adjust myself, ready to send this cat packing.

"It's gonna be that type of night, huh?" Gravel and grit scrape off my tone.

"I actually wanted to talk to you." Her soft voice snuffs out the flame of desire.

"Ah, shit. Here we go."

When her fist lightly punches my arm, the kitten meows at me for tipping sideways and dislodging him. "Knock it off. This is genuine."

I rub at the sore spot. "Apologies. Please continue."

Frankie huffs, but settles deeper into the cushions. "I've been on my own for so long. Those dark roads are shitty company. It sucks having no one to miss. I don't want to be alone anymore."

My blink is slow. The math isn't mathing. "But this isn't about sex?"

She pinches the bridge of her nose. "You're my boyfriend, okay? I'm making it official."

"Ohhhh," I breathe. "You really like me."

"And for the record, this is exclusive. If you so much as look at another woman—"

"I won't," I cut in.

"But if you do, I'll—"

"Chop off my balls," I finish for her.

Frankie gives a sharp nod. "Damn straight."

"Well, if I catch a guy anywhere near what's mine—"

"I'll punch him in the throat." She mimics the action to avoid any confusion.

Offense grunts out of me. "But his balls are safe?"

"Figured you'd do the honors of crushing those."

"It's a deal." I grab her hand, threading our fingers together. "We're doing this."

"Afraid so, honey."

I falter, letting my jaw unhinge. "Honey?"

Her shrug is completely unbothered. "I'm stuck with you, right? Might as well call it what it is."

"Damn, that's almost sweet."

She plops a kiss on my cheek. "You're welcome, honey."

"Gotta admit, I don't hate it."

"That's a first," she laughs.

"Never hated you," I grumble.

Her palm squeezes mine. "You have a weird way of showing it."

"A man has to protect himself when attacked from all

angles." I glance at a lump along the seam of her leggings, willing to bet there's a knife stored in a secret compartment.

"Seemed too good to be true." Frankie hums thoughtfully and studies me for a moment. "I never thought I'd have this."

My heart strums to a faster beat. "I didn't plan on ever having it again."

She gazes at me like her wheels are spinning over something heavy, but it's not ready to be spoken aloud quite yet. "What's something you've always wanted to do, but haven't had the chance?"

I grin at the choice of topic. "Ride a motorcycle."

"No way!" Her loud blurt startles Tux, but he just curls himself into a tighter ball. "You've never been on a motorcycle?"

"Thought about buying one when I was younger. Once Ronnie was born, it didn't seem practical."

"Such a good dad," she croons.

"Babies and bikes don't mix."

Frankie rolls her eyes. "Depends who you ask."

"How old were you?"

"Too young to remember. Like Ronnie and her horses."

"We're all a bit reckless in our own way," I chuckle. "Okay, your turn. What's something else you haven't done but want to?"

She chomps on her bottom lip. "Promise not to laugh?"

"I'll do my best."

Her gaze drops to our clasped palms. "I've never had someone hold me without expecting more. Could you do that for me?"

My tongue swells and I can't get a word out. "You want to… cuddle?"

"For fuck's sake. Forget I asked," she growls. "We're about to have a bad misunderstanding and those never end well."

Before she can leap off the couch, I'm cinching an arm around her waist and tucking her into my side. The cat screeches, turning into a damn loofah. He darts off in a hissy fit that would usually impress Frankie. But instead, the feisty redhead is deathly still against me. I'm not even sure she's breathing. Her rapid pulse is a spooked animal about to flee. My hand coasts along her rigid frame, trying to ease her into it. A sputtered exhale loosens in the strain in her limbs. After another minute of sturdy coaxing, she slumps against me.

"Are you good?"

Frankie's next breath is raspy. "Yes."

"Is this okay?"

Her nod is slow but noticeable. "It's… nice."

"What you wanted?"

She swallows audibly. "Even better."

My grip tightens slightly. "I'll hold you whenever you allow it."

"Might happen often if this is how it feels." She tilts her head back until our eyes connect. "Don't tell anyone about this."

"Wouldn't dare, menace." I reach for the remote and hand it to her.

"Smart man." Frankie snuggles closer while changing the channel. "Just soak it in, stud."

Some cheesy dating show appears on the screen. Not that I'm paying much attention one way or another. My focus is consumed by the woman in my arms and the dreamy smile curling her lips. I toy with her fingers just to touch her in more places.

Her sigh of contentment might as well be a siren's song. "Who takes care of you?"

"Are you offering?" I shift us lower on the couch into a more comfortable position.

She hums her approval and nuzzles against me as if I'm her pillow. "Thinking so. This feels right."

My chest expands on a long inhale, filling my lungs with relief. "Does that mean I get to take care of you?"

"That's up to you, honey." Frankie pats my abs, which flex under her caress. "But I'll tell you what. I could fall asleep like this."

And then my cheek rests on her forehead, connecting us at another point. "Don't let me stop you."

When I wake up in the morning, I'm by myself on the couch and the house is too quiet. Even the animals aren't making any noise. It reminds me of the desolate months when happiness didn't bounce off the walls. I'd become accustomed to the silence and assumed that's how it would remain.

But now, my heart lurches in the stillness. I can't wait for my girls to get home. Their near-constant eruptions of chaos are the only cure for my battered soul.

CHAPTER THIRTY

Frankie

"**G**O FASTER!" RONNIE SQUEALS IN THE BACKSEAT when I press a touch harder on the Passat's accelerator. "Turn on the boosters!"

"Gonna get me arrested at this speed," I tease her. As if this snail of a sedan that Byron forces me to drive is capable of breaking the law.

"Hurry!" Her little legs straighten to push against the passenger seat like that will get us moving quicker. "We gotta win the race!"

I scoff, tightening my grip on the steering wheel. "Nobody can beat us."

The tires are silent as I whip into a parking spot. This snoozer couldn't burn rubber if I set it on fire. But what's most important is that Ronnie arrives safely. See? I'm maturing.

"We're here!" My voice is entirely too chipper for seven-thirty in the morning.

She wanted to get to school early today for breakfast. I didn't question her even though the options are usually flimsy and floppy and not appetizing. It must be the novelty of it. Byron was still passed out on the sofa when we left. I didn't have the heart to wake him. Maybe he'll still be dreaming by the time I get back and I can reward him. Gosh, I really am becoming a better person. Who would've thought? Certainly not my old crew.

"Chop, chop. We've got places to be." Such as riding a certain cowboy before the sun completely rises.

Ronnie scrambles to open her door. "Don't leave me!"

A cloud of mist puffs from my mouth as I hoof it around the trunk before her feet even touch the snowy pavement. "I'm not going anywhere, kiddo. We're stuck together."

"Daddy too?"

I smile while ducking into the car for her backpack. "Yep, he's along for the ride."

She slides her tiny hand in mine as we walk to the school's entrance. "Do you love him?"

"Meh." I tip my head from right to left. "Maybe a little."

Her gasp is a rowdy burst of excitement. "Do you love me?"

"Lots," I admit while my pulse begins to gallop. That's the closest I've come to fully saying it.

"We're a real family," she murmurs under her breath. "I knew it."

Flutters fill my stomach until I have the urge the skip,

which is completely ridiculous. I might be giddy, but that's taking it to an unhinged level I can't accept. At least not yet. If trashy reality television has taught me anything it's that this is the honeymoon phase when everything feels shiny and bright. Much can go wrong, especially for a jaded crook like me.

But I allow Ronnie's joy to fuel my own. We stroll along the sidewalk as if rainbows and unicorns surround us. My spirits are warm and toasty despite the cold. All that matters is the future we're building together.

Except there are obstacles in our path.

Two recognizable stains on society are standing beside an unmarked van as if they're about to offer candy to kids. There's a jail cell with their names on it. My grin melts into a scowl. These assholes have to be the dumbest criminals on the planet.

Their already unfortunate faces are bruised and mottled. Whatever Dennis did to them must've hurt, but it missed the mark of finality. I won't make that same mistake.

But first, I need to get Ronnie out of their sight. My hands tremble slightly as I loop the straps of her bag over her arms, settling the weight on her shoulders. Ice fills my veins when I kneel on the frozen ground in front of her. A crease appears between her delicate eyebrows.

She tips her head at that adorable angle and I suddenly want to cry. "What's wrong, Frannie?"

"Nothing," I say too quickly. "I'll just miss you."

Her features pinch tighter. "You'll see me at the bus stop later."

My nod is jerky. "Have a great day, okay?"

Ronnie stares at me, burrowing into the depths of my conflicted soul. "Don't forget to feed Tux."

I offer a wide smile, but it's more phony than the couples on *Too Hot to Handle*. "What about Darla and Dottie?"

"Duh, silly. You know their schedule."

"Of course," I reply dutifully. "And I have to give Greta seventy-five pats on the neck."

"Don't skimp out. She'll tell me." With two fingers, Ronnie points from her eyes to mine as if she's watching me.

"Got it." And then I trace along the length of her nose, swooping off the end to drop a tap on her chin. "Love you, kiddo."

Her eyes go round. "You did it."

"Is that okay?"

She lunges forward to wrap me in a hug I'd willingly suffocate from. "I love you sooooo much. Will you let me call you Mommy soon?"

I hold her tight, squeezing my eyes shut against the watery sting. "Really soon."

Ronnie pulls away and her expression is almost blinding enough to blot out the trouble behind us. "Thanks for loving me and Daddy."

"Thanks for showing me how," I whisper.

"Welcome," she chirps and begins backing toward the doors. "Gotta go! Byeeeee."

My reason for compassion trots off, turning once more to wave at me. I return the gesture and up the ante by forming a heart with my hands. Ronnie giggles while trying to copy the action. When she disappears around the corner, red tints my vision.

I stand and whirl to confront the dumbass duo. The edges that little girl has softened now sharpen into deadly points. My shoulders square as I strut forward with malicious intent. These morons are messing with the wrong bitch.

"Rough week at the office? Damn." My cringe is way over the top while I inspect the damage to their mean mugs.

The older one who likes to believe he's in charge grunts at me. "That was touching, Frankie. She clearly means a lot to you."

My expression hardens into stone. "Leave her out of this."

"I don't think we will," he drawls. "Unless you cooperate."

"Are you threatening me?" I tip my head back and let a shrill cackle fly free. "Good fucking luck with that."

His beady eyes narrow. "We've got a couple men that were just locked up in county thanks to Dennis Benson and his sleazy cop buddies."

"Awwww, did they forget about you? That must be really upsetting."

"Didn't take 'em but a day to join forces with your brother."

"How unfortunate for them," I sigh. The legal system should really pick up the pace and move my brother to maximum security prison already.

"Walker seems to think you'll come to your senses

and agree to this job. You owe us. Veronica will stay out of harm's way."

"She will regardless," I snap. If they don't think I'll end their miserable existences to protect hers, they're more stupid than I originally thought.

"Just one job," he coaxes.

"As a start, right? That's how you lure me." I study my nails, cleaning an imaginary smudge off the middle one. "You need to learn to respect a woman's wishes. I'm not interested."

The criminal well beyond his prime scrubs at the greasy whiskers on his jaw. "We brought someone to convince you."

When the two step aside, the air crackles around me for a second. Just as suddenly, my body bows under the brutal force of the unexpected attack. I just got sucker punched straight in the gut. That's the only way to describe Jaxon Steele appearing like a mirage.

"Hey, Frankie." The man who I used to consider a partner in actual crime smirks as if I'm the problem.

Memories are a tidal wave crashing over me until I struggle to breathe. I haven't let him cross my mind after wallowing at Sip in the Stacks, licking my wounds like a neglected stray. My gaze flicks over him now. Based on appearances alone, I landed in a much cushier spot.

"Are you fucking serious? You abandoned me and teamed up with these losers?"

His shrug couldn't care less about my outrage. "They had more to offer."

"Ouch," I hiss. "That'd burn if I didn't label you as a traitor."

He laughs, but it lacks humor. "Come with us."

"No."

"C'mon, Frankie. Admit that you miss it."

My nose wrinkles at his filthy jeans and ripped shirt. "I don't."

Jax's features look even more ragged when he frowns. "Why are you pretending to go legit? You'll never be satisfied as a housewife in the 'burbs."

I roll my eyes skyward. "Nice try, but I'll still pass."

"Why settle? Nothing beats the adrenaline of a hustle. Once a thief, always a thief."

My glare is a serrated blade. "Your argument is weak. Much like your loyalty."

"I'm sorry about running off, but I always planned to find you again. We're a team. Let me prove it to you." He beckons me forward as if I'm an obedient hound.

For whatever reason, I pause to contemplate my choices. Intrusive thoughts are illogical like that. Past and present collide in a gruesome battle for control. The perceived disappointment from Byron and Ronnie induces nausea. It's tough to shake the queasiness of admitting a relapse.

But Jax isn't completely wrong, which I hate to admit. It might be fun to be part of a con, just for old time's sake. The devil on my shoulder steeples his fingers and I exhale heavily.

"What's the job?"

His haggard expression lifts in victory. "It's a simple in and out. We just need you to crack into the safe."

I stare at these crooked men and something clicks. A slow smile curls my lips. It feels like destiny or some other divine intervention.

"Okay, I'm in."

CHAPTER THIRTY-ONE

Byron

I READ FRANKIE'S MESSAGE FOR THE TWENTIETH TIME as if the text will change. It's been almost three hours since it appeared on my screen, commanding me to blindly comply. As if I'm the type to surrender that easily. She's left me little choice in the matter, though. The fifteen I've sent in response remain unanswered.

That doesn't prevent me from trying again.

I manage to wait a full minute before my fingers are furiously typing another attempt.

She doesn't listen. There's no evidence that my texts are even going through. Her phone is probably off. That's why I can't track her location. The car is still parked at the school where she must've left it.

My legs set me in motion, pacing back and forth next to the road. Ronnie should arrive any minute. I need to calm the fuck down or she'll freak out. That won't be beneficial for anyone.

Agitation snatches the reins and rips the hat off my head. The urge to toss it flexes my arm. Instead, I exhale heavily and drag a hand through my hair.

It's probably nothing. I'm overreacting. My mood has been off since I woke up alone after the best night sleep I've had in years. Frankie is capable of defending herself. But this isn't the first time the woman I love stopped responding.

That gives me pause. Love? I don't love Frankie. And it's a massive stretch to find any comparison to Nina's death. My mind is playing tricks. Shit, I need to get myself together.

The squeak of worn brakes alerts me that the bus is here. My mind whirls. When did that happen? I paste on a grin that I hope Ronnie won't see straight through. She bounces down the stairs with the usual pep in her step.

"Hey, cupcake. How was school?" My knees creak when I crouch to greet her.

"Sooooo fun!" Ronnie runs into my open arms, giving me a much-needed hug. "We learned about the solar system. It's super duper huge. Like we can't even see it all!"

"Really? That's out of this world." I don't have to fake

my enthusiasm. This is familiar and natural, allowing me to focus on cooling off.

She nods as we begin the trek to the house. "Did you know that Jupiter is the biggest planet?"

"No way! It must be massive."

"Yep! Where's Frannie? I wanna tell her."

This scene, on the other hand, is entirely too familiar. My smile slips ever so slightly. "She's not home. There's something she had to do."

My daughter hums thoughtfully. "Like what?"

"I'm… not sure." Hesitancy chops my statement into pieces.

"Maybe she's getting us a present."

"Why would she do that?"

"To be nice, duhhhhh."

My eyes narrow at her. "Watch your tone, sassy pants."

"It's prissy," she corrects.

"What do you mean?"

"Frannie says my pants are prissy. I never ever wear sassy pants. That'd be silly, Daddy."

"My mistake," I mumble.

Ronnie does a twirl when we approach the driveway. "I can't wait to see what she gets us."

"Don't get your hopes up." At this rate, I'm crossing my fingers that she'll be back for bedtime.

"It's gonna be special," my little girl continues as if I hadn't spoken. "Like a pink umbrella or sparkly picture frame 'cause she loves us."

"Ronnie," I sigh. "Don't pressure her to say that she

loves you, okay? She needs to tell you on her own when she's ready."

"But she is ready," my daughter insists.

"I'm not so sure about that."

"Yes-huh," she insists. "She told me so. Her finger swooped down my nose and tapped my chin. Just like you do it."

My stride falters and I stop in my tracks. "When?"

"At drop-off this morning," she chirps. "Frannie was actin' kinda weird, but I guess she just had jitters in her tummy. Loving someone is a super big deal. My tummy gets flip-floppy too. Oh, and I think she was cryin' a little bit. But those were happy tears."

Meanwhile, my stomach plummets to my toes. I break out in a cold sweat. Why would Frankie tell Ronnie she loves her on the same day she pulls a disappearing act? None of this makes sense.

"Are you sure?" I ask in rushed tone.

"Positive!"

Without further information, I'm left to assume the worst. She got spooked. Someone took her. There was a fight and she got arrested. That spiral leads nowhere fast.

I check Frankie's location again just for something to do. When her dot appears on the map, I almost drop my phone. That blue circle blinks like a beacon. She wants me to find her… in the middle of nowhere.

The area is beyond the outskirts of town. It could be a warehouse or some other large building. Either way, it reeks of that biker gang. Dennis assured me they were taken care of, but it's not uncommon for a few stragglers to crawl out of an attack like cockroaches.

Now, it's a question of if Frankie went willingly or by force. The answer will determine how I respond. I also need to know what I'm walking into. Maybe she needs reinforcements.

A frigid chill whips across my face, reminding me that I'm standing still. At least I have a direction to follow. That loosens the strain in my chest. I'm able to take my first decent breath in hours.

"Hey, cupcake?"

Ronnie pauses drawing a stick figure in the snow. "Yes, Daddy?"

"How would you like to visit Paisley and Brody? I need to have a chat with Uncle Dennis."

Her lips twist. "What about Frannie?"

"She'll be back soon enough." Even if I have to haul her home over my shoulder, kicking and cursing.

"And then she'll be my mommy?"

My momentum putters to a halt. "Did she tell you that too?"

"Yep," Ronnie states with conviction.

Words fail me, much like my sanity where that woman is concerned.

We're going to have a serious conversation. I just have to find her first.

CHAPTER THIRTY-TWO

Frankie

J AX AND I ARE FOLLOWING THE TWO CLOWNS DOWN a dank warehouse corridor. Lights flicker to the sound of static and water dripping. It's giving very low budget film vibes.

Rot burns in my nostrils. That might be my internal conflict staging a protest or unidentifiable sludge dripping off the walls. Whatever it is should redirect me to the straight and narrow. Unfortunately for me and my delayed conscience, I'm committed to seeing this through.

"I need to tell you something," Jax murmurs softly to prevent an echo. His tone almost carries a note of concern.

"It's a little late for confessions." Especially when I've already plotted his demise.

"Frankie, this is serious. It might get messy. I don't want you to get caught in the middle."

A stale snort rips from me, bouncing off the concrete fortress. "Since when?"

"I'm a cop," he blurts.

My boot catches a ghost hole and I stumble. "The fuck you just say?"

Jax winces as my voice carries, but the bozos we're tailing don't hear me. "I've been undercover since the start."

A bomb explodes in my brain. I gape at him with my mouth hanging open, bound to catch flies and gangrene. But then his words repeat. Once more for good measure. This is too much.

I start to laugh. Loudly. The amusement just pours out of me. It quakes through my whole frame until I'm folded in half.

He gives me a firm shake. "Will you shush?"

"You shush!" I whack him across the stomach, grinning like a maniac when he doubles over. "That's what you get for lying."

"It's the truth," Jax rasps while straightening to boldly face me again. "I'm sorry I couldn't tell you sooner, but that would've compromised the case. Kinda defeats the purpose, Franks."

My hands tighten on the bag strapped to my chest. It's armed to the teeth. I never leave home without it. The daggers are about to come in handy.

"I'm gonna stab you in the dick," I seethe.

Jax hunches forward slightly like that will protect him. "I'd rather you didn't."

"You deserve far worse."

"That might be true, but my intentions are decent."

"Really? So, what's the grand plan? You're gonna hang us"—my arm waves at the goons ahead as if I care what happens to them—"out to dry for a crime we haven't committed yet? Really solid, asshole."

"No, I never wanted you to be a part of this. That's why I ditched you after the compound was raided. It seemed to all work out for the best when Byron hired you."

My eyes narrow into sharper points than my entire knife collection. "You've been keepin' tabs on me?"

He has the audacity to smirk. "Part of the job, whether you're my target or not. How's the nanny gig? Can't say I ever would've guessed that."

"You and me both," I mutter before remembering that I'm mad at him. "Quit trying to distract me. You're a snake."

He holds up his hands when I aim a blade at his throat. "Whoa, whoa. Think about what you're doing, Frankie."

"Don't worry about me."

"I'm not the enemy."

"I disagree. We were friends, or so I foolishly thought. Lying bastard," I spit.

"We are friends," he reiterates. "You're like a little sister to me, which is why I care where this leads. Put the knife down."

"Why would I do that?"

"Because you're smarter than this," Jax states calmly. "It would also save me the trouble of disarming you."

"As if you could."

His eyes twinkle. "Wanna bet?"

I want to argue and beat him in a fight. Years of experience strongly suggest I shouldn't bother trying. Steam spews from my flared nostrils. At least now I understand how he was always so damn skilled at hand-to-hand combat.

With a flick of my wrist, the dagger is tucked into my bag. I discreetly turn on my phone while my fingers are in the vicinity. The rapid-fire buzz of silent notifications isn't that easy to ignore.

My arms cross over the noise and I tap my foot for an added precaution. "Happy?"

His nod is quick. "You will be too."

"That remains to be seen."

"As I was saying," Jax drawls. "There are a lot of big players in this game. James Keller was a pawn meant to get me higher in the ranks, but then he died. I stuck around to sniff out these bikers. It took months to determine they're a dead end."

"Wow, great detective work." I slow clap.

He scowls. "It's a process to get accepted by a criminal organization. Plus, paperwork is a bitch."

"Uh-huh, I almost care enough to keep listening."

"What're you two ladies gossiping about?" The bellow ricochets at us like rancid morning breath.

"That's my cue," I chirp. "If you'll excuse—"

But Jax yanks me back before I can even take a step. "Fuck off. We're having a meeting," he yells at them in return.

"Shouldn't we be included?" It's the same voice from earlier.

"No," Jax clips. "We'll be along shortly. Find something to do."

"Don't like that guy," comes out as an offended mutter, but they don't say more.

"Wait," I say as a thought occurs to me. "If these losers are getting you nowhere, why am I here?"

Jax sighs. "Those bikers wouldn't take no for an answer. They have a serious hard-on for you."

"Obviously," I purr.

His upper lip curls at my attempt to pamper my pride. "When they insisted that we pick you up, I knew it was my time to strike. I figured you'd just turn on your signature charm, flip us off, and walk away. I'm curious as to why you got in the van."

"To eliminate the threat." I slice a finger across my throat.

Jax's stony expression isn't impressed. "You're not a killer."

"I'll be whatever it takes if they try to use Byron and Ronnie against me."

That gives him pause. "You care about them," he murmurs.

"Yeah, so?" I shrug it off as if my heart hasn't kicked into acceleration mode.

"I'm glad you found a place to settle. That's what I wanted for you."

"Like I care about your approval," I snap.

"Well, you have it regardless."

"Okay, for real," I sigh. "What're we doing here?"

"We aren't doing anything. Feel free to go." Jax juts his chin in the direction we came from.

"Unlike you, I don't leave my team behind." My nose crinkles. "Not that we're a team anymore."

"I'm just going to apprehend these small-timers before moving on. There's no need for you to get your hands dirty. In fact, I'd strongly advise against it."

"Where are you going next?" Why I'm asking is a better question.

He eyes me closely as if he's not going to tell me. "I'm on the hunt for Jimmy Benson."

Shock betrays me, widening my eyes before I can act normal and uninterested. "Byron doesn't know where he is."

"Don't fret, Frankie. I'm not going to shake down your boyfriend."

My gut clenches. "Why would I believe you?"

"There's someone else willing to bait the trap." But his lips are sealed after that.

"Why are you telling me all of this?"

Jax shrugs. "Maybe you'll actually believe me someday. I want you to trust me. You were never part of the plan."

I let out a wary, weary exhale. "I can't believe you're a cop."

"I can't believe we're still standing here."

"Well, you look like shit," I fire in return.

"Part of the disguise." He smooths a palm down his stained shirt that has more holes than a slice of Swiss cheese. "Let's get this over with. Stay out of my way."

"Cocky jackass." I'd love nothing more than to take him down several notches.

But then he's on the move. Jax sticks to the shadows like a predator about to pounce. Before they even hear his approach, he has the first dumbass in a sleeper hold. The second goon whirls around just as Jax kicks his legs out from under him. Both guys are down and done for within seconds.

Dammit, Jax's smug attitude is warranted. I even have the urge to applaud his methodical attack. It was very efficient. I guess that's what he was trained for.

"Wow." I can't keep the awe out of my voice. "You'll have to teach me how to do that."

His smirk is entirely too confident, taking me back to simpler times. "Join the force."

And with that, I'm smacked with a dose of reality. "Absolutely not."

Jax looks me over as if I could've been harmed in the one-sided scuffle. "I was lying, by the way."

"About what?"

"People can change. You were always meant for more than a life of crime. I'm glad you found it."

My nose stings and I drop my gaze. "That almost means something."

"Get outta here before I haul you in." He whips out two pairs of cuffs from his jacket pocket.

"Yeah, it's about that time. This was… enlightening." Not to mention cathartic. An old, festering wound now has the chance to heal. "See ya around?"

Jax gives me a stern look. "Not if you stay out of trouble."

"Unlikely," I laugh.

"Take care of your new family, Franks. It's a good look for you."

Heat burns my eyes in an embarrassing display of emotion. I turn away before he can catch me blubbering. My hurried stride doesn't drown out Jax's call for backup. A bitter huff scraps from me. That piece of traitor trash was a cop all along.

Winter greets me with a burst of cold wind as I step outside. I inhale the fresh air, allowing my eyes to slide shut for a moment. The crunch of furious footsteps snaps my gaze open. My attention locks on Byron's full-speed approach.

"Hey, boyfriend," I croon. "Did you get my bat signal?"

"Cut the shit, menace," he growls.

The clench of his chiseled, bearded jaw is visible beneath the darkening sky. It's almost tempting enough for me sprawl on the ground in offering. But then I remember Jax's cover is at risk of being blown.

I block the entrance with a starfish formation. "You can't go in there."

Byron presses himself flush against me. "Why not?"

"It's… dangerous."

That gives him pause. "Are you hurt?"

I bite my inner cheek. "No."

"Did you hurt someone?"

My scoff is affronted. "No."

"Gotta give me answers," he rumbles low. "Or I'll bust that door down and get them myself."

"It's been taken care of," I evade.

Which isn't good enough for him. "Dennis told me that two of the bikers escaped. Are they in there?"

The truth expands in my chest, but I force it down. "I'd rather not say."

The demand for destruction steels his towering stance into a dominating force. "Move."

As a last-ditch effort, I launch myself at him. I'm whisked into his arms as if this ploy was choreographed. Byron's palms cradle my ass while I cinch my legs around his waist. In a downward swoop, I fuse my mouth to his and proceed to kiss the suspicion out of him.

Warmth floods me immediately. It's potent and intoxicating. That spicy, woodsy scent of his goes straight to my head. I feel my lashes flutter against the feverish onslaught. If Byron wasn't holding me, I'd melt into a puddle at his feet.

He groans while swiping his tongue out to tangle with mine. I fist the front of his shirt, yanking us impossibly closer. We fight for control and I get lost in the motions. My hips buck against him, grinding into his belt buckle. Byron clenches his fingers until his grip is almost painful. I nip at him, hoping we both leave a mark.

"Let's have sex," I murmur against his lips.

He grunts when I smash my breasts into him. "Just want to distract me."

"No," I mewl. "Need you, honey."

My hand glides down, wedging into the snug space

between us. I stretch my fingers in an attempt to undo his jeans. There's too much blocking me. My nails claw at him, unable to get a grip.

"If I could just—" But my statement stalls when Byron comes to an abrupt halt.

The dingy walls of the warehouse blink into view. I realize too late that he's carried me to the scene of the non-existent crime. Panic clutches my throat until I notice Jax is slumped on the ground. My former friend is looking just as knocked out as the other two.

"Dammit," I cry. "You outmaneuvered me."

Byron is vibrating with desire or rage. Most likely the latter. "What the fuck, Frankie?"

"It's not what it looks like," I rush to say.

"Did you do this?"

"Uh-huh, yep. All by myself. Okay, we can go now." I rock against him, trying to move us along.

"Menace," he rasps. "Why don't I believe you?"

"Not sure, but that's a you problem to sort out later."

Byron's shrewd awareness rips into my defenses. "I thought you didn't hurt anyone."

My nose rubs along his. "I didn't, thank you very much. They're just taking a little nap until the cops arrive."

He considers my honesty while his focus slides over the men. "You took all three of them out?"

"Hey!" I pin him with a nasty glare. "Your lack of faith in me is really sexy. I'm super turned on right now. Be a good boy and fuck me on this dirty concrete."

"Frankie," he deadpans. "I'm trying to get a handle on this situation so you don't get arrested."

"Mhmm," I breathe. "You're the one who got me tossed in the back of a squad car."

Byron jostles me as if trying to convince my logic to wake up. "This isn't the time for jokes."

"How do you figure? They're alive. The police will arrive any minute. It's fine." I clasp his cheeks in my palms. "But we won't be if we don't leave right now."

His hard gaze is about to argue. "I want you to tell me how you got involved in this."

"The details aren't important, but our future is. Please take me home."

"Promise me that this won't touch Ronnie."

"I would never let any harm come her way." Conviction clangs in my icy tone.

Byron's stare burrows deeper into mine, still searching for more. "Did you do this to protect her?"

My eyes slide to Jax who appears to be fighting a grin. Such a shit. I should throw him under the bus. But something stops me. Maybe it's a sign of forgiveness. I might be truly healing. Or the fact that he's actually on the right side of the law. I'm still pissed about that.

"They came to her school," I tell him. "That was their last mistake. I wasn't about to let them get away again."

He holds his silence for a long time, but then the fight bleeds from him on a loud exhale. "Thank you, menace," he finally says. "Thank you for doing whatever it takes to keep her safe."

"Always, stud. No limits." I wrap him in a hug that fills me with warmth. It's a comfort only he provides. "And don't worry. I've got your back too."

"Does that mean you're sticking around permanently?"

A sudden shyness creeps in, burying my face in the crook of his neck. "If you'll have me."

But Byron doesn't let me hide. His thumb and forefinger grasp my chin, tugging until our gazes meet. "I do without question, but I think we need to change your job description."

Laughter sputters from my cheesy grin. "Are you about to fire me?"

"Think of it as more of an upgrade."

"To what?"

"Mine," he murmurs against my smile. "Pretty sure Ronnie has her own title picked out for you."

My belly swoops and I almost giggle. Gosh, I'm turning into a sap. "It's a deal."

"And now," Byron gives me a gentle kiss. "I'll take you home."

CHAPTER THIRTY-THREE

"AND THEN THE PRINCESS DROPPED HER SWORD. There was no more pain or suffering. Her broad smile lifted to the sky in thanks of those who fought before her. She'd slayed the dragon and saved the prince. The kingdom was secured once again," Frankie finishes reading and closes the book.

Ronnie sighs happily from under her mountain of blankets. My little girl gazes at her more-than-a-nanny with enough adoration to make my heart swell. The redhead gazes right back at her with equal affection, if not more. The bond they share is truly something to behold.

Which is why I'm standing in the hallway, watching them like a stalker. If they're aware of me spying, I haven't been called out. The dogs are quiet and sprawled on the floor. Tux is curled up on Ronnie's pillow, feeling right at home. His demonic green eyes narrow at me as if I'm the intruder. That little shit can fuck off. Those girls were mine first. I'm not going anywhere.

After finding Frankie at that warehouse earlier, I haven't let her out of my sight. The fear of losing her sunk in its claws, spreading a poison capable of destroying me. My unresolved abandonment issues shook me to my core. But I fought against the darkness and won.

Doubt drifts away in the breeze from the overhead fan. Whatever Frankie did today was unfinished business like she said. We're leaving it at that for now. I'm choosing to trust her. That hasn't steered me wrong. All that's left to do tonight is confess my feelings. By the sounds of things, that's a popular choice this evening.

"Are you ready to be my mommy now? You've already taken my sadness away." Ronnie's voice is heavy from the pull of sleep.

Frankie sweeps hair off my daughter's forehead before dropping a kiss there. "We need to talk to your dad about that."

"He says it's okay," my little girl insists and I almost laugh.

The redhead hums thoughtfully. "When did he say that?"

"I dunno, but we're gonna live happily ever after."

"Just like that?"

Ronnie nods. "And ride off into the sunset. You gotta hold on tight. I don't want you to fall off. Giddy-up, new mommy!"

A flicker of hesitation crosses Frankie's expression and

she glances at the framed picture on the nightstand. "Do you think your real mom would approve?"

"Uh-huh, I can have two. One is up in heaven and the other is down here. That's you," she whispers. "But both of you are in my heart."

The redhead's bottom lip begins to wobble. "It's tough to argue with a perfect explanation."

"More happy tears?"

"This"—she motions to her flushed face—"didn't happen until I met you."

Ronnie's tired eyes blow wide open. "Wow, does that make me special?"

An agreeable noise comes from her. "The only exception, remember?"

"Your little loophole," she breathes.

"Which is the only reason I'm co-hosting your birthday party. How many other kids will be there?" Frankie cringes while waiting for the answer.

"I invited my whole class!" Ronnie giggles.

"It's going to be the end of me," the redhead groans.

"Don't worry, Mommy. I'll protect you from the meanies!"

"Same, kiddo. Forever and always. Okay, time for bed." Frankie slides a finger down Ronnie's nose, swooping off the end and landing with a tap on her chin.

My daughter is quick to repeat the motions on her adopted mom. "Love you lots."

"I love you more than my wildest dreams imagined."

"What? How is that possible?"

"No clue, but you conquered the odds."

"Do you love Daddy too?"

"Yeah," she whispers softly. "I love your daddy very much."

Ronnie's squeal wakes the dogs who look at me to confirm or deny danger. It's my heart that's at risk of exploding. This conversation is the cure my broken soul didn't realize it needed.

"He loves you bigger than the whole galaxy!" My daughter flings her arms wide, startling the cat.

Frankie drops her jaw. "That's too big. Are you sure?"

"Positive. Go ask him!"

"I'll think about it, but only if you fall asleep really fast." After giving Ronnie a hug, Frankie stands and flicks off the lamp. "See you in the morning. It's the start of whatever comes next."

"Mhmm," my little girl mumbles, already drifting off.

Frankie tiptoes from the room to where I'm waiting for her in the hallway. "Enjoy the show?"

"Immensely." I hook one of her belt loops and tug until her chest is flush against mine. "You love me, menace?"

She bites her lip and nods. "But don't get too excited. I have no idea how to love someone properly."

"Not true. I just witnessed a very emotional display. Ronnie saw something in you from the start. It was your ability to form an inseparable connection and love her unconditionally when no one ever taught you how." Which reminds me that we might be disturbing her. Without releasing Frankie, I shuffle us to the kitchen and lean against the counter.

The woman in my arms exhales the weight of needless worry, trusting me to support her. "She's easy to fall for."

I tighten my hold. "What about me?"

"Took a bit more persuading," she quips. "But you get bonus points for raising a really great kid."

"I've done the best I can. You're going to help me finish the job."

"That's what it's looking like," she sighs and loops her arms around my neck, stretching to give me a soft kiss.

My gaze feasts on her, finding it almost hard to believe we're here in this place. "History almost had me convinced that it was repeating itself, but you were coming back to me."

She clucks her tongue. "Told you that you're stuck with me, honey. You'd be wise to believe it."

"Three of the people meant to love me the most have left. But now there's you," I rasp.

"I'm not going anywhere. Do you trust me?"

"Yes."

"Is there room for me in here?" She taps the space above my heart.

My hand rests over hers on that spot, feeling the beat begin to race. "You've given me a reason to have faith in love again. It flutters just for you, little menace."

"Fucking butterflies," she laughs.

I tuck some hair behind her ear, about to do something I've never done to a grown woman. There's a ledge straight ahead, beckoning me to take the leap. My thumb coasts down the slope of her nose, lifting off the tip, and ending with a bump to her chin.

"I love you." My voice cracks like a pubescent teenager. "All that other fluffy shit too."

Her inhale catches, but then she's repeating the action back to me. "You make the fluffy shit appealing."

"I'll take that as a compliment."

"You should," she coos and escapes the cage of my embrace. "Now, if you'll excuse me, I have to pet Greta seventy-five times."

My eyebrows lift. "And why's that?"

"Didn't have the chance earlier and I've received a stern reminder from the boss." She tips her head toward Ronnie's room.

An idea forms, slanting my mouth into a smirk. "That's actually where I was headed."

"Convenient." Frankie takes my hand in hers, leading us to the foyer to get bundled up.

I zip her coat slowly, sad to see her curves covered. But they'll be in my grasp soon. Until then, we huddle close while stepping outside to face the elements.

Quiet nickers greet us when we enter the barn. Frankie goes straight for her horse's stall. The metal latch slides free, bouncing an echo off the wood. She pushes the door open wide enough for her ample assets to squeeze through. After yanking off her gloves, she begins gliding her palms along Greta's neck.

"Didn't think you were serious about petting her," I murmur while resting along a beam.

"A few things you should know about me, stud." Frankie's gaze flicks to me. "I don't break promises, go back on my word, or cut corners. Ronnie's wrath is something I never want to deserve."

I grunt and scrub over my beard. "That's very honest of you."

"Don't act so surprised." She appears to contemplate something for a moment. "Do you think I'm a thief?"

"Not anymore." I chuckle when she glares. "You're recovering."

"Did I steal your heart?"

"Can't steal what's freely given."

Her nod is slow and calculated. "Am I allowed to be Ronnie's mom if I'm not married to you?"

My gut clenches. "You can be whoever you want to be, menace. Labels are just that. We'll figure it out as we go."

Frankie's swallow is audible. "I don't want you to think I'm trying to replace your wife."

"I don't think that. Besides, it's not possible. I'll always love Nina, but she's my past. Memories are all I have left of her. You're my future. Whether we get married or not, I want you by my side."

Her consistent strokes along Greta's neck come to an abrupt halt. "You want to get remarried?"

My eyes rove over her as if she's not buried in layers. "I didn't want to until you arrived on the scene."

"Awww, you love me." Giddiness bounces from her voice.

"Sure do," I reply. "I also love open communication in a relationship."

"That's probably important," she agrees.

I allow my unwavering stare to delve deeper. "Are you ever going to tell me what happened in that warehouse?"

Her gaze slides off mine. "I got closure."

"For what?"

She shrugs. "A part of my past that really stung, but I refused to admit it."

A tightness knots in my chest. "I don't like secrets, menace."

"It's not mine to tell. Can you respect that?"

I blow out a heavy exhale through clenched teeth. My boots carry me to the gap in the stall door where I extend my arms overhead, bracing against the top board. Frankie's attention burns into my change of position. A slow heat crawls over me as she shamelessly ogles.

"Like what you see, menace?"

"You're really fucking hot," she blurts. "It's horrible for my concentration."

"Good thing I'm not paying you to keep track of my daughter," I drawl with extra sarcasm.

"That reminds me," she murmurs. "You should probably stop paying me. It's kinda icky in our situation."

"There's nothing icky about our situation." I resent the very notion.

Her eyes roll. "As if I was cashing those checks. I'll keep testing your credit card's spending limit, though."

"Please do," I laugh while mentally tallying how many times she's pet her horse by this point. "But it's gonna cost you."

"Oh yeah?"

"I'll need an answer. A real one this time. What's something you've always wanted to do, but haven't had the chance?"

Her smile is wistful, capturing the whimsy of the question. "Love someone enough to surrender my soul."

A rough cough scrapes from me. "Damn, I think you've been watching too much reality television."

She huffs. "Jerk."

"Your jerk," I retort.

"Seventy-five. I'm done." Frankie swipes along Greta's neck once more. "Your turn."

"I'm interested in petting your pussy, not your horse."

She shakes her head while brushing her palms together. "The question, stud. What's something you've always wanted to do?"

The truth rushes forward in an uncontrollable surge. "Grow old with the woman I love."

Her gaze leaps to mine while her breath hitches. She walks forward until our boots bump. "Here's to hoping that can be arranged."

I cup her cheek in my palm. "Will you let me make love to you?"

She leans into my touch. "Gosh, that's really romantic."

"Do you hate it?"

Frankie leaves me hanging for too many seconds. "Not even a little bit, but let's try it to confirm."

CHAPTER THIRTY-FOUR

BYRON GUIDES ME TO THE END OF THE AISLE WHERE there's a staircase. The wood steps creak beneath our climb that delivers us to a large, open space. Square bales are stacked from floor to ceiling, but there's a section near the front that's empty.

"The hayloft?" I can't recall visiting this part of the barn before and spin in a slow circle.

Byron approaches me from behind, settling his hands on my hips. "It's comfortable."

My head rests on his chest and I glance up until our gazes connect. "I'm failing to see how getting poked by straw will be pleasant."

He grinds into me, revealing how hard I get him when we've barely touched. "You're about to get poked by something bigger than straw."

Desire burns through me to pool in my lower belly. "I thought making love was supposed to be slow and sensual."

"Doesn't matter how fast we go. I'm still filling you to the brim. And look." He tilts my chin to the oversized skylight above. "We're going to make love under the stars without freezing our asses off."

My butt rocks against him to the pulsing thrum that's beginning to consume me. "When does that start?"

He sweeps my hair to the side and peppers kisses along my jaw. "Right now, menace."

And then his wall of muscle disappears. Byron stalks to a trunk in the corner that I didn't notice. Its rusty hinges squeak open and he digs inside. A patterned blanket is in his grip when he straightens to stride back to me.

"Why do you have that in the hayloft?" Seems like a nightmare for fabric of any kind.

His brown eyes gleam in the low lighting as he spreads it out on the floor. "Ronnie likes to have tea parties and picnics up here. Pretty sure you've attended a few."

That detail slipped my mind in the heat of this moment. A swoop flips my belly. "Gosh, you're such a good dad. It's almost unbelievable."

His lips kick up into a smirk. "I'm also a really good boyfriend. After I'm done dicking you senseless, you'll be completely infatuated with me."

I wrinkle my nose. "Not on your daughter's play blanket."

He grunts as if I've offended him. "This is new. I've never had a reason to use it."

"Saved for a special occasion?" My heart drums to a chaotic beat when his smolder blazes into me.

"Can't think of a better one," Byron rasps. "C'mere, baby."

One of my brows ticks up. "Baby?"

"Pairs well with honey. We're sticking together for always." He extends an arm toward me.

All I have to do is take it. The distance between us closes at a tortuous pace, giving my sanity a second to recover. It's been through a lot of adjustments lately. Once I'm within reach, Byron pulls me tight against him. Our mutual affection is a feral beast that's about to be sated.

We shed layers like thick, armored walls crumbling down. Discarded clothes pile on the floor in a rush to expose our scars. With each article dropped, I feel exposed but seen. Byron's fingers unclasp my bra and the final barrier is tossed away. We stand bared to each other—loved and accepted with our flaws on display.

After he guides me down onto the blanket, I bury my nose in the woolly fibers. "It smells like home."

Byron lowers himself on top of me, propping up on an elbow as I lift my bent legs to bracket his hips. "What's that smell like?"

My lashes flutter shut as I give myself permission to be vulnerable. "Your addictive cologne that reminds me of the forest in spring. A healing caress I hadn't felt before. Hazelnut coffee that you brew to barista quality. Dirty talk that's so filthy it makes my toes curl. The warmth of your smolder on a lonely night. Things we've never done but will together. Everything you've given me."

"Damn," he breathes. If I'm not mistaken, there's a slight shine in his stare. "That's…"

"What you mean to me, but there's plenty more where that came from."

Byron gulps. "Not sure I can express myself quite as eloquently."

"Don't have to use words. Just show me." With my ankles crossed behind his ass, I give him a gentle pull for encouragement.

The tip of his cock slips along my arousal, nudging my slick entrance in greeting. "Ready?"

I nod, but give him verbal confirmation too. "Yes."

Byron pushes into me with care and control, making my body accept every inch he has in excess. The twinge from him stretching me steals my breath and I gasp. His lips slant over mine to take advantage of the opportunity. It's a chaste kiss, but binds us tighter. Static crackles and buzzes wherever we touch. The contact is magnetic.

Once I'm split apart beneath him, a calm sensation floods in. It's the long-awaited sunlight after a lifetime in darkness. We're joined completely. He's all I see and feel. My tongue sneaks out to taste him, inhaling his signature scent along the way. My senses are consumed.

That's when Byron pulls all the way out just to slide back in. The thick length of him filling me in a single stroke is climax-worthy. I cry out and cling to him. He repeats the motions, getting into a steady rhythm. His groan is guttural and already bordering on desperate, meeting the thrill sparking under my skin.

A blissed-out smile forms, whisking me away into a dreamy state. "Damn, my good boy really loves me."

"That's it, baby." He strokes my cheek with such reverence, a lump clogs my throat. "Your love is stunning. It glows from every part of you."

I tremble when he glides deep. "Fuck, why does it feel so good?"

"Your guard is finally down. I'm in all the way."

"Gosh, that's erotic and romantic. I'm doomed," I whine.

Chemistry like this is a myth, or it was until now. Our connection buzzes in my veins and I clench around him. Byron jolts, breaking stride. The disjointed gait makes this even more significant. We're in this together.

His tempo evens out again, driving me higher with every thrust. The blanket under me cushions the steady friction. He's right—this space is comfortable. The air is stagnant but not stale. There's a clean quality that's either from the organic feed or the purging of our suffering. I breathe it in deeply.

My nails drift along his sides, tempted to dig in and never let go. It's just that euphoric. Byron's hands collect mine, fingers threading together, as he tugs my arms straight overhead. This brings us impossibly closer. Our noses and foreheads brush with each gentle stroke.

I capture his gaze with mine. "Does love always feel like this?"

"You tell me. I want to hear more of those thoughts you've kept locked away. Spill them for me," he urges on a lazy entry.

"It's more than sex." I arch against the restraints he's created. "We're sharing our souls."

His chuckle is seduction wrapped in kinky fantasies. "Just like that, menace."

"Your turn," I insist.

"It's never been like this," he admits. "What I feel for you is truly indescribable. It's like you've brought me back to life. Given me a new purpose. I'm overwhelmed by you."

The naked adoration in his tone wobbles my bottom lip. "Is it weird that I want to cry?"

"Let it out," Byron croons. "I'll be here to catch you."

A single tear tracks down my temple, freeing a drop of pain. Several follow the same path. The purifying drizzle provides room for clarity to reach me. A choked exhale escapes next. This was always going to happen. We were meant to be here.

With that realization, I submit to the throb hammering in my core. Each spike of stimulation prepares to obliterate me. Byron's pace increases to feed our lust. We still haven't hit the peak, but it's looming just ahead.

Strain pinches his features. "Is this enough for you?"

"More than I can handle," I mumble. "You're fixing what you didn't break."

His lips brush against mine. "Give me all that sweetness."

I nip at him. "Don't get used to it."

"Think I will, menace."

My legs cinch around his waist and I start to buck into his steady movements. "Finish it, stud. And then you'll have to scoop me off this floor. I won't be able to walk."

"Fuck, baby. I love you," Byron whimpers in my ear.

That fragile sound is what undoes me. The orgasm hits me like a teetering force. I'm hovering over the edge, tipping into oblivion. White light streaks across my vision as the first quakes take hold. Pressure bears down on me until it's difficult to breathe.

Byron shoves into me a final time, succumbing to his own release. Our ecstasy collides in a frantic crash. I gasp while the relief surges to electric heights. The impact is intense and blinding. Spasms twitch through my limbs as he struggles to support his weight. In the end, we hold each other close through the revival.

"Thank you," I mumble weakly. It feels like my muscles are replaced with jelly.

Byron drops a sloppy kiss on my mouth that's lax with labored exhales. "Told you the dicking would be good."

"You weren't lying." My palms rove over the expanse of his back. "That's a love worth believing in."

CHAPTER THIRTY-FIVE

FRANKIE BLOWS OUT A LONG, SEEMINGLY CALM exhale. "I need a cigarette."

My chuckle rises above the balls of energy bouncing around us. "You don't smoke."

"Now is a great time to start. Whose idea was this?" Her dagger-like nails stab in the direction of the party bus as if she wants to pop the tires.

"You watched the episode of *Peppa Pig* with her. Nothing else would do after seeing that."

"It's too much," she whines. "Did she really have to invite her whole class? And did they all have to be available? Twenty-seven kids is a crisis waiting to happen."

"There's no need to kick up such a fuss. We've got almost as many adult chaperones."

"Easy for you to say," she mutters. "You're father of the century."

Warmth spreads through my chest. "Welcome to the rest of your life, menace."

"I didn't agree to this level of insanity." Frankie waves at the birthday celebration that's just getting started.

"Should've read the fine print," I chide.

"Have you met my mommy?" Ronnie's animated voice carries over the crowd as she points wildly to the redhead beside me. "That's her over there. She's the best! When I'm old enough and my daddy says it's okay, my new mommy is gonna let me get tattoos and she's gonna buy me lotsa knives. A girl's gotta protect herself you know."

Frankie probably doesn't realize that her scowl flips into a smile worthy of a beauty pageant. "Okay, fine. It's not that bad."

"Other than your influence on her," I chuckle.

"I warned you that I'm not cut out for motherhood."

"That's a bunch of bullshit and you know it. But maybe you'll let me put a baby or two inside of you to really test the theory." I loop an arm around her waist and tuck her into my side. "Can you imagine? The best of both of us."

"Or the worst."

My grin rises to meet her grumbled response. It wasn't a rejection. "Either way, they'd be better than other people's children."

"Got that right," she huffs.

Primal satisfaction rumbles from my gut and squares my shoulders while I cast my gaze across the guests. "Well, how about that. Chance decided to show his face."

Frankie narrows her eyes in his direction. "Who's he staring at?"

"Gemma," I grunt.

Red hair whips me as her gaze leaps to mine. "Paisley's sister? No shit."

"There's something going on between them. It might be an interesting story."

"Poor soul." Her bland tone doesn't sound the least bit sympathetic. "He looks roped in rawhide."

The bus driver chooses that moment to descend the stairs, beckoning everyone inside. "All aboard! The Foxy Lady is departing shortly."

An explosion of noise and hazardous amounts of sugar content erupts from the kids. The ground quakes with their excitement. Even the adults have extra pep in their step as they approach the neon pink party wagon. Meanwhile, Frankie's complexion has paled significantly.

"If I don't survive, I'm going to haunt you." She shudders as if preparing for the ghostly role.

"Wouldn't expect anything less."

"C'mon, Mommy!" Ronnie races toward us and tugs on Frankie's arm. "Sit by me. Please, please!"

Any evidence of upset thaws from the reformed ex-con's frigid posture. "Of course, kiddo. I'd love that." But then Frankie's green eyes slice a glare at me, revealing the fire burning in their depths. "You're still going to pay for this."

"I look forward to it, menace." My lips slide into a smirk as I fall into step behind them. "And for all our years to come."

EPILOGUE

MY FINGERS SLIP WHILE I TRY TO SECURE ANOTHER knot. "Quit struggling."

Byron bucks beneath me, not going down without a fight. "This isn't consensual."

I scoff and tighten my hold on his bound wrists. "As if you're suddenly concerned about consent."

But just for the sake of avoiding triggers and safe words, it's very possible for him to escape. This situation is like a pebble compared to a mountain. I'm not under any illusion to claim otherwise. He's enjoying this whether he openly admits it or not.

Which the smug grin on his dirty mouth proves. "What's something you've always wanted to do, but haven't had the chance?"

Frustration sparks in my veins and I resume my feeble

strategy of binding him to the headboard. "That didn't give you permission to flush my pills."

"I was just trying to give you what you wanted," he croons.

"You twisted my words after a moment of weakness. Now," I snap. "Hold still."

"What's in it for me?"

"Be a good boy and find out."

His hips flex under me, giving solid approval from his arousal through the blanket. "I'm in the mood to be bad."

"Unfortunately, you're not in control. Remind me of that pesky line you like to yammer?" I tip my head, pretending to think it over. "This will go a lot smoother if you cooperate."

Before Byron can submit to my whims, the bedroom door creaks open. "Mommy?"

The soft voice halts my attempts at retaliation as I flip my position to face Ronnie. "Hey, kiddo. What're you doing awake?"

The horror in my voice is warranted. This is a scene no adult ever wants a child to witness. I'm straddling her dad's lap with rope in my hands like a devious cowgirl. It's a small miracle that we're somewhat dressed. Scantily-clad is better than stark naked.

"I had a bad dream," she mumbles. "Can I sleep with you?"

"Ummm." I peer at Byron from over my shoulder. "Is the tent still erected?"

He grunts while lowering his bound wrists. "Deflated faster than a popped balloon."

Relief sags the strain in my spine and I turn to smile at Ronnie. "Sure, kiddo. We were just getting tucked in."

Her footsteps shuffle across the carpet. "Were you camping?"

I send her a quizzical look in the dim glow from the lamp. "No?"

"Then why do you need a tent?"

Byron's chuckle is gruff beneath me. "Mommy has a wild spirit that likes to take us on pretend adventures."

I laugh, but the sound is strangled. "We were just… messing around."

Once getting a closer glance at us, Ronnie pauses her approach. "Why is Daddy tied up?"

He unravels the last of knots and tosses the rope to the floor. "That's a good question. Care to answer, menace?"

"Not really," I mutter.

"Is it 'cause he was tryin' to sneak a bedtime snack?"

I'm already nodding along. "Mhmm, yep. That's plausible and much more appropriate."

She frowns at me. "But Daddy doesn't like bedtime snacks."

"Good point, cupcake."

"Depends what he's offered to eat," I whisper under my breath.

"I'm craving something very specific," he replies just as quietly.

Ronnie's lips squish in concentration. "Like what?"

"A bun in the oven." Byron rests his arms behind his head while I get more uncomfortable in the hot seat.

It's only then I realize I'm still astride him while carrying on a conversation with our little girl. I climb off him and sprawl out in my usual spot as of late on the king-size mattress. That leaves plenty of space between us for the innocent child who I can only hope isn't traumatized. Ronnie leaps into the allotted space without an ounce of hesitation or mental scarring.

After getting situated on a pile of pillows, her angelic features study mine. "Why were you tying Daddy up? I want the truth."

My lips roll between my teeth. "Gosh, those prissy pants are inquisitive tonight."

"Frannie," she sighs, losing her patience with my stalling techniques.

"He wasn't listening," I blurt.

She gasps. "Why not?"

"That's not quite true, cupcake. I was actually listening too carefully," Byron interjects.

Her head cocks to one side, eyes still pinned on me. "Huh?"

It appears I'm on the hook for this snafu. Might as well come clean. "Your daddy wants to put a baby in my belly. Can you believe that? It's not like you want to be a big sister."

But Ronnie's expression is lit up like Christmas morning. "Oh, oh! I want a little sister. I do, I do! Please, Mommy!"

Byron's chest is shaking with laughter. "Gosh, menace.

You're really clueless about kids. Every only child wants a sibling, especially when they're young."

The error in my explanation smacks me with an ignorant dose of humility. "Thanks for the words of encouragement, Daddy."

His eyes heat on me as if he wants to give me more than his chocolate smolder for dessert. "Whenever you're ready, baby."

Which reminds Ronnie what's at stake. "Let's tie up Mommy and put my little sister in her tummy!"

My stomach clenches and I slip beneath the comforter for protection. "Um, no. That's not how it works."

Byron's smirk is the definition of smug. "You did this to yourself."

Ronnie rips off the covers I've buried myself under. "How do we get a baby in there?"

My arm slides across my middle as if that will divert her plans to get me pregnant. "I'm not sure. Let's discuss it in the morning."

Her pinched expression looks like she wants to argue. "I'm not gonna forget."

My exhale waves a white flag in surrender. "I don't imagine you will. Ever."

Byron claps a palm over his mouth to muffle a bark of laughter. "This is more entertaining than reality television."

"Hush," I scold.

Ronnie sighs happily. "I'm tired now."

In unison, Byron and I stoke down the slope of her nose, ending the practiced motion with a tap on her chin. She smiles as her eyes slide shut. Across our daughter's sleepy form, my hand claps his to connect us as a family.

"Love you," he tells us.

"Love you," I echo.

"Gonna have the sweetest dreams," Ronnie murmurs. "My little sister can't wait to meet me."

That's technically the end, but I have a few bonus scenes from *Tangled in Trouble* for you. Get them free here!

Curious about Chance and Gemma? Their story—*Roped in Rawhide* is releasing next.
Here's an exclusive sneak peek.

Chance

On Ronnie's party bus…

MY HEART IS IN MY THROAT AS I CREEP ALONG THE narrow aisle. Kids are screaming. Parents aren't even trying to quiet them down. There's a funky smell in the air and a sticky residue on the floor. It's a sensory overload, but all I see is her. All I've ever seen is her.

Which is why I pause beside her seat. There's no moving on from a woman like Gemma Keaton. Not that she was ever mine to begin with.

That doesn't stop me from staring. I've been doing a lot of that since she returned to Cloverleaf Meadows after transferring to a closer college.

My gaze devours her shamelessly, roving over her glossy hair and soft features. She's so damn beautiful. It hurts to look at her. But that ache in my chest is most likely from the damage I've done. What I wouldn't give to rewind the clock.

My gaze lowers. Gemma's arms are crossed loosely over her waist. At least until she notices where my attention has wandered. She tugs at her left sleeve, covering the scars peeking out. I furrow my brow at the defensive action.

"Did you need something or are just going to stand

there?" Gemma's glare finds me gulping over countless excuses.

Every single one of them is a waste of breath. It's going to take a lot more than flimsy apologies to fix what I broke. If there's even anything left to fix.

"You look really beautiful," I blurt.

She snorts. "Flattery will get you nowhere."

"Are you saving that spot?" I point to the empty space next to her on the bus seat.

"For anyone but you," she clips.

A wince pinches my face as if I have any right to be bothered by her hostility. It's a brand I've worn since we were seventeen and my actions ripped us apart.

"I miss you." My gaze drops to her delicate hands that I've never gotten to properly hold. "I miss our… friendship."

That offensive term ridicules what we used to share, and what we could've been.

The unshed tears in Gemma's eyes couldn't agree more. "Should've thought about that before you ruined it, bronc."

You can pre-order *Roped in Rawhide* today!

Have you read the other two standalones in the Cloverleaf Meadows series?

Buckled in Barbwire is Brody and Paisley's story. Read this enemies to lovers, marriage of convenience, one bed, age gap romance here!

Saddled in Secrets is Colton and Bianca's story. Read this older brother's best friend, morally gray bodyguard, grumpy x sunshine, he's been yearning for years romance here!

Want another grumpy single dad? Jake Evans will give you all he's got! Enjoy this excerpt from *Wrong for You*.

"If you want to keep your hands, I suggest you refrain from touching her." It's a miracle my voice remains level.

Bleary eyes try to focus on me. "This your girl?"

"She's my everything as far as you're concerned," I snarl.

The asshole takes a breath and squares up like he wants to challenge me, but one look at my face and the tipsy groper wisely retreats. My glare follows his stumbled stride to the bathroom. Good fucking riddance.

Harper whirls to confront me. The lit fuse in her gaze sparks my arousal. When we finally get to fucking, our combined passion will be explosive. My body thrums in anticipation of joining hers.

"What do you think you're doing?" Her sharp tone rises above the thumping music to smack my wayward thoughts.

"Saving you." My possessive tendencies belong to her. It's no surprise that my protective side manifests for her too.

"From what?" She pauses to scan the crowd, fake concern replacing the fire in her expression. "Dancing?"

"Did you want him pawing at you like a feral cat in mating season?"

Her hip cocks to the side. "I was about to handle it."

"How?"

"A sharp elbow to the ribs usually does the trick." She demonstrates and narrowly misses the person behind her.

The storm wreaking havoc on my composure regains momentum. I go rigid as more failures against her pour down on me. "Are you often in situations where you need to defend yourself?"

"Why does it matter to you? I'm single and free to dance with anybody I like."

"Well, I don't like to see my friends treated that way." That casual title is wrong for her on too many levels to count.

Harper catches the distaste curling my upper lip. "Oh, please. That bullshit is stinking up the bar. Ginger and Callie aren't far if I require reinforcements. Stand down, buddy."

"Too late. I'm already off my stool."

She clutches her forehead with a groan. "We just had this conversation. You weren't going to intervene, remember? It was your grand plan."

"There's an adjustment period," I grumble. And I'm a total fraud.

Her smile is pure satisfaction, as if she predicted this exact event. "Having regrets the second another man's hands land on my ass?"

I clench my jaw against the impulse to immediately agree. "What'd you think about my peace offering?"

Or—more accurately—fuel for her blaze.

"Weak at best. These panties aren't dropping." Harper tugs at her fastened jeans. The truth is in her alert awareness. She's sober, which is how I prefer her for this altercation.

I prowl further into her space. "Are your panties pink? The thong I peeled off you—"

She claps a palm over my mouth. "Knock it off, Jake. That's behind us, remember?"

My fingers circle her wrist to remove the gag before I lick her soft skin. "I'm not so sure about that anymore."

Want more? *Wrong for You* is available now.

ACKNOWLEDGEMENTS

Hey again! I'm hoping that if you've made it this far, Tangled in Trouble was a win for you. That's what I wish for the most whenever I release a book. It's a deeply emotional experience to write a book, let alone publish it for others to read. That part never gets easier, but the fact you chose to read one of mine really makes a difference. Thank you for spending your precious time with Byron, Frankie, and little Ronnie. It means more than I'll ever be able to describe.

Next, I need to thank my husband. You're the grump to my sunshine. The inspiration for my heroes. Not only are you an incredible husband, but you're also the best dad to our kiddos. I'm extremely lucky to be living a fairytale life with you. I love you tonnes, honey. You're stuck with me for always.

Huge hugs of gratitude to Heather and Shain. I couldn't have done this one without the two of you. Thanks for lounging on the couch with me and binging cheesy dating shows. Our friendship is the type that's tough to find, but we did it. I can't wait to keep doing this author gig alongside you both for years to come.

Many thanks to Allison for always being down to meet for a "work" lunch. We definitely get plenty of plotting done. You make this job a lot less lonely and I'm grateful to have you not too far down the road.

I also need to give endless snuggles to Kate, Leigh, Renee, Jackie, and Jodie for all you do. This career can be tough and I'm very fortunate to have such encouraging friends. Thanks for brightening even the darkest days.

Thanks to Alex with Infinite Well for editing my words to make them spotless. And to Bryanna for doing such an awesome alpha read. This book wouldn't be what it is without you two.

Major thanks to Candi Kane PR for always hootin' and hollerin' about my books. I'm so thankful for your promo services, but even more grateful for your friendship. I appreciate you very much!

I have to gush about Stacey from Champagne Book Design. You always know just what to do to make my interiors perfect. My books are beautiful because of you. Thanks for always fitting me in. You're the best!

My gorgeous cover is thanks to Neptune Book Cover Designs. Your talent is extraordinary and I'm so happy to have some of your work for my books.

All the love to Harloe's Hotties—my reader group. These are my people. My safe space. The reason I'm excited to write books and shout about them. Your support means the world to me. I'm extremely grateful to each and every one of you. Same goes for my review crew, influencers, bookstagrammers, betas, and YOU for picking up this book. You're all the reason I get to continue doing this job. Keep reading for me!

Cheers to book baby number twenty-five. YEEHAW! If you loved Tangled in Trouble, and want to do me a small favor, please consider leaving a review. What you have to say matters. Even one sentence helps new readers find my books.

Thanks for everything, and until next time.
Happy trails!
xx
Harloe

ABOUT THE AUTHOR

Harloe Rae is a *USA Today* & Amazon Top 5 best-selling author. Her passion for writing and reading has taken on a whole new meaning. Each day is an unforgettable adventure.

She's a Minnesota gal with a serious addiction to romance. There's nothing quite like an epic happily ever after. When she's not buried in the writing cave, Harloe can be found hanging with her hubby and kiddos. If the weather permits, she loves being lakeside or out in the country with her horses.

Broody heroes are Harloe's favorite to write. Her romances are swoony and emotional with plenty of heat. All of her books are available on Amazon and Kindle Unlimited.

Stay in the know by subscribing to her newsletter at
http://bit.ly/HarloesList

Join her reader group, Harloe's Hotties, at
www.facebook.com/groups/harloehotties

Check out her site at www.harloerae.com